PRAISE . . ..
IT HAPPENED AT TWO IN THE MORNING

"With Alan Hruska you're guaranteed a nonstop pace, witty dialogue, and characters you care about. *It Happened at Two in the Morning* was my must-read thriller this year and—wow!—he delivered."

— Peter Lovesey, award-winning author of the Peter Diamond series

"A legal thriller that really thrills. It hits hard and keeps you off balance until the last page. I couldn't put it down. "

— Phoef Sutton, *New York Times*–bestselling author of *Heart Attack & Vine*, *Crush*, and *15 Minutes to Live*

PRAISE FOR
ALAN HRUSKA'S THRILLERS

"Beautifully written and beautifully imagined, this dark, spiraling, Kafkaesque nightmare might be the best psychological suspense you'll read this year—or this decade."

— Lee Child, *New York Times*–bestselling author of the Jack Reacher novels

"An erudite legal thriller."

— *Library Journal*

"Vividly real and quite compelling."

— *Booklist*

IT HAPPENED
AT TWO
IN THE MORNING

ALAN HRUSKA

PROSPECT
·PARK·
BOOKS

Published by Prospect Park Books
2359 Lincoln Ave
Altadena, California 91001
www.prospectparkbooks.com

Distributed by Consortium Book Sales & Distribution
www.cbsd.com

Library of Congress Cataloging-in-Publication Data
Names: Hruska, Alan, author.
Title: It happened at two in the morning / by Alan Hruska.
Description: Altadena, California : Prospect Park Books, [2017]
Identifiers: LCCN 2017023442 (print) | LCCN 2017027860 (ebook) | ISBN
  9781945551185 (ebook) | ISBN 9781945551178 (softcover)
Classification: LCC PS3558.R87 (ebook) | LCC PS3558.R87 I84 2017
(print) | DDC 813/.54--dc23
LC record available at https://lccn.loc.gov/2017023442

Cover design by Howard Grossman
Book design & layout by Amy Inouye, Future Studio

ALSO BY ALAN HRUSKA

Pardon the Ravens

Wrong Man Running

Borrowed Time

ONE

Tom Weldon looks out on the lights of the city. Squinting, he imagines a moon-sparkled bay. *To be anyplace but here,* he thinks. The hour is late, but lamps still flare—from office towers, such as the one he's still working in.

At the desk in front of him, a senior partner of the firm, Harrison Stith, attacks Tom's draft with the stub of a red pencil. Each slash, to Tom, is like the drawing of blood.

"Tom Weldon, Tom Weldon," the senior man says, as if lamenting the junior's very existence.

"Yes, Harry?" says Tom. He's long-legged and wary, with craggy features uncommon in a young lawyer, and the wavy brown hair of someone too busy to have it cut at a shop.

Harry stares at Tom's name among the attorneys listed as "of Counsel" on the brief. "Should be an 'e' at the end, don't you think? Should be Well*done*. Know why it's not?" He sits back in his chair, with plump cheeks and thinning hair, comfortable in his condescension.

"Probably was at some point," Tom says.

"Not your name, fella. Your performance. Here. At the firm. You know why—regarding your performance—we cannot say well done?"

"We…?"

"The partners."

Tom slides into the wing chair facing Stith directly. "Are you firing me, Harry?"

"We don't fire people. You know that."

"You're passing me over."

"In the vernacular, yes."

"At two in the morning, you're passing me over?"

"It's not quite two," Harry says. "And it's not just my judgment."

"You waited to tell me until we finished this brief? At two in the morning!"

"You had to be told," Harry says soothingly.

"That here, at this firm, I'm a dead man?"

"That's a fair summary, yes."

"I might be the best lawyer *in* this firm."

"Not for our purposes, no."

He stares up at Tom blankly. In the setting of his desk, his big leather chair, and the cityscape behind him, Stith looks like a figure in a diorama.

"Let's take the present situation as an example," Harry says.

"Of what? Your duplicity?"

"Your perfectionism, Tom. Why are we still here at two in the morning? Why, in fact, was this brief not sent to me until eight o'clock tonight? I don't know what you think you're writing. Or, for that matter, for whom you're writing it."

"We could have filed what I gave you," Tom says. "You haven't changed it *that* much."

"No, not that much," Harry acknowledges. "There wasn't time."

"To dumb it down."

"To reduce the risk that our particular judge, who is not genetically blessed—"

"With a brain," Tom notes.

"With a functioning one, yes, that's the point—will think we're talking down to him."

"What about the client?" Tom asks.

To which Harry restrains a guffaw. "The client? Give me a break."

Tom looks about him again, at Harrison Stith's living room of an office, and then back at Harry himself. Ironies abound. Stith is a man of long, stately, patrician lineaments, and lineage, lecturing Tom Weldon—equally long, but scruffy in looks *and* background—on the unwisdom of producing elegant work. Tom rises from the wing chair. "Are we done here?"

"You're leaving me with this? Now?"

"Now it's yours. You can take my name off it."

"I want you to file it!" Stith says."

"You mean stay here another two hours? Retyping and printing what you've done to my draft?" Tom smiles. "Give *me* a break." He leaves, with Stith sucking the air.

———

Elena Riles waits for the reaction of five actors, a dramaturge, and two staffers of Playwrights Community, who, despite the late hour, have just workshopped her play. Actually, everyone waits on the dramaturge, Neil Offinger, who is also the Artistic Director of the institution. Neil, a small man of bent features, ordinarily speaks in institutionalese, as if his sentences were crafted for a grant application. When giving notes on a play, his remarks are briefer, though no less obscure.

"I think …" Neil muses, and everyone leans, literally, his way. "I think … it has moments, but it's rather long, don't you know."

Elena makes a face. "Too many words?"

"Well, that would account for its length, yes."

"Like *Don Giovanni* having too many notes."

"Are you comparing yourself to Mozart?"

"The comparison was to the royal review, which is what, it seems, I'm being treated to here."

The dramaturge is unfazed by the sarcasm. Indeed, he seems to fancy the allusion. "There's another thing. Your work's a bit … derivative, don't you know."

"My *play?*" Elena says, standing. *"Derivative?"* Though scrawny and short, she's somehow imposing, with her covergirl face framed by unstylish dark curls. She wears a denim skirt, tank top and overblouse. In a much earlier age, artists would have been commissioned to paint her in gowns.

"Calmly, Elena."

"Derivative of fucking *whom?*"

He looks around. "Anyone on this? Let's hear it. Todd?"

The actor whose name is Todd looks up, appearing stressed. "I dunno. Beckett? Pinter?"

"Yes, well," Neil says. "A lot of that."

"This is bullshit," says Elena.

"Now, now," soothes Neil.

"You defend that!"

"It's just a note, my darling, and everything in due time. Anyone else?"

People look sleepy. Sitting around a battered wood table on hard folding chairs, they also look as if they want to go home.

"We started too late," Elena says. "Everyone's tired."

"I'm afraid discussion of the other plays did exceed the time allotted."

"You booked too many, Neil. For one night, ridiculous. And mine last."

"Yours was the longest. And we have only the one room, darling."

"Oh?"

"I'm just saying."

"No, you're not *just* saying. You're implying."

"Perhaps we should dismiss the cast. Schedule discussion for when everyone's fresh, has the time to think more about it."

Elena starts to leave. "This is really bullshit."

"Elena!"

"I'm not buying you another room."

"No one's suggested—"

"Y'know, Neil. You've got a lousy hand, and you just over-played it."

———◦◦◦———

Robertson Riles, a handsome man of unimposing physical stat-ure, gruff style, and immense wealth, waits in an unlit office for his daughter to call. The office building, which he owns through a personally controlled REIT and leases to his firm, Riles Whitney & Co., sits on a side street in the west end of Hell's Kitchen. It's an architecturally undistinguished steel and glass structure, except that it's taller than any building within blocks. As a result, Riles enjoys an unobstructed view of the rest of Manhattan from the top floor. In the darkness of his space, the city lights float up like clusters of the galaxy. Riles owns many other shafts of those lights, and the feeling of pro-prietorship is deeply satisfying. His daughter's tardiness pro-duces quite the opposite effect.

There are issues to discuss. He has two sons-in-law in the business; however, they've already demonstrated their inca-pacity to lead it anywhere but into Chapter 11. Elena has the genes, if she would but use them. And while he badgered her into business school, she's remained adamantly opposed to joining the firm. Tonight, he means to corner her again on the subject. She said she'd be late. He said, "Try to make it before sunrise."

"Why tonight?" she asked.

"Just be here," he said. "I'll wait."

If not tonight, he thinks, she'll have another excuse for tomorrow—and the next day. It's important that he speak to her now.

For one thing, he's about to launch the biggest and possi-bly bloodiest takeover fight of his life. The target, whose stock he's been secretly buying for months, is General Technology & Media, headquartered on Sixth Avenue in a dark glass building as tall as his own. His rival for that prize is Jockery Holdings Inc., which occupies the entirety of the building adjacent GT&M's—twin peaks disturbing the perimeter, and serenity, of his view. Riles's company will be the "white knight," since he has a relationship with GT&M's largest stockholder. But, at the opening of the market that day, an as yet undisclosed "black knight" bought a block of GT&M shares even larger than the tranche seized by Jockery Holdings. Riles wants Elena in on the battle if for no other reason than to learn the rules of the "kill," how it's best done—and the thrill of it.

For another thing, there is churning in him this night a feeling of more than normal disquiet. He believes himself to be an extraordinary person, but one susceptible to extreme whimsies and premonitions. He's learned to honor these. It's not that his whimsies are always gratifying or that his premonitions always come true. But either signals that something important is about to happen in his life that his consciousness hasn't picked up on yet, some opportunity, or threat; something he damn well better be ready to pay attention to. And call to the attention of the person who matters most to him.

As for his promise, that he'd wait all night for her call, he thinks he might have to make good on that too, when, finally, his private line rings.

"Dad, I'm leaving. Five minutes. Seven max."

"I'll be downstairs," he says.

He delays a few moments. It's that disquieting premonition. Sharper now, more pronounced. It's not opportunity, but danger. As if it might be the last night of his life.

———⟐———

Tom Weldon traverses an empty and relatively dark street. No cabs to be found, he's bound for Tenth Avenue. He's not overly fond of this walk; it's uphill and uninteresting, crammed with low grungy buildings and graffiti-scarred walls. Then he arrives at the block where the one skyscraper incongruously looms. It's the ostentatious home of Riles Whitney & Co., standing out like a beacon.

The street is the one Tom normally takes, having just a bit gentler uphill slope and, given the Riles building, a little more activity, though he expects none at this late hour. Just as he passes the entrance, however, several surprising things happen almost simultaneously. None other than Robbie Riles, a recognizable gray-haired figure who famously owns most of the company, strides out of his skyscraping castle. Then a young woman, turning the corner from Tenth Avenue, begins waving as Riles appears. And, most unanticipated, a cab signaling empty, passing her, heads directly toward Tom.

Tom runs forward and waves, not at Robertson or the young woman, who passes him on the other side of the street, but to flag the taxi. It guns by him too, halting abruptly in front of the building, and proves not to have been empty at all. Two men jump out of the vehicle; one grabs the young woman and tries to shove her into the back seat. The other goes for Riles, who is already swinging his arms at his assailant. Instinctively, Tom hurls himself at the woman's captor, which is almost the last thing he remembers. The very last thing he remembers is being hit by a punch delivered professionally to the left side of his head.

⸻

Near the top of Time-Warner Plaza on Columbus Circle in Manhattan, in one of the most expensive condominium apartments in the world, a bald man of considerable height and an overall thickish, sleek appearance lies without sleeping next to a beautiful woman half his age. She generally calls him Rex, though that's not his name, and professes to be in love with him. He accepts both the sobriquet and the displays of affection. His own displays are delivered less warmly but in marketable form. The arrangement suits both of them. As does the fact that most nights she's there she sleeps easily while he lies awake. He'll sleep eventually. But four hours is all he needs.

One of his mobiles gyrates on the night table. Rising from bed, he takes the phone with him to the window. "Yes?" he says softly.

A calm male voice on the other end says only, "It's done. First phase."

"Thank you," Rex says and hangs up. Always good, he thinks, to be courteous to everyone, even, or maybe especially, to henchmen.

His bedroom complex, a wraparound windowed corner suite, frames views of the park to the east, and of downtown and the Hudson River to the south. He can just make out the top few floors of the Riles Whitney building southwest of him. He smiles, contemplating the corporate commotion no doubt already going on there as he settles himself back into bed. Relaxed by this thought, he feels himself sink into his mattress. Like a drug, he thinks, drifting off into slumber. A job well done *is* like a drug.

TWO

Tom awakes in the dark with a very bad headache, barely able to move. Or breathe in air pungent with sweat but curiously laced with perfume. Feels like he's been sleeping on a garden hose. His shirt and suit jacket are sodden. Raising his head slightly, he sees someone sitting across from him. A bar of light streaks her face—though not enough light to identify who she is. He thinks he knows who, however.

"Where are we?"

"I think it's a potting shed," she says.

He struggles to an upright sitting position to feel for the wall. It's two feet away, and it's stone. He reaches overhead. His sensation of inadequate headspace is confirmed. Then he feels beneath him. "This *is* a hose."

"Brilliant," she says.

"But this shed's not a potting shed," he points out politely. "A potting shed would be made out of wood."

"You really give a shit? It's a cage. For us, it's a tiny stone cage."

"There's a door behind you; you've tried it?"

"No," she says. "I've just been sitting here stupidly for an hour waiting for you to wake up."

"Would you mind if I try?" He's still trying to be as gracious as possible in the circumstances.

"Be my guest," she says, edging out of the way.

Steel construction, no give whatever. He sinks back into his coiled nest.

"They stole my wallet and cards," she says. "Even took my BlackBerry."

"Mine too," he says, trying to sound caring.

"I had a lot of private stuff on that."

"Hmm," he says, mind now fully on an appraisal of their prison. Obviously too low to stand up in. If it were empty, enough room to lie down in and spread his arms and legs—but it's not empty. Besides the girl, there's that hose and a rake. No immediate use for either presents itself.

He twists around. A narrow slot near the top of the wall behind him appears to be their one source of light and air.

The girl has become strangely quiet.

While struggling to take off his jacket, he says, "I saw you waving to Robbie Riles."

"And?"

"So you know him?"

"He's my father."

"Ah," he says.

"Meaning?"

"Meaning, of course, that might explain what we're doing in here."

"You're thinking kidnapping," she says.

"I'm thinking that's the most likely explanation, yes."

"And you're just what?" she says. "The innocent bystander? Who the fuck are you, anyway?"

"Tom Weldon."

"Doesn't really tell me that much."

"There are other clues," he says. "Like I'm wearing a suit, having worked until two o'clock in the morning."

"So you're a lawyer."

"Got it in one."

"Coming from Eleventh Avenue?"

"We just moved there," he says, then reflects on the irony of his still using the first-person plural pronoun with regard to that firm. "The far west of Manhattan is the new frontier."

"Bad place to be at two in the morning."

"As it happens, I'd say, yeah."

She says, "Did you *see* what happened?"

"To your dad? Sorry. Didn't."

Silence.

He says, "You have any idea who they are?"

"Not a clue."

"Well, whoever," he says. "They'll just want the money."

"No doubt."

"They obviously don't want to kill us," he says. "They could have done it by now. Curious, though. Why they just left us *here*."

He looks around again. "Don't you think it's odd?" he says. "Two men go to all this trouble, grabbing us, commandeering a taxi, taking us all the way out here, wherever this is, sticking us in this shed, and then not bothering to tie us up? Indeed, why the hell did they leave us with anything else in here—even a garden rake?"

"'*Indeed?*' You talk like that all the time?"

"Yeah. I'm a lawyer. Let's try the rake."

"Where? In that slot behind you?"

"Where else?" he says, wedging it in there.

He struggles with it for a few seconds.

"What's happening?" she asks.

"Not very much."

"Try slamming it, then."

"Okay," he says skeptically.

"Try it!"

Pushing back against the coiled hose to get the maximum leverage, he thrusts the rake like a spear, bashing the steel end against the top of the wall.

"And?" she says.

"I think something—a stone—came loose."

"No fucking way!" she says excitedly.

"Way, indeed," he says, prying it looser with his hand.

"Hit it again!"

He does. Two stones fall outward and let in a flash of sun. They stare at the light. Then Tom starts frantically smashing the rake head to the wall until more stones come loose.

"Let me have your jacket," she commands.

He shuffles it to her, and she drapes it over the opening. Pushing her head through, she thrusts her shoulders at the wall, and the whole thing gives way. Hastily they clear the stones and scramble over them.

"Fucking out of there!" she exclaims, bounding to her feet.

Achingly, he rises next to her.

It's the middle of the day, sun high in the heavens. They find themselves in a dirt yard of what was once a large farmhouse. All that's left now of house, barn, and outer buildings are charred ends of timber and ashes. Barren fields stretch seemingly for miles. A well, fifty feet off, is enclosed by a stand of birches.

"Insurance fire," Tom says.

"How do you know?"

"Just has that look. This place was once prosperous."

"I gotta pee," she says. "There's no privacy."

"Behind the trees," he suggests.

"Not much privacy there!"

"I won't look."

"I can trust you?"

"You have a choice?"

"No, you bastard," and she storms off.

He laughs and turns his back on her.

THREE

The Acting District Attorney, Mike Skillan, has the perpetual scowl of someone expecting the worst. He's a large, square man in his early fifties, with good bones in a fleshy face. His cheap haircut, close on the sides, leaves a clump of black hair on the top flopping over a wide forehead. He wears a white shirt, rep tie, cordovan shoes, over-the-calf socks, and the pants to a very good suit, bought during his life in private practice. The suit jacket is draped over the back of his desk chair.

In an arc of chairs confronting his desk sit several high-ranking members of his office, including the redheaded, squirrel-nosed chief deputy, Joe Cunningham, who is invited to start things off. "Has all the markings of a slam dunk," Joe says.

"Or a frame," notes Mike.

"Her gun," Joe points out.

"In her apartment. Left there. Conveniently."

"In the bottom of a garbage bag," Joe says. "She ran. Something spooked her. Before she could throw it out. But there's more here, Mike."

"Bet there is."

"First, the relationship, father, daughter? Stormy," says Joe. "Page Six. Yet she's still the heir, heir*ess*. Which is pretty good motivation. And the second thing … I'll let Foster do this."

Eyes on Foster Donachetti, head of the trial division, narrow face, hooked nose, saturnine and svelte. A former partner of Mike's, he's a man of many suits, made in London, with a perfect gray, double-breasted pinstripe chosen for the day. He says, "The gun wasn't registered, wasn't legal."

"Even less reason, then, to believe it was hers," Mike says.

"Except," Foster says, in an argument-ending tone, "we have the guy who sold it to her. Victor Contrares, gun merchant to the stars."

"Really?" Mike says, still thinking something's amiss.

"Singing very prettily is our Victor."

"How'd we find him, connect him?"

"He found us," Foster says. "Walked right in. This morning."

"Said he supplied?"

"That was the proffer," Foster says. "Of course, he's lawyered up."

"Why'd he come in at all?"

"We would have had him, he says. He could hear footsteps."

"I don't know," says Mike, not persuaded. "Whatta they want?"

"Immunity. Transactional only. Fair deal. Which we gave him."

Mike frowns but nods. "Corroboration?"

"Phone records. Three calls, her to him."

Mike sits back. "Okay, book her," he says.

"She's gone," says Joe. "Of course she's in flight. More confirmation."

"So find her."

"Obviously, the cops are looking, tristate, PA, elsewhere. Big alert."

The door swings open. Sammy Riegert, works for Donachetti. "You should hear this. Cops got a call. Young woman, her boyfriend's missing. Guy named Thomas Weldon. Called her from work at two in the morning, said he'd be right home. Never showed. Work for him was Forty-Ninth and Eleventh. We're guessing he walked right into the shooting."

"You don't guess, Sammy. Whatta you got?"

"Phone records. Fourteen calls between Weldon and Elena Riles last two months."

Chorus of whistles.

"Okay," Mike says. "We want both of them. Him as a material. Anything else?"

FOUR

Julian Althus stands uncomfortably behind the desk in Robbie Riles's old office. Seated before him is the Riles Whitney outside counsel, Harrison Stith.

"I realize, Harry, it's the corporation you represent, not me personally."

"That's true," Stith says. "But until a conflict arises...."

"And it might never, you're saying."

"Quite probably never."

"Given a confluence of interests," says Julian. "The company's, mine."

"Such a ... confluence," says Harry, "is more likely than not, I think."

Julian laughs. "Always liked you, Harry."

"Thank you, Julian. Fully reciprocated, I'm sure."

"Shall we go for a walk?"

Without further invitation, Julian makes for the door. Harry, much like a loyal dachshund, jumps up and follows.

———✦———

In Central Park, Julian strolls briskly toward the underpass to the Sixty-Fifth Street transverse. Harry keeps pace, which isn't easy for him. Though both men are of an age, Harry's pre-dinner routine features martinis, whereas Julian frequents a gym. He's a tall man with an athletic step, a high smooth brow, and light straight hair blown every which way in the wind.

"You don't mind this, do you, Harry? Getting out in the air? Little exercise?"

"Delightful," says Harry.

"At a thousand an hour, or whatever it is you fellows now bill?"

"Worth every penny."

"So what are the steps?" Julian asks.

"To the accession?" Harry says, already huffing and puffing. "Well, of course, it's not automatic. Requires board action. Appointment of a nominating committee. Then their nominations for the post. Not necessarily for a full slate, just CEO. But one would expect others now to tender their resignations to give the new CEO—you, if that's the result—flexibility. So, as a practical matter, it will be a new slate."

"And the election of the nominating committee?"

"Usual way. Wouldn't be inappropriate for you to put forth some names."

"Safe names."

"Naturally," Harry says.

"No one would be surprised by this?"

"Only by the opposite."

"And Elena?" Julian asks. "The sole heir to his controlling interest?"

"The cops think she did it."

"Yes, that's already leaked, hasn't it? Somehow I find that inconceivable."

"Hmm," says Harry. His sources have told him something even more surprising, if that's even possible, about his associate Tom Weldon. But there's no point, he concludes, sharing that with Julian now.

They stroll for a while in silence.

Finally, Stith says, "Are we walking back as well?"

"Why, Harry? You've reached the point of no return?"

"We are getting rather far away."

"You're hoping, maybe, for a limousine waiting on Seventy-Second Street?"

"Is there?" Harry asks.

"No limo," Julian says, upping the pace considerably.

Harry stops. Julian then does too and smiles sympathetically. "Not in shape?"

Harry, breathing hard, says, "Why in the world did we have to come out here for this conversation anyway?"

"Because, Harry, the air out here isn't bugged."

FIVE

At an abandoned farmhouse, Tom and Elena stop to look at the sign. It's the third such farm they've come to, each with the same placard, placed by the same bank with the same message. In effect it says, Want this property? We've foreclosed on the mortgage. You can buy it at auction.

"Colonial Bank," Tom says. "That's one of yours, right?"

"Not mine," Elena says indignantly.

"Well, your dad's."

"The firm he works for," she says.

"Rather the other way around, isn't it?"

"What're you, giving me grief?" she says, staring up at him, her hair all frizzled and in disarray. "I'm starving, dying of thirst, drop-dead tired, and you're picking a fight? I did not drive these people from their homes. And how do you know so much about it, anyway?"

"The law firm I worked for? Represents Riles Whitney."

"So you're the guys who foreclosed on all these farms we just passed."

"No," he says. "That's done locally. The original strategy— get these farmers in over their heads, then steal their land— that sort of thing's hatched in New York."

"By my dad, you're saying."

"Actually, I doubt it. CEO might have to approve such a plan, but it's not likely he conceived it."

"You don't really know what the fuck you're talking about."

"Probably right," he says.

She turns toward the house. "Let's go in. Maybe there's some food. At least water. And maybe the phone works."

But the doors, front and back, are locked.

"So?" he says, not liking it. "Break a window?"

"You've never done that?"

Tom finds a rock in the weeds, walks back up to the front porch, smashes a window. They both pause to examine what he has wrought.

"Yeah, okay," she says, "if you clean it off, so we don't slice ourselves up getting in."

He unlocks and raises the window, swipes his jacket at the windowsill, then they both climb inside. They're in the dining room, still furnished, with a dusty old table, chairs, breakfront, all sitting in stale air. The living room is tiny, with ratty furniture, some stuffed, some spindly. They can smell a dog, though none is in evidence. The phone is dead, but there's an old portable radio in the kitchen, which Tom turns on.

"What?" she says.

"News," he says, finding a local station. He listens while she turns on the water tap, lets it run. Then she opens all the cabinets, the old refrigerator, goes into the pantry, comes back with a frown.

"We're in Pennsylvania," he says. "This is coming from Allentown."

"And what? You think they'll have a story about us?" She cups her hand under the faucet and drinks, then ducks to drink some more. Wiping her mouth, she says, "Try it. There's nothing to eat."

He does, drinking lengthily.

"So what do we do?" she says. "Just keep going?"

"Of course."

"Can't be every farm went belly-up."

"Of course not."

"We keep walking, bound to find one."

"Bound to."

"Except I'm pretty wiped," she says.

"So let's grab some winks."

"Jesus."

"What?"

"*Winks?* People still talk that way?"

"Some people," Tom says, laughing. "Come on. My guess is they left the beds."

"Beds. Plural. Got that right."

As they start upstairs, the news intervenes. Robbie Riles is dead. Shot dead in the street. Then: "The police in six states are searching for his daughter, Elena Riles, and her alleged accomplice, Thomas Weldon."

They look at each other. She screams, *"What?"*

"Steady."

"Steady?"

They listen for more details. "Miraculously, on a Manhattan street, there were no witnesses, at least none who has stepped forward. The murder weapon, however, was found in a routine search of the daughter's apartment. Mr. Weldon's girlfriend reported him missing, and a connection was discovered between him and Ms. Riles."

They look at each other stupefied. "What the fuck!" she says.

"Easy."

"I don't know what to feel."

"You're in shock," he says.

"I didn't even like him. I wished him dead. Probably thousands of times."

"You obviously don't mean that."

"No. Yes. I don't know."

"You don't," he says. "I can tell."

"I'm not crying."

"You're in shock."

"I'm not in shock," she insists.

"You wouldn't know."

"I know *that*. As to everything else, I'm confused. I shot my own father? And you're an accomplice? I don't even know you."

"True."

"What kind of connection?" she says. "Have you been stalking me or something?"

"No offense, but until today I'd no idea of your existence."

"Something is really fucked up here."

"That's one way of putting it," he says.

"How would you put it?"

"No, your way's good."

"And you've got a girlfriend," she snaps.

"Had," he says.

"They said *have*."

"I was supposed to move out tonight."

"Great timing."

"Yeah. Whole thing, great timing."

"Let's get out of here," she says.

"Can't sleep?"

"You kidding? I don't know what I'm doing, but sleep is not one of the things in my range right now."

"Okay."

They leave through the front door. Standing on the porch, she says, "I can't believe this. He's dead. I used to think he'd never die."

"Everyone dies."

"That's *really* brilliant, thank you."

"Sorry."

"No," she says. "Anything you say right now will really piss me off."

"I understand."

"No, you don't. Shit. I don't know what to do with myself."
Then she sits on the porch steps and cries.

SIX

Yasim Maktoum views Lower New York Bay lovingly from his bench in Battery Park. The weather is soft, the air salty, the passersby determined on whatever their course, as if freed by the sun to fly in light clothing. Across the water, at the far horizon, a ferry approaches, bringing or returning more passengers to this island. *Come ahead!* Yasim thinks. *Why would you not? It's the best place in the world!*

Yasim vastly prefers living and working in Manhattan, with a weekend house in Rye, to living and working in Dubai. He's loyal to his emir and the Emirates, especially since his substantial income depends on their continuing prosperity. And he's quite valuable to both—one might say indispensable—given his now-intimate knowledge of American banking and bankers. But he's also lived here long enough, patronized enough restaurants, frequented enough clubs, soirees, theaters, etc., to consider himself a real New Yorker.

His contentment is jarred by an older man sporting a tailored suit and a pointed beard, who strolls in from a path behind Yasim and wanders off to the railing, about thirty yards away. There, the man seems either lost in his own thoughts or fascinated by the tide lapping the seawall. He's an olive-skinned man of middle height and middle age—and quite obviously of Middle Eastern heritage. After a while, in which the man shows no interest whatsoever in Yasim, he turns and makes his way directly toward him, across the geometric pavers of the promenade. "Rashid," says Yasim, coolly, in greeting.

"Yassy, my son," says the older man, taking the seat alongside him.

"I am not actually your son, nor do I bear to you either the resemblance, affinity, or disparity of years that would make such a relationship likely."

"So you're not pleased to see me."

"I know why you're here," Yasim says.

"We want you to come home."

"Yes, that's what I said, I know."

"What is more," Rashid says, "we think you should leave immediately."

Yasim looks out over the water.

"You've been here too long," Rashid says. "Just forty, but nearly half your life in this country."

"Don't you people understand? No one suspects me."

"They will."

"Maybe," Yasim says, his voice rising. "If I suddenly go racing off."

"True. That might hasten the suspicion. But then you will be safe."

"I'm irrelevant. The Emirates won't be safe."

"Safe enough," Rashid says. "From questioning."

"You mean safe from the questioning of me!"

Rashid nods.

"You think what?" Yasim says, his high voice already ridiculing what he's about to say. "You think they'd torture me?"

Rashid shrugs.

"Idiot! They don't torture people here."

He gets a look of disbelief.

"Not for something like this," Yasim amends. "This wasn't a terrorist act."

"Depends on one's interpretation, doesn't it?"

"There is no one, Rashid, no one in the entire UAE, as qualified to handle this situation as I."

"I don't dispute that."

"Because I know the scene, I know the people!"

"To be sure."

"Yet you would not only prevent me from handling it, you would compromise my position, the Emirates's position, the position of the entire UAE, by throwing blame in a direction it doesn't now go. I leave peremptorily, as you suggest, someone in law enforcement immediately says, 'Aha!'"

"You are not as sophisticated as you think."

"Oh?"

"For example," Rashid says, "you wanted to have this meeting in your office."

"You think they're bugging my office. See, you know nothing. You're influenced by the movies. To get a wire placed here, you have to go to court, show probable cause. It's a difficult process which they don't even bother with for someone like me. I'm totally above suspicion. I'm a notorious pro-American. They come to me for help, and I give it. Happily. Freely. Because it serves our cause for me to do so. And besides, I have our office swept every single day. Before I get in."

"I've no idea, Yassy, whether the Americans are bugging your office."

"So?"

"I do, however, know that we are."

In a moment of hidden hysteria, Yasim tries to review every conversation he's ever had in that office.

"Easy, dear fellow," says Rashid.

"Why would you tell me this?"

"Have you anything to fear?"

"Words may be misinterpreted."

"Depends on who's listening to the tapes."

"You?"

"Who else?"

"So I repeat," Yasim says. "Why tell me now? And why lead me away to the park?"

"You think *I* want this conversation listened in on?"

Yasim was beginning to understand. "You want something from me."

Rashid laughs.

"What? What is it? How may I be of service?"

"You think you're the only one, dear fellow, who prefers living in New York?"

———

Sun's low, road's straight, landscape's barren.

"It'll be dark soon," Elena says.

"We have another hour, at least."

"Then what do we do?"

"You're trudging," Tom says. "We might get somewhere if you'd actually walk. And not spend so much time at these abandoned farms."

"I found food at the last one."

"Half a jar of peanut butter."

"Exactly," she says. "And I can't go faster in these shoes."

Abruptly, she sits on the side of the road. On both sides, farmland stretches, not entirely flat but totally uncultivated. He's about to complain about their stopping here, when he sees her tears streaming.

"What?" he says gently.

"I was wearing running shoes. I changed for my dad. I promised him a talk at his club. It was already too late, but I changed anyway."

Tom can think of nothing to say.

She says, "So what are we rushing for anyway?"

"A farm that isn't abandoned? A town, maybe?"

"We'll see a car first."

"One that'll stop?"

"Yeah," she says. "What are they doing, driving past? What do we look like, murderers?"

"Listen," he says.

They do. The sound's faint, but it's growing. Then they see it, materializing from the dusty haze of the road.

"Oh, God," he says.

"What's that, a cop car?"

"I think so," he says, peering hard.

They watch it get closer.

"Y'know," he says, "just as well. Sooner we straighten this whole thing out...."

The car arrives and stops. Seaversville PD marked all over it. A male and a female officer emerge with their car radio blaring. Tom and Elena can hear the report. It's all about them.

"So, you two lost?" The woman. She's in charge. Slight, snippy, a bit bulgy in the hips, and suspicious of them.

"We're the two your radio's talking about," Tom says.

"Yeah, figured. Seymour," she says to the other cop, a hairy behemoth whose cap rests on the protuberances of his eyebrows and whose belt bristles with cop paraphernalia.

Seymour says, somewhat gutterally, "Hands on the top of the car, you guys."

"Hey, look you," Elena says. "We need help, not abuse."

The lady cop draws her weapon. "Do what the man says."

"Jesus!" says Elena, slamming her hands on the car roof.

Tom, following suit, says, "Isn't this a little hasty? The gun-drawing bit? We really look to you like dangerous fugitives?"

"According to the reports I'm getting, mister, you two just gunned down an innocent man."

SEVEN

Mike and Dottie Skillan have long looked forward to this night, a celebration of their twentieth wedding anniversary. And Mike isn't the sort of public official to let the demands of the office interfere with his personal plans. They've booked at Le Bernardin. After dinner there's a room waiting for them at the Pierre. During dinner, they have Dottie's favorite topic of conversation: Michael's career.

"Big opportunity, this," she says.

"For what?" he asks. "Self-destruction?" It's an act; she knows it, and he knows she knows it.

"To look wise but prosecutorial, sweetheart. Gubernatorial. Presidential!"

He smiles. They are very well suited to each other. His physical ideal might run to small skinny women, but she is he in female form. And not only in a broad-faced, big-boned way. They have the same tastes, from colors to types of entertainment to variations of sex play, about which both of them are avid. They think the same things are funny. And most important of all, they have the same object in life: his elevation to high office. The one difference between them, and it's not small, is that he's far from sure he's willing to do everything required to achieve such a goal, whereas she has neither doubts nor qualms on the subject.

"Aren't we getting a bit—"

"Ahead of ourselves?" she says. "I think not. What's needed, of course, is to stay ahead of events. To shape them. Which you are ideally situated to do."

"The girl may be innocent."

"Then don't overcommit. The pose you should strike is as one who weighs both sides judiciously before coming down hard."

He laughs. "You should do PR."

"I do do PR, darling."

"And very well too."

"You do see the opportunity."

"To fuck up. I see that."

"How can you fuck up?" she says. "You don't indict her unless you're absolutely sure."

"Are *you* absolutely sure?"

"Well, no one likes her," Dottie points out.

"That's not the question."

"Pretty damn close. And look at the evidence. Already. The gun! The fact she bought it illegally! Her secret liaison with this lawyer who just happens to come along! Then they both flee. I mean, how much do you need, for crissakes? What are they fleeing *from*, if not their crime? And she stands to inherit billions!"

"Which she would have done in any event," Mike notes.

"Some people are more impatient than others."

"Enough to kill a parent?" he says. "In the street?"

"She obviously wanted to make it look like a robbery."

"Which is why no money appears to have been taken."

"You can't know that," she says.

"There were hundreds of dollars in his wallet."

"He might have had thousands."

"If she were trying to make it look like a robbery, why would she leave anything?"

"So as to make it not look so obvious that she was trying to make it look like a robbery."

He laughs indulgently at this.

"Their relations were notoriously strained," she adds.

"Look, baby. Robbie Riles had strained relations with half the civilized world. Because he himself was barely civilized. He was a landlord to thousands, a moneylender to nations, and the owner of an international financial scandal sheet. More people hated him than Stalin."

"Including his daughter."

"Some evidence does point to her, which is why we're picking her up. But there's not quite enough yet for an indictment."

"Except by the press," she says.

"The press, of course, is happy to indict anyone."

"What more could you want?"

"Fingerprints, for one."

"The gun was in her apartment!" she says.

"And we'll have the prints any minute."

"On the gun?"

"There are prints on the gun. We need to match them to prints identifiable as hers."

His cell phone rings. "Yes?" he says, muffling the word with his hand cupped over his mouth and the phone. He listens. "Good," he says. Then turns to his wife. "We have them, the prints. They match."

"Wow," she says quietly.

"It's pretty strong."

"Maybe you should get back to the office."

"Joe can handle it," he says.

"*Joe?* Let Joe get in front of the cameras, instead of you?"

"Then I'll get the cameras up here?"

"In front of Le Bernardin?" she says. "A five-star restaurant?"

With wry amusement: "You want me to go back downtown? Tonight?"

She stares at him as if to say, *If you're joking, I'm not laughing.*

He turns around. "Waiter! Check please."

EIGHT

On the way to the Seaversville police station, Seymour, who is driving, and his superior officer, who is watching the fugitives in the back seat, consider their strategy for the evening.

"We should call Hollister," says Seymour.

"Did that. He's not exactly communicating at the moment."

"You mean he's drunk?" Seymour says.

"Draw your own conclusions."

"Well, it wasn't me who talked to him, was it, Becky?"

With alarm showing on her face, she resorts to a deep whisper. "Was it, *who*? You're calling me by, *what*? In front of the—" She jerks her head back.

"You used *my* name!" he whispers back.

"That's entirely different."

"Sorry, Sergeant."

"Keep your head in the game, Seymour. And consider what we're gonna do with these prisoners."

"Do with 'em? Oh shit. We only have the one cell now."

"That's the problem," she says. "However—"

"You gonna put 'em both in the same cell?" he whispers. "Man and woman?"

"They look pretty cozy to me, actually."

"I don't like it," he says. "I wanna be on record, I don't like it."

Her whisper is now sibilant. "What would you like, eh? What's your alternative? We let one go?"

"No. Course not."

"So?"

"When they getting picked up?" Seymour asks.

"In the morning. First thing."

"Okay," says Seymour. "So we put the guy in the cell and guard her in the office. Handcuff her to a chair or something. Chairs are bolted to the floor."

"We're not fucking handcuffing a woman to a chair. Not on my watch."

"What then?"

"They killed together," she says. "They've been running together. They're both going in the fucking cell."

The car pulls up to a one-story cinderblock building in the middle of the one-street shopping area of the Pennsylvania town. Tom and Elena, both handcuffed, are taken from the car and led into the building. As they enter a small front office with three desks, a television left on is blaring an impromptu news conference being given on the street at One Hogan Place by Deputy Chief New York District Attorney Joe Cunningham. Becky, Seymour, Elena, and Tom all stop in their tracks and listen.

"The prints on the gun match hers," says Cunningham. "That's all I can tell you at the moment."

At least three reporters ask at once, "So you'll indict?"

"That's District Attorney Skillan's decision."

"And the guy, Weldon?" asks the beat writer for the News.

"We're waiting on Mr. Skillan."

"So where is he?"

"Heading here as we speak."

"You're here, he's not?"

"All right guys. I know what you want. Forget it."

The four in Seaversville watch Cunningham push through the crowd to get into the building.

"Show's over," says Becky, and directs them into the cell room in back.

Two cells, a solid wall divider, but one cell is gutted and missing a door.

Elena glances at the reconstruction scene and says, "You putting us in the same cell?"

"Just until the New York van gets here," Becky replies. "You got a problem with that?"

Tom jumps in, "No problem."

"You?" Becky asks Elena.

Elena looks at Tom. "We'll see."

They're herded inside the cell, with Becky covering, her pistol drawn. The cell door is slammed and locked. Then Becky directs both to extend their arms through the bars for Seymour to remove their cuffs.

"You can drink the water," Becky says, heading out, Seymour trailing.

"Other amenities?" Tom asks.

"Sure," says Seymour. "There's a cot."

"What happens when we have to use the toilet?"

Becky stops in the doorway, making Seymour halt too. "Look, you two. We know you're ... together, so to speak. So, best for everyone? You're adults, work it out." The two police officers leave.

Tom and Elena look at each other. "This is ridiculous," Elena says. "The sooner we get back to the city—"

"Don't think so," says Tom. "I seriously doubt it's going to be wonderful back in New York."

"Maybe not wonderful, but we'll straighten it out. Throw on the lawyers. Common sense. No one's gonna believe I shot my own father."

"They already believe it."

"That's the press," Elena says.

"The guy we just heard? Joe Cunningham. He's the Chief Deputy DA. He believes it."

"He's a moron," she says. "And probably a pol who thinks

he's gonna get something out of it."

"Maybe. But he's hardly acting in a vacuum."

"So what do *you* think?" she says. "*You* think we did it? We were there, we should know."

"They found the gun in your apartment," he says. "With your prints. How'd that get there?"

She blows her cheeks out. "Someone's framing me. Obviously. It's the guys who kidnapped us. Or whoever they're working for. After they blindfolded me, they stuck something in my hand for a moment. You missed that. You were unconscious."

He looks at her as if to say, *I didn't have to see it.*

"I'm in a frame," she expostulates. "It's what I've been saying."

"Deep frame," he says. "*That's* the point. And not just you. Someone's gone to the trouble of creating records of phone calls between us. You have any idea how hard it is to do that?"

"Some, yeah."

"And my guess—that's only a small piece of it. For example, those two clowns, Becky and Seymour, were looking for us. They knew exactly who we were when they found us. How'd that happen? This is a boondocks town in Pennsylvania. New York puts our names out on a general tape to a bunch of states along with a bunch of other names, none of which does any boondocks town pay the slightest attention to. Unless they've been tipped. And who knew enough about our whereabouts to give special warning to the police department of Seaversville, Pennsylvania?"

"Hmm," she says. "You sure about this?"

"And a lot of other things. Like tomorrow morning, before we're shipped back to New York, there's got to be an extradition hearing. We have a right to counsel on that hearing and a right to be there. And until that hearing is held, Pennsylvania cops have no right to turn us over to New York cops. So what the hell is the story about we go directly from a PA jailhouse into a New York van?"

"So you're saying what? The cops are in on the frame?"

He shrugs. "Something's happening. Something bad. Your father was a very powerful guy. Whoever's responsible for shooting him is probably equally powerful. And there's probably a whole lot more evidence. Maybe even a witness."

"Jesus!"

"You don't think they could manufacture a witness?" he says.

"No, I'm totally getting it."

"And if we go back to New York, while we're trying to dig ourselves out, where do you think we're spending our days?"

She looks sick.

"Rikers, probably," he says. "Where you wouldn't be *too* conspicuous. Billionaire heiress?"

"So what are you saying now?"

"I don't think we ought to wait for the van."

"A fucking prison break?" she says. "Who the hell do you think we are? Bonnie and Clyde?"

"Shouldn't be that hard. And this isn't exactly a prison."

"Okay, mastermind. Say we do that somehow. Then what's next?"

"We get lost in America?"

"Living on what?"

"What we earn?" he says.

"Jobs? Without social security numbers?"

"There are ways."

"Sounds great," she says. "How long? You're gonna say, until they find the actual murderers, but until they find us, they won't even look. So if I gotta chose between living some dingy kind of life forever and trying my hand at staying outta Rikers and breaking the frame—how do you think I'm leaning?"

"All right," he says.

"All right what?"

"You're not going, I'm not going."

"Why?" she says. "What's stopping you?"

"My plan requires two people."
"You got a plan? Already?"
"Of course."
"And what about for when we get out—*if* we get out?"
"Got a plan for that too," he says.

NINE

What the fuck you doing, Joe?" Mike Skillan, in his office, rips off his jacket and slams it down on his chair, which Joe correctly interprets as a sign to stay standing.

"I got ambushed, Mike. On my way into the office. Right after I called you. They already had the story. Had had it almost an hour. They knew about the prints."

"*I* didn't know about the prints then. How the fuck did *they* know about the prints?"

Joe heaves a sigh. "Beats the shit outta me, Mike. But they fuckin' well did. You can check. Sammy was there."

Mike doesn't like this, he doesn't like anything about it. "In the future—"

"I know, Mike. I got blindsided. No more answering questions, unless you tell me to do it."

Mike picks up his jacket, drapes it on the back of the chair, sits, stares at his assistant who's still standing. "Y'know the worst thing about this? It's forcing our hand."

"Pretty fat hand, Mike."

"And will probably get fatter. Know why?"

"I'd say because she did it, and is an amateur. Probably panicked and started leaving clues all over the place. Sorry Mike. Not buying into that 'she may have been framed' theory."

"So let's think again," Mike says. "How'd the press know about the prints before you found out?"

"A leak in the lab," Joe suggests. "Don't worry, I'm on that."

"Good. And while you are, also check out exactly who the information went to, in what sequence, and at what time."

"News like that," Joe says, "could spread fast in the department. Maybe dozens knew before I did."

"So find out."

"This some kind of witch hunt?" Joe says, voice getting cautious. "Guys talk to the press here. Always have. We're not gonna stop it. Let me issue some new directives, scare people a bit, but I really don't think we're so porous in general we need to start tying people to stakes."

"I'm not talking about random leaks to the press."

"Oh, shit, what? Conspiracy theory?"

"That's right, Joe. That's one of the things possible. And to me, at least as plausible as a young woman with no record of mental illness or crime suddenly shooting her father in the middle of the street."

Joe frowns. "Dammit, Mike. The case against this woman is fucking overwhelming."

"A flood. Right. Probably, in two minutes, a tsunami."

"That's what I'm saying."

"When're we getting the daughter here?" Mike asks. "I'll wanna talk to her."

"By noon. Latest."

Sammy bursts in. "We have a witness," he says. "Eyewitness. To the Riles killing. Thought you should know right away."

TEN

Elena screaming for five minutes brings both cops back into the cell room, whereupon Becky screams back, "What the hell you screaming about?"

Elena clamps down immediately. "This guy," she says. "I want him outta here."

"Oh yeah? Why's that?"

"He's groping me, what do you think?"

"I don't believe it."

"Exactly," says Tom. "It's bullshit. She's hysterical."

"Oh yeah? Wanna see the bruise marks?" says Elena to Becky. "Let's go into the ladies room, I'll show you."

Becky looks uncertain.

"I'll tell you, Sergeant. I get outta here, I'm going right to the press. The jailhouse in Seaversville? They lock men and women together in cells!"

"All right,' says Becky. "You come out here with us. You're not gonna like it."

"Because why?" says Elena, heading toward Becky. "You're gonna chain me to a pipe or something? Or to one of those steel chairs? This is a jailhouse where they chain women to chairs?"

Becky halts her with a jab to the shoulder. "Then you," she says, pointing to Tom.

"What?" he says, all innocence.

"Out here."

"*I'm* getting chained now? Pretty damn sexist."

"Get out here!" she commands, unsheathing her pistol.

He obeys, leaving the cell. Seymour slams it shut on Elena and locks her in. With Becky waving the gun nervously toward the doorway, Tom leads the procession to the outer room.

The rest goes amazingly easily.

Becky points to a chair; Tom sits in it. Seymour bends to start cuffing Tom's leg to the chair leg. Becky starts shouting at once, "Dammit, Seymour, the arms first!"

Too late. Tom yanks Seymour's gun from its holster while at the same time shoving the distracted, squatting man's shoulder, bouncing him on his butt.

As Seymour makes a move to get up, Tom, himself rising, says, more calmly than he feels, "I just shot a billionaire, Seymour. You think I'd have any qualms about shooting you?" Then, swinging the gun toward Becky with menace, "Or, for that matter, you?"

She stands there, too angry and frightened to speak. But dangerous with a gun still in her hand.

Tom summons a convincing laugh. "You think they would've hired an amateur for the job I just did? And having done it—for me, you two are just collateral damage." He aims Seymour's gun at her forehead.

Becky carefully lowers her weapon to the floor.

Tom says, "I'd like you, Seymour, to take those cuffs and attach the sergeant to the chair you'd intended for me." And into their stupefied faces he yells, "Now!"

Tom supervises their carrying out his directions. "Above the crossbar, Seymour!"

Gesturing with the pistol toward the back room, Tom says, "Before cuffing you, my friend, let's release the young woman, shall we?"

One last glance at Becky as she glares at the floor.

Mike and Joe, through the two-way, watch Sammy Riegert question Horace Moon, nighttime janitor of the Riles Whitney building and alleged witness to the shooting of Robertson Riles. Horace, a slender middle-aged man in a good but frayed suit and rumpled shirt and tie, waits attentively for the next question.

"So let's hear it again," Sammy says. "Every detail. What you saw and heard."

"After Mr. Riles went out of the building?"

"Right," Sammy says. "You say his car wasn't there?"

"Didn't see it."

"You know his driver?"

"Not really," Horace says. "I know what he looks like."

"And he wasn't there?"

"Didn't see the man."

"So what did you see?"

"A girl with a gun."

Sammy shows him a newspaper photograph of Elena walking the street with some punk-looking guy. "Ever see her around before?"

"Yeah, that's her, I think."

"The one with the gun who came over to Riles?"

"That's right," Horace says.

"Then what happened?"

"She shot him."

"Just like that?"

"Seemed so."

"How much time elapsed between her walking over to him and her shooting him?"

"No time. She just did it."

"How far away were you?"

"Oh … thirty, maybe forty feet."

"You wear glasses?"

"They're reading glasses. For distance, I see just fine."

"So was there anyone else there?"

"Yeah, this guy in a suit."

"This guy?" Sammy says, showing him another photo.

"That's him."

"And?"

"They took off."

"What did you do?"

"When I stopped shaking?" Horace says. "Went to my room in the basement."

"What took you so long to come forward?"

"Figured it out, finally." Horace says. "Trouble I'd get into if I didn't seemed worse than the trouble if I did."

Foster Donachetti picks his moments. He glides into the one open chair next to Mike Skillan in front of the two-way. Jacketless, in the dark room, he still looks dressed up. "That's the good news," he says, referring to the witness, Moon.

"All right," says Mike. "What's the bad?"

"The suspects? Flown, if you can believe it. Somehow managed to bust out of the lockup in Seaversville, PA."

Mike laughs. "Sure digging themselves deeper. "Who's out looking?"

"Allentown, Wilkes-Barre, Scranton, others."

"Shouldn't be that hard to find." He heads towards the door.

"Where you going?" Joe asks.

"If you need me," Mike says, "really need me—I'm at the Pierre. But it better be earth-shattering."

ELEVEN

The sun rises through the back window of the truck—an eighteen-wheeler loaded with canned beer. Tom and Elena bump along in the cabin, listening to some unknown country and western singer wailing about not getting laid. Roy, their driver and ostensible benefactor, who just picked them up off the road, sings along in a decent basso, radiating bonhomie. He's a giant—they could tell even though he's sitting—but he's got a bad back, which is a serious disability for a truck driver. His seat is outfitted with back supports and magnets, and sudden moves make him wince. The truck carries enough canned beer to supply a city, he tells them. "City of Cincinnati, yep," says Roy over the road noise and the music.

"Good luck for us," Tom says, studying the man's large, puffy, bearded face.

"Big coincidence, then, my going to Cincy?"

"Sure is."

"I say Ohio, and you say us too?"

"Happens."

Roy gives out a loud guffaw and snaps off the radio. "Hey! Guys! Who you kidding? I know who you are."

"Oh yeah?" Tom says. "Who's that, then?"

"You being coy?"

"No, Roy, just cautious."

"Okay. Who, then, was it broke outta the Seaversville jailhouse last night? Am I right, or am I right? Who then's all over the friggin' airwaves?" His self-satisfied smirk is illuminated, and made gruesome, by the new light of the day.

"If you thought that was us," Tom says, "aren't you taking a big chance?"

Another loud laugh. Then, low-voiced, condescendingly, "I don't think so."

"Well, we're certainly grateful for the lift."

"I'll bet. This is like your getaway car." Roy now smiles with some secret thought. "How 'bout the girl? She grateful too?"

"Sure am, Roy," says Elena.

"Good," Roy says. "So here's the deal."

"Not just a favor, then," Tom says.

"Sure it's a favor. But there's a way you can pay part of it back. I happen to need twelve thousand dollars. If it wasn't a favor, I ask for twenty-five, minimum."

"You do this often, then?" Tom asks.

Roy looks confused.

"Your having a standard rate, I mean," Tom says.

"It's worth a helluva lot more than twelve thousand, what I'm doin' for you."

"Pretty expensive, Roy. It's just a lift."

"I could stop. You could get out."

"Don't think so."

"Price is now twelve-five."

"Make it anything you want. We don't have that kind of money on us."

"Hey!" Roy says. "No problemo! We are fortunate to live in a digital world." He lifts one hand off the wheel, as if delivering a sermon. "Been an invention, man! Called a wire transfer!"

TWELVE

Teddy Stamos is a short man with a jutting jaw and large nose. He walks with a nodding cadence and a forward tilt. As a result, he makes a pugnacious appearance, as if cutting a swath, or searching for something to pounce on. And while his suit is exquisitely cut, and his haberdashery expensive, he creates the impression of an overdressed frog.

This, at least, is how Lowell Jockery sees him, as the man comes bobbing into his office, though Lowell knows Teddy is competent, even creative, at what he does. Stamos founded and still heads an international firm of private investigators, which Jockery has had frequent occasion to use. Creativity is not normally a hallmark of such a profession, but the matter now involved requires it. What's more, the present part of that job is of such a sensitive nature that Jockery trusts no one but himself to assign it, and no one but Stamos to carry it out.

"So, Teddy," says Lowell without preamble, "what think you today of General Technology & Media Corporation?"

"After four down quarters, I'd say it's ripe, LJ. Quite … ripe."

"And whom would you identify as the most likely swallower of that plum? Apart from ourselves, of course."

"Robbie Riles was said to be keen. But, of course, he's gone."

"He is, yes," says Lowell musingly, as if he'd just thought of that too. "And what about Julian Althus?"

"I should think equally keen but far less powerful and certainly more distracted. At the moment, by the succession."

"Be good, Teddy, if you could find more with which to distract him."

"Althus?" Teddy asks.

"Well, say, the GT&M shareholders. About Althus."

"Hmm," says the little man. "More."

"You're not following?"

"In a general way, yes. Of course. But specifically … not quite yet, LJ. As usual, you're some steps ahead of me."

"Well, the man he's replacing was just shot down in the street."

"Riles. So he was," Teddy says, as if enjoying this sharing of news. "They're thinking it was the daughter and her lover."

"So they are," Jockery says. "And so it probably was. But are they the only ones with a motive? And who's to say they were acting alone?"

"Oh, I see."

"Yes, I thought you would."

"Indeed, Julian Althus *is* a likely suspect," Teddy says.

"Isn't he though!"

"So I'll get going on this."

"We don't need that much," Lowell points out.

"The merest suspicion…."

"Would do nicely, yes."

"And the timing?" asks Teddy.

"Yes, timing is key. Assemble the information as quickly as possible. And the ability to use it, of course—witnesses and so forth."

"The ability to strike when we need to."

"Exactly," Jockery says. "When we know he's in and in favor of the acquisition."

"Oh, LJ, this is brilliant." Teddy rises from the chair, which has the peculiar effect of diminishing his height—at least any appearance of it. But his broad face takes on the smile of the practiced flatterer. "If I might just say, LJ—"

"Don't, Teddy. No need."

As Teddy bows himself from the room, Lowell's secretary puts through a call.

"Rex, darling," gushes a female voice. "You left this morning without planting a single kiss on my glorious bod!"

THIRTEEN

"So this is how it's going down," says Roy, having pulled over on a back road in the middle of miles of cornfields. He twists around to fish a laptop from behind his seat. "Either me dumping you on your asses in this godforsaken spot, then calling the cops on the tail end of my bye-byes, or you emailing your banker right now, wire transferring the twelve five, I of course giving you my account number, etcetera."

Elena says, "That is pretty high tech of you, Roy."

"Yeah, well."

"Trouble is," says Elena, "I don't have the money."

"You're a fucking billionaire!"

"See, people make that mistake about me. It's my father who's got all the money. Had, anyway. I don't take from him. I'm a writer. I don't have a dime."

"This is total bullshit!" says Roy.

"No, I believe her," says Tom.

"You shut the fuck up."

"Calm down," Tom says. "I have the money."

"Do you?"

"I do. But how can we trust you?"

"Me? Easy. What fucking incentive do I have to turn you in? In fact, I tell on you, then you tell on me, the money incriminates me—it's a lose-lose."

Tom looks at Elena. She shakes her head. He says, "Okay. Let me have the laptop."

"You'll do it?" Roy says, a little surprised.

"Just watch me."

Roy, looking skeptical, nonetheless hands it over.

Tom's fingers flash.

"You need the transfer info," Roy says.

"Just a sec." Tom types some more, clicks on "send," then hands the laptop back to Roy, who retrieves the sent message.

"Who the hell's Perry Rauschenberg?"

"My lawyer," says Tom.

"I thought you were a lawyer."

"I am. But lawyers need lawyers. You know what they say. A lawyer who represents himself has a fool for a client."

"Oh yeah?"

"That's the fact."

"And what the hell's this?" Roy says with considerable outrage.

"That's me telling my lawyer to charge you with attempted extortion, which is a felony, if you do what you're threatening."

Roy, with the face of a sullen child, says, "You didn't have to do that."

"I know. I could have just given you the money. But Roy, you were beginning to piss me off. So y'know what? *Now* it's lose-lose for you."

"Get the fuck outta my car."

"You got it, man," Tom says, reaching over Elena to open the cab door. Then to her, "Go, go!" And they scamper.

Revving the motor of an eighteen-wheeler can make a horrible groaning noise, with the gravel kicking up like a sandstorm. Tom and Elena dive out of range, but as Roy's truck barrels out of sight, she seems wistful.

"Maybe we should have given him the money," she says.

"Don't think so."

'We're in the middle of nowhere again."

"Not quite."

She points at the bleak horizon of corn. "So your point being what? There are working farms here? Big deal. We're escaped cons! What are we going to do? Walk into some house and say, Hi folks, can we please use your telephone?"

"No, I think we should get out of the area, probably out of Ohio."

"Terrific idea," she says. "Your helicopter or mine?"

"I thought we might take the train," he says.

"The train," she repeats dully.

"About a mile back, there was a crossing. We drove over some tracks."

"You've some reason to believe that trains still run on those tracks?"

"Only one way to find out," he says.

"We stand there and wait."

"Exactly," he says.

"A passenger train, no doubt, will come right along. With a dining car. Maybe we can get business class."

"I wouldn't count on that, no."

"So you want us to hop a freight," she says.

"That's what I'm suggesting, yes."

"Assuming one actually arrives."

He shrugs.

"And is moving slowly," she says, "with a door open."

"That would be convenient, yes."

"With no desperate characters hovering inside."

"We're pretty desperate ourselves," he says, "if you think about it."

"I don't have to think about it."

"So, let's go?"

"We have an alternative?"

FOURTEEN

Yasim is lunching with Birdie O'Shane in a suite at the Sherry-Netherland on Fifth Avenue. Both wear hotel terry-cloth robes; they have just bathed after indulging in an hour of voluptuous sex. Birdie is one of the reasons Yasim wants to stay in New York. For a UAE official in high power, she is acceptable, barely, as an occasional trophy escort in Manhattan but would be impossible as an openly kept mistress in Dubai.

Yasim spreads a slice of duck pâté onto a toast wedge and hands it to Birdie, then admiringly watches her eat. She has fine, white, even teeth, conferred by genes, not orthodontists. She is also tall—half a head taller than he—slender and blond. Arabic women of high birth aren't slender; few are tall; and none, of course, blond, by nature or otherwise. Birdie, he thinks, isn't terribly bright, but to Yasim this is also a virtue. He has little idea, long term, what he will do with her. He knows only he would regret losing her now.

Birdie works at the consulate. Yasim hired her. That's how they met. At the time, he felt a need to have a young Western woman of statuesque beauty in the building to enhance the cosmopolitan aura he was attempting to create. He preferred a British accent, and mentioned in the interview that his ad had required this.

"But it didn't say," she noted, "that I had to *be* English. I'm an actress. I can do any accent you please."

Not very well, as it turned out. But in the end, it didn't

matter. She spent a week slaughtering BBC posh, until Yasim said, "Just be your own dear natural self." By that time she'd already taken her clothes off for him.

Yasim dips an outlandishly large shrimp into cocktail sauce and bites off a bit of it. His mobile gyrates in his bathrobe pocket. He sneaks a peek. No one from the Emirates, for whom he's on call 24/7. "I'll have to go to Dubai for a while," he says.

Birdie's role, played flawlessly, is that she's built a life around Yasim, which is far better than the dodgy sort of jobless existence she'd been leading before. "How long is a while?"

"Not very long."

"That's not an answer."

"Only one I have, sorry."

"So take me with you."

"You wouldn't like it."

"Really?" she says. "The pictures look great."

"They're for the tourists."

"Oh, I know. But we could stay in those parts."

Yasim laughs at her innocence.

"You have a home there?" she asks, as if the thought had just come to her.

"I keep a flat."

"Oh yeah, what's it like?"

"Very functional."

"How many bedrooms?"

"One plus a spare."

"So you're married, after all? Is that why I can't come with you?"

"I'm not married, and I'm not going over there for pleasure. I'm going there so that I may stay here. And I plan to be there for as little time as I need to in order to ensure that."

"They want you to leave the consulate?" she says with alarm.

"There's at least one person with that idea. And he's now here. I'm going back to find out whether anyone over there is actually entertaining the same notion. And if they are, to stop it from going any further. Do you understand, darling?"

"Of course. So maybe I could help."

"You can. But here."

"You want me to work on that guy?"

"I want you to watch him for me. And one more thing. You remember three nights ago?"

"Sure."

"Where were we?"

She looks mystified as to why he's asking. "At the Hotel Du Pont. In Wilmington, Delaware."

"Working late, right. Did I have any phone calls, or did I make any?"

She shakes her head, now looking a little frightened. "I can't remember."

"I want you to remember. I didn't. Remember *that*."

"Okay," she says uncertainly.

"And two nights ago?"

"Two nights ago?" she repeats. "I wasn't with—"

"Same place, same answer."

"Okay."

"You may be asked those questions while I'm gone."

"What's this about, Yassy? Who's gonna ask?"

"Anybody. Cops, anyone."

"Cops?"

"Don't worry about it."

"Why would cops … what the fuck happened two nights ago, Yassy?"

"A man got killed, someone who loaned lots of money to the Emirate of Dubai and was about to call the loan."

"How much money?"

"What difference does it make? Several billions."

"So they think you killed him?" she says. "Is that really why you're going back?"

"On the contrary. They don't think I had anything to do with it. That's why I have to stay here. That and you, my darling."

"So why would the cops be coming around? To me?"

"Routine. You work for me. But I'm not sure they will. I simply want you prepared."

"Prepared is good, but I'm smarter than you think, y'know."

"I think you're very smart."

"No, you don't," she says. "You've got me down as a ditz. For example, if the cops asked about your getting calls in Delaware, I'd have said, 'Oh, no. He always turns his phone off when he's with me.'"

"You know, sweet, what you tell the cops can be made public."

"So?"

"You like your job?"

"I could lose my job?"

"Going public with our affair—"

"Oh, I get it."

"So…."

"I am a ditz."

"Of course you're not. I simply want you to know, I'm striving for both of us."

"I see, Yassy, I do. I'd say or do anything for you!"

"I know you would," he says, and almost believes it.

FIFTEEN

Tom and Elena, sitting on the north side of the tracks, watch yet another long train speeding past. The line is in use, which is the good news. But the cars going by are neither open nor sufficiently sluggish for them to attempt climbing on. They've chosen a relatively straight stretch of track, giving them a view due east of about a fifth of a mile until the track bends into a tunnel of foliage.

"Great idea you had," Elena says.

"You mean the one about catching a slow-moving freight train?"

"That's the one, yes."

"It would seem to require," he says, "a bit more patience than you have."

"More than you'd expect from my condition."

"You're pregnant?"

"Very funny," she says.

"Hungry?"

"Starving, on the edge of extinction."

"In that case...."

"What?" she says. "You're hoarding food?"

"Hoarding?"

"Tom, do you have food?"

"I can see you're desperate," he says, retrieving a sandwich from the right side pocket of his suit jacket.

She stares at it with disbelief. "Where'd you get that?"

"It's Seymour's."

"You stole Seymour's lunch?"

"I did," he says, handing it to her.

"Did he have only the one sandwich?"

"No, there's another."

"Well, eat it!"

"I'm not close to death."

"You eat that damn sandwich," she says, "or I'm not eating mine, and I *am* close to death."

Laughing, he pulls the other sandwich from his left side pocket, but then scrambles to his feet. "What's that?"

Elena also stands, listening.

Then, plainly, there's rumbling on the tracks.

"It's moving slowly," she says in almost a whisper, at the same time rewrapping and handing back her sandwich. He stuffs both back into the pockets from which they came.

Then the train emerges on the bend, indeed moving slowly and, indeed, with several doors wide open.

The train approaches. "Which car?" she calls, starting to run alongside the tracks.

"Just pick one," he says, following.

They position themselves for the leap.

"You go first," he says, running faster, "and I'll kind of push you up."

"Okay, but you damn well better get on the same car!"

"Okay. This one!" he yells over the din and clattering of the train. "There's a handlebar at the side!" Elena grabs hold, and there appears in the doorway of the car a grizzled geezer who reaches down to yank her up. Then, as Tom hoists himself onto the train, the old man flashes a knife at both of them.

SIXTEEN

Julian Althus's secretary signals her boss. "Sir, there's a Mr. Theodore Stamos on line one. Are you available?"

He has to think about that.

"Sir?"

"Tell him … never mind, I'll pick up." He does. And says curtly, "Yes?"

"Mr. Althus?"

"Speaking."

"This is Theodore Stamos."

"What can I do for you, Mr. Stamos?"

"I run a private—"

"I know who you are. Why the call?"

"I'd very much like to talk to you."

"We seem to be in the process of doing that."

"About Mr. Riles's death."

"Who are you working for, Mr. Stamos?"

"I'm afraid I can't tell you that."

"Then I don't see why I should continue this conversation."

"Because—and you should believe this—it can only be to your advantage."

"Oh, yes?" Julian says skeptically. "How so?"

"Well, the DA's people will be upon you quite soon."

"Upon me? And how do you know such a thing?"

"That's my business, Mr. Althus, knowing things."

"And the questions they'll ask me? You know those too?"

"The important ones, I do."

Julian, rising, carries the phone to the window. "Where are you now?" he says, looking down.

"In the lobby of your building, sir."

"Perhaps …" Julian reflects on the people scurrying about on the streets. "No, wait. There's a diner, near the corner of Fifty-Second and Ninth Avenue. I'll meet you there."

"You'll recognize me?"

"I told you. I know who you are."

"And I you, sir."

"Then why did you ask?"

"It's my way of learning things," Teddy says. "To know that you recognize my face as well as my name—that's a useful bit, sir."

"You're a dealer in bits?"

"Oh, I am, sir. Most definitely. The bits do add up."

—⁓—

Teddy is seated facing the door in the farthest booth from it. There's a full cup of coffee in front of him. His hand rises slightly at the wrist in a coy little wave as Julian enters. The executive sits across from the private detective and observes him, as if studying a specimen beneath glass. "Pretty brash of you, calling me," Julian says.

"I suppose. But the shortest distance between two points—"

"Is a straight line, to be sure. But what is the point of your points, Mr. Stamos?"

"Teddy. Please."

"Very well." Julian's mouth twists in distaste. "Teddy."

"I know you'll soon be visited by the Manhattan District Attorney's office; I know why, and I know what they'll ask you. You'd like to know what I know. I'd like to know what you know about the killing of Robbie Riles. I'm of course suggesting we barter the information, a simple quid pro quo."

"All right … Teddy. You go first."

"I spill everything I know, then trust that you will too?"

"Precisely."

"It's not how we do it."

"No?" Julian says. "Why not?"

"We haven't established trust."

"And how do we do that?"

"It's a sort of striptease," says Teddy.

"Oh, yes?"

"I give you a bit, you give me a bit, then I give a bit more, and so on."

"I see."

"I've done this before, you know."

"I'll bet you have."

Teddy laughs. "The DA wants to know what you know about how and why Robbie Riles got killed."

"That's not much of a bit," Julian says.

"Okay. The guy they're sending to interview you is Sammy Riegert. He's in the trial division. Works for Foster Donachetti. Pretty high up."

"Which my secretary could have found out when she scheduled the interview."

"So now you have it sooner."

"I don't even know yet that it's true."

"Trust me."

"I thought the point of this exercise was to earn it."

"And what would you like? I keep feeding you information until you tell me at the end you know nothing?"

"We're wasting time, Teddy. The fact is I *don't* know anything. I can only guess why Robbie was shot, as can you, but I don't know. Likewise, I don't know who shot him. And since I wasn't there when it was done, I've little idea how it was done."

"It's pretty clear the daughter did it."

"Oh, really?"

"With a male accomplice."

"If you say so," says Julian in a bored tone.

"Okay, I'll give you this, gratis. You know the accomplice is a lawyer. In fact, he works for the firm that's your outside counsel. And what the DA is interested in is whether they were acting alone or with some additional accomplice. Someone who might not have been there on the night, so to speak, but backed them in some way, was part of this. And they suspect that someone might have been you, Julian. That's why they're coming to see you. So you see, that's pretty good information. I get paid a lot of money for information like that."

"Why gratis, then?"

"Maybe, after all, you caught me in a festive, Christmassy sort of mood."

"It's July."

"For me, Julian, the reality is … giving to one's fellow man is always in season. Especially if the fellow in question is about to become CEO."

SEVENTEEN

I want all your money, and I want she should take all her clothes off," says the hobo to the frightened pair huddling in the far corner of the railroad car. He's a short bearded man in a purple T-shirt that seems in the dim light to say "Beni" over the picture of a cleaver.

"Forget it," Tom says. "It's not gonna happen."

"I want that!"

"You can want all you like."

"You see this knife?" says Beni, thrusting it in their direction.

"Yeah, I see it," Tom says, shrugging out of his jacket and wrapping it around his arm. "But you come near us with that knife, and I'm gonna take it from you. You wanna know why? Because I'm bigger and stronger than you and not whacked out on drugs. And when I've got the knife, then what are you going to do?"

The hobo thinks about that, his face furrowing in sunbaked grooves. "I'll cut ya!" he says and jumps forward a step.

"I'll cut you worse!"

Which seems to confuse him.

"You get back, Beni!"

The train rumbles on, farmland, woods. They're out in the country, and it could be any country. The man lowers the knife. "You got any money?"

"Not a dime," Tom says.

"What the fuck good are yer?"

"We can give you a sandwich."

"Oh, yeah?"

"Oh, yeah. Pretty good too."

Elena says, "You're giving him your sandwich?"

"I thought we might split the other one."

"While this bum gets a whole sandwich just 'cause he has a knife?"

"He's obviously starving."

"That wasn't his first thought."

"You're right." Tom turns back to the hobo. "Okay, new terms. I'll give you half of my sandwich for information. Like where's this train going?"

"You said a whole sandwich."

"Sorry. We don't like your manners, so the terms have changed. Half a sandwich and you're lucky to get that."

"Son of a bitch."

"Life *is* a bitch," Tom notes, "but it's a lot easier if you're nice to people. And you'd better hurry. That offer could be withdrawn any time."

"Kentucky."

"This train's going to Kentucky?"

"Damn straight. Ashaway."

"Oh yeah? What's there?"

"Never been. Steel mill, I think."

"Okay. You give me the knife, I'll give you this delicious half sandwich."

"Hey! I ain't givin' you no knife! You said nothin' about that."

"That's the deal, mister. You give me the knife, I'll give it back to you when we get off or you do."

"Fuck that."

"As you wish," says Tom, handing a full sandwich to Elena, taking a half for himself and laying the other half within its wrapping on the floor of the car.

They start eating, the hobo squatting, looking on.

"Hey, this is really good," says Tom. "Ham and cheese, but-ter and mustard!"

"Sure is," sings out Elena.

Beni watches the sandwich being consumed.

Some small town rattles into view, then disappears out the corner of the open car door.

Beni rises and comes toward them with the knife extended. Elena gives a start. Tom, grasping her upper arm, squeezes it slightly. He goes on eating; the hobo approaches. Eye to eye, Tom and Beni, with Tom finishing his half sandwich, Beni standing there, staring, still holding the knife. As Tom reaches for the other half on the floor, Beni grabs his wrist with one hand, lays the knife in front of him with the other, then swoops the treat up for himself.

At least Tom gets a good look at the man's T-shirt close up. It says not simply Beni, but Benihana. *How such a man comes upon such a shirt is one of those mysteries,* Tom thinks, *that will simply have to go unsolved.*

The man trundles off with his prize, squats once more, and in three bites consumes it. Elena picks up the remaining half sandwich, breaks it in two and hands half of it to Tom. He gives her a look of new appreciation.

EIGHTEEN

Sammy Riegert scares most people. He's a no-necked, large-shouldered young bull of extreme intensity, barely contained by a conference room or his cheap blue suit. Yasim, by contrast, presents an exterior of calm. If he seems ruffled at all, it's by the presence of Rashid, who insisted on being there for the interview and now stands menacingly at his back.

"So you knew Mr. Riles personally?" Sammy asks.

"Of course," says Yasim. "Most of the work on these loans was done by his subordinates and lawyers, but he made occasional appearances, and we had reason to talk from time to time."

"Just you and him?"

"That's right."

"And can you tell me what these conversations were about?"

"They *were* confidential."

"The man's dead," Sammy notes.

"Quite so. But the obligation of confidentiality is one I owe to his company."

"So you're not claiming any sort of diplomatic privilege."

"Possibly. Such privileges do exist."

"Let me understand your position here, Mr. Maktoum. You're not the UAE Ambassador to this country."

"That would be Mr. Adoub," Yasim says. "He's in Washington."

"You're—"

"Vice-consul, in charge of the consulate here in New York."

"But you're also an employee of Istithmar, the investing arm of Dubai."

"That's correct."

"There's no conflict in those positions?"

"On the contrary. What's good for Istithmar is good for Dubai and hence for the UAE."

"But in your discussions with Mr. Riles, you were acting in your business capacity."

"And in every other capacity I possess."

Sammy wonders what he's doing there, interviewing this guy. And he's not the only ADA with that concern. Just before leaving his office he was buttonholed by Joe Cunningham, who, when told where Sammy was going, shook his head with rueful disdain. "What the fuck," said Joe. "It's a goddamn waste of time. You ever see a cold-cocked case like this. Prints on the murder weapon? Eyewitness? I mean what the fuck we doin'?"

"I'm just following orders, Joe."

"Yeah, you do that, man. And you come equipped with a mind of your own, right? So what's that good brain tell you?"

"I'm wasting my time interviewing this guy."

"Right. So you'd better get on with it."

Sammy pushes himself to do just that. "Reports were circulating, were they not, that Mr. Riles was unwilling to give a further extension on his companies' outstanding loans to Dubai?"

"There were stories, yes."

"Were they accurate?"

Rashid steps forward. "Is Mr. Maktoum a suspect in this matter, officer?"

"You can call me Mr. Riegert, or ADA Riegert, but 'officer' doesn't quite fit. I'm not a cop. And no, Mr. Maktoum is not a suspect. He might be a witness. That's what I'm trying to ascertain."

"Obviously," says Rashid, "the daughter did it. With an accomplice, it appears."

"You must know I can't comment on that."

"Look," says Yasim. "It's public knowledge Robbie Riles was threatening to call his loans, which would have triggered defaults under *all* the Emirates's loan agreements, so that every other lender would also have called. It's all been in *The Wall Street Journal.*"

"And this would have been bad for Istithmar, Dubai, and the UAE?"

Yasim laughs. "Ruinous."

"So after you talked to him, to Riles, what was your impression? Was he about to pull the plug?"

"I really couldn't say."

"Well, what did *he* say?"

"You know, it really doesn't matter what he *said*. Any more than if we'd been sitting around a poker table. The question you should be asking is whether his personal best interests were served by calling the loan. If yes, he would have done it. Not otherwise."

"And?" Sammy asks. "Were they?"

"I couldn't possibly know that. I don't have nearly enough facts. His affairs were more complex than most governments'. And far less transparent."

NINETEEN

Excuse me, sir," says Tom to a passing senior citizen with a wild tuft of white hair. "Where's downtown Ashaway?"

The older man stops, readjusts his glasses, and gives a laugh that sounds like a shout. "You're standing on it, son." And then takes off.

Elena says, "He thinks we're stupid."

"He's probably right."

"Hasty judgment," Elena says. "At least as to one of us."

"Let's see," says Tom, "because I brought you here, and I think this town may be perfect."

They look out upon a small square park of brown grass, scraggly trees, and a couple of benches. In the middle of the lawn stands a large copper plaque, mounted on granite. It memorializes the fact that Ashaway, Kentucky, was the birthplace of a not terribly famous left-handed pitcher for the Cincinnati Reds. The four surrounding streets look mainly residential but do contain one storefront bank, two shops, one small restaurant, a diminutive courthouse and, on closer inspection, a town hall. Indeed, on still closer inspection, some of those residences appear to be lawyers' offices. But, if there's any activity in this town, it isn't going on in the square. At least at this time, which is mid-afternoon.

"So what's our next move in this brilliantly conceived plan of yours?"

"Take a bench?" Tom suggests.

She nods, they head for one and plunk down, then look around at their surroundings from this different perspective. Doesn't change a thing.

"I'm hungry," she says. "I'm tired. I need a bath, and I need to sleep."

"In other words," Tom says, "we need money. Now that we're in an actual town, do you have any way of getting some? Like in the next half hour?"

"Now that I've lost my cards? And without tipping off somebody as to where I am? No."

"Nobody you can trust?"

She thinks. "Not really. You?"

He thinks, shakes his head.

"What about your girlfriend?"

"Puh-lease," he says.

"Wire transfer from your friendly bank?" she asks with a bright false smile.

"First thing they'll be checking."

"S'wat I thought," she says.

"S'way it is."

"So we're fucked."

"Maybe," he says. "But there are options."

"Oh, yeah?"

"We rob the bank?"

"That's not amusing."

"No," he says. "It's not. But it is an option."

She turns on him, and he laughs. "There's nothing funny about this," she says.

"You're right. So. Only one option, which was the plan. Risky as hell, but doable." He gets up and starts moving. "We should walk," he says over his shoulder.

She pops up after him and hustles to catch up. "Where the hell you going?"

"Around the square."

"That's a contradiction in terms."

"Don't be so literal," he says.

"If you were coming back to that bench, what'd you need me for?"

"For your judgment."

"About what?"

"The best law office."

"You want a lawyer? From Ashaway, Kentucky?" she says in tones of mounting incredulity.

"No. I'm hoping to find a lawyer who wants a lawyer. An associate. Someone to do his thinking, research, and writing for him. I'm highly credentialed."

"As a fugitive, right. And nuts. A lawyer is the most likely kind of guy to turn us in."

He stops in front of a four-story town house bearing a plate on its door that reads, "Law Offices of Magnan, Magnan, Dickstein, and Angelino."

"What do you think?" he asks her.

"Too many names. And I think this whole idea is crazy."

"Desperate times, desperate measures," he says. "We have no place to sleep, as you just pointed out. We're hungry and it's not even dinnertime. We need baths, new clothes—"

He starts walking again. "We should keep going," he says, and she jogs to keep pace.

Another brownstone, another plated door, but paint peeling everywhere.

"What do you think of this?" he says, stopping again. "Only two names."

"Too shabby. Too little business to need help."

They move on.

She says, "You know what the odds on this are?"

"It doesn't matter. We get turned in, we get turned in. We are not equipped to live off the land, eating grass and finding the right kind of mushrooms. At least I'm not." He turns toward her.

"Don't look at me," she says.

"Didn't think so. And if we go door to door, asking people if we can wash their cars or cut their lawns, the chances of getting reported are even higher."

He stops at another plated door. Law Offices of Horatio Downs. "How 'bout this one?"

"I don't know," she says.

"Relatively fresh paint. Single practitioner."

"I don't know, Tom. It may actually be less risky if we try calling someone."

"I'm going in."

"Shit. And what am I supposed to do?"

"Come in with me."

"What?" she says. "Why?"

"You'll see. Let it play out."

TWENTY

Horatio Downs is dictating a brief to his secretary, Josephina. They are both in their early seventies, he but a year older than she. She is the only secretary he's had during the past forty-two years, and while he's always called her Jo, she still calls him Mr. Downs.

"You know, Mr. Downs, most lawyers these days type their own briefs, letters, and such on desktop computers or laptops."

"I'm aware of that, Jo."

"And have you considered developing that facility?"

"I have, indeed."

"Would put you right up there with modern-day attorneys."

"That it would."

"So?"

"So, if you're ready, Jo, shall we get started?"

"Of course, Mr. Downs."

He makes a harrumphing sound, sorts out the notes on his desk, puts his head back in thought, in composition mode, when two people suddenly appear in his doorway: a lanky young man in an open-collared shirt and rumpled suit, and a petite young woman in a white blouse and blue denim skirt that look dirty and slept in.

"If this is a bad time," says Tom.

"For what?" says Horatio.

"You see," says Jo. "Every proper law office has a reception-ist. If you did your own typing, and I were sitting out there...."

Horatio waves this off. "If you're looking for a lawyer," he says to Tom, "I'm awful busy right now. Pretty booked up."

"Could you use the help of a magna from Yale who was editor-in-chief of the *Law Journal*?"

"Ha!" says Horatio. "And that's you? Or is it she?"

Elena says, "No, I'm a receptionist."

"It is I, sir, yes," Tom says.

"Then I couldn't afford you."

"I'd work cheap."

"Not cheap enough."

"Room, board, and pin money?"

Horatio squints. "That's pretty cheap."

"As I said."

"What's the catch?"

"We're wanted for murder in New York, and would like to hide out in Kentucky."

A big grin spreads across Horatio's mouth. "Now that's original."

"I thought the best approach would be candor."

"No doubt."

"My friend here is Elena Riles. I'm Tom Weldon. Elena's dad was shot two days ago. The police seem to think we did it."

"Did you?"

"Certainly not," Elena says.

"Would I have read about this?" says Horatio.

"We're all over the tube," Elena says.

"I'm not a TV watcher. But there was a story, as I recall… two young desperados escaping from some jailhouse in Pennsylvania."

"That would be us," Tom says.

"You seem awfully proud of it."

"It did take some ingenuity on our parts."

"I doubt that much was required."

"We'd never done it before," Elena points out.

"Well, in that case," Horatio says with a smirk. "So what's the deal? I'm supposed to hire you under fictitious names, pretend I've no idea who you really are, and harbor you as fugitives?"

"No pain, no gain," Tom notes equably.

"The gain being your probably very short-term services?"

"I'll do your research, write your papers—briefs, memos, opinion letters, whatever—and Elena, who has a first-class mind, very organized and efficient person, will assist Miss—"

"Mrs.," Jo says. "Mrs. Downs."

Tom's mouth opens and shuts. "Of course. I'm sorry. I should have realized."

"Why?" says Horatio. "We don't, half the time."

"In all events," Tom says, "we will provide highly motivated service."

"I dare say you would. And as a lawyer, I assume you know the risk we'd be running."

"I do."

"And yet you ask us to take it."

"I put it out there."

"Why do the police think you killed her father?"

"We're being framed. By whoever did kill her father. The same people who kidnapped us."

Horatio smiles. "You were kidnapped too, were you?"

"You think we made that up?" Tom says.

"Probably not. Too fantastic. You may not be the genius you say you are, but anyone could concoct a better story than that."

"Good," Tom says. "Glad you believe it, because it happens to be true. And if you trust that judgment, brings the risk way down."

"Assuming you escape the frame."

"No, if we escape the frame, the risk evaporates."

"Hmm."

"Meaning you'll do it?"

"On condition," Downs says.

"Name it."

"On my desk is a memo I wrote on interviews with my client, the Ashaway Steel Company. They're pretty unpopular in this town right now, having folded their tent and moved to Covington. The employees want a class action for wrongful discharge and other such things. Here's the complaint in the case, our answer, and motion for summary judgment. And here's my opponents' answering brief. I need a reply brief two days from now. Have a draft on my desk first thing in the morning. I like it, you're hired."

"In one night you want a brief you can file?"

"I was gonna do it before you barged in."

"Okay. Fair enough. But we'll need one thing."

"You want to be paid beforehand?"

"Food money," Tom says, waving his hand between Elena and himself.

"She eats too?"

"Yeah, the both of us eat," Elena says.

Horatio snorts. "Here's fifty bucks. Plenty for two at Gene's, which is the restaurant on the square."

"We might be recognized there."

"Yeah, you might. And you might as well find that out now."

TWENTY-ONE

In Brooklyn, there are many characterless streets on the outskirts of distinctive neighborhoods. Teddy Stamos now drives on such a road between Fort Greene and Park Slope. It's inhabited mainly by working-class Arabs. He is tracking a person of such status and descent, who is known as Morrie Khalil, and who, until recently, was the driver for Robbie Riles.

Getting Khalil's address wasn't difficult. Lowell Jockery himself once rode in Robbie's car and recalled the oddity of Robbie's having an Arab driver with the name of Morrie. The rest was hacking, and Teddy employs the best. The Transportation Department of Riles Whitney & Co. listed a Maurice Khalil.

Parking in Brooklyn, impossible for most, is also easy for Teddy. A no-parking spot across the street from Khalil's house is perfect. All one needs is what Teddy has: a placard from the New York City Department of Film that allows parking at such spots all over the city.

Teddy climbs the stoop of a two-family dwelling and rings the bell. While waiting, he looks out over the street. Low narrow houses on both sides, clad in aluminum siding or fake brick, minimum or no space between them. Typical outerborough residential. The sidewalks are treeless and dotted with garbage cans, their overflowing state a ripe reminder of the inequality of city services.

The door is opened by a plump, youngish, attractive woman of Arab ancestry and modern dress. "Yes?"

"How do you do?" Teddy says. "I'm Theodore Sullivan, I work for United States Immigration, and here are my credentials." He flashes a badge that would have borne inspection had she made it.

"We have no immigration problem," she says curtly.

"None that I know of, ma'am. I'm looking for your ... husband?"

"Yes?"

"Who may have information about someone who does have an immigration problem."

"Who?"

"I can't say, ma'am. But that information is very likely to come out in my interview of your husband."

"He's not here."

"Do you happen to know where I might find him?"

"No," she says and closes the door.

Teddy is not daunted. He does his research, engages surveillance, and rarely wastes time. Which means he would not personally have driven all the way to Brooklyn unless he knew in advance where Khalil spent his time when not working and not at home. So he makes directly for the neighborhood park, which is only a few blocks' walk. And there, sure enough, is Khalil, waiting on a park bench for a chess game, and just getting off a cell phone conversation, doubtless, Teddy thinks, with his wife. Khalil picks Teddy out immediately and laughs.

Teddy, flashing his badge, sits next to him on the bench. "Your wife mention I was looking for you?"

"She did," Khalil says, affecting a cool manner. He has the physiognomy for it: large head and enormous beak of a nose tilted insouciantly to one side. And out of livery, he wears jeans.

"So you're thinking," Teddy says, "if he knew enough to find me in the park, why didn't he come here first, thereby eliminating the risk that the wife would sound a warning?"

"I was thinking that, yes."

"I can always find you, Morrie. This way I learn something additional. Which is whether you have something to hide."

"Which you would have concluded, if I ran?"

"Exactly."

"No one loves talking to Immigration. Even people with nothing to hide."

"Yes," Teddy says, "but I'm not from Immigration. And you probably expected that as well."

"So who are you," Morrie says, "a cop?"

"That's who you were expecting?"

"Why don't you just tell me who you are, and what you want?"

"Someone who can do you a good turn."

"Someone who likes to play games, that I can see."

"I'm not, actually, such a person, nor of course a cop. But I am truly someone in a position to enrich your life."

"Oh yes?" Morrie says. "To the tune of say, what?"

"Patience."

"I do nothing illegal."

"Be calm," Teddy says. "I'm a private investigator. What I'm here to propose is perfectly lawful. Indeed, all I want you to do is your duty as a citizen."

"I am a citizen."

"I know that."

"And now my patience is gone."

"This involves possible testimony."

"Yes?" Morrie says. "Ha!"

"You have a problem with that?"

"What happened happened."

"So you know what this is about?"

"Of course I know. I was Mr. Riles's driver. He was murdered. Private investigators do not otherwise arrive on my doorstep."

"You seem like an intelligent man."

"Of course I'm an intelligent man. You think I could have driven for Mr. Riles for ten years if I wasn't?"

"Was it that long?"

"I expect you know exactly how long it was."

"And you're now driving for Mr. Althus?"

"Okay," Khalil says. "Let us stop. Who are you working for? Why do I have to tell you anything?"

"You don't. That's the beautiful thing about this. I'm not trying to force you to do anything. I simply want to give you a large amount of cash on two conditions. One, that you tell me the story of that night, the night Mr. Riles was killed, and two, that your memory of that night happens to help my client."

"Who is?"

"That, of course, is the one thing I can't tell you."

"How 'bout your real name?"

"Yes, that I can tell you. I'm Theodore Stamos, head of the agency bearing that name, which you might have heard of."

Khalil shakes his head.

"Well in this age, you can learn all you need know about me at your keyboard. Which is that I'm a perfectly reputable individual, running a highly prestigious agency."

"How much money?"

"Depends on the value of what you have, Morrie."

"So what's the minimum?"

"If you have anything usable at all, ten thousand dollars."

"And if I tell you the facts and you can't use it—still, I've given you information. I've given you my time. There ought to be some money for that."

"Let's say, then, a hundred dollars."

Khalil scoffs. "A hundred dollars. I'd make more than that in a game here."

"Two-fifty, then. Just for your time. And the jackpot? If we put you on the stand—if the stuff's good enough to use in court? Fifty thousand dollars. You could use that?"

"How can I trust you?"

"I'll trust you," says Teddy, taking out his wallet. He quickly fishes out two one hundred dollar bills and a fifty. "Earnest money," he says. "Now can we get started?"

"Not here," Morrie says.

"What's wrong with here?"

"Just come, man. You ask too many unnecessary questions."

TWENTY-TWO

The sole waitress, who declares her name to be Nancy, stands poised with a pad to allot Tom and Elena a very few seconds before dealing with demands in the rest of the room. She's a woman near fifty, built in two distinct halves: the top meager and flat, the bottom lavish and protuberant. "Stew's good," she says. "It's lamb. Made fresh today."

"I'll have it," says Tom, "with the vegetable soup."

"And the little woman?"

"I beg your pardon," says Elena with incipient outrage.

Tom intervenes. "My wife'll have the stew also."

Nancy swivels and leaves, shouting their order in the direction of the kitchen.

"My *what?*" Elena cries indignantly. "My *wife?*"

"Safer," says Tom.

"I'm not doing it! The hell with that!"

"Listen to me—"

Nancy returns. "Hot rolls? They're real good."

"Sure," Tom says.

"Say," she begins, "you guys just passing through?"

"No, we're working for Horatio. Just started."

"Hey, that's great! New couple in town."

She's off again.

Tom says, "See? New couple. *That's* natural. Two young singles who aren't a couple? What the hell they doing in a town like this?" Tom pauses to grab one of the rolls Nancy left in a basket on their table. "Can't say we're just passing through. We're likely to eat here every day."

"Married," Elena says with disdain.

"I'm sure you could do a lot better."

She makes a show of looking him over. "You're not completely hideous."

"Just marginally."

"Stop fishing," she says. "I hate stew."

"Look around you."

She does. Stew guzzling at every table.

"Eat what the natives eat?" she says.

"Always best."

"So," Elena sighs, "where we sleeping tonight?"

"Horatio's got a sofa," he says.

"Okay," she says. "So where you sleeping?"

"Don't think sleeping's on my agenda tonight."

"You're writing the brief," she says.

"Kind of a life-or-death project, don't you think?"

"So how do I help?"

"By being very, very quiet."

"That's easy then," she says. "I'll be sleeping."

"That's why I asked you to be quiet."

"What?" she says.

"Never mind."

"What are you saying, I snore?"

"I haven't said a thing."

"*What?* So you're saying that I snore? I don't snore!" she says defensively.

"Only a bit."

"You're lying!"

"If it pleases you to think so."

"You're fucking lying!"

"I guess your boyfriends never mentioned this?"

"There's nothing to mention!"

Nancy plunks down the two bowls of stew. "Bet you two're newlies, right? But you fight like old marrieds." With a chuckle and a wink, she leaves.

"You see," Tom says. "You got a con going, you gotta sell it."

TWENTY-THREE

Mrs. Khalil opens the door. "You bring him back here?" she exclaims to her husband.

Morrie leads Teddy inside. "Better than out in the open."

"People could see you bring him back here!" She lowers her voice. "They could be watching."

"Then it doesn't matter where I bring him, does it. And don't be so paranoid."

They are standing at the end of a small living room, and Khalil nudges the short man toward a small sofa with large tufted cushions. Teddy sits, Khalil nods, and Mrs. Khalil leaves the room.

Morrie says, "You want me to talk? I have to be sure. It's not that I have anything to say that's incriminating, but words on a tape or a disk, who knows how they can be scrambled."

"So you're worried, what—I'm wired?"

Morrie shrugs.

"So, fine," Teddy says, getting to his feet. "Frisk me."

"Not good enough."

"Really? Not good enough? Whaddya want?" Teddy says. He makes a deprecating sound. "A strip search?"

"That's right."

"You gotta be kidding."

"I'm not kidding. That's the deal."

"What are you, a fag?"

Khalil rolls his eyes. "I look like a fag to you?"

"Well, then you're out of your mind. I'm not going to do it."
Khalil sits, on a chair facing the sofa, and Teddy descends
once more into the cushions.
Morrie says, "I know what you want, Mr. Theodore Sta-
mos. Only one thing it could be. I'm not an ignorant man.
I know about takeovers. I know how they're won."
"Oh, yes?" Teddy says. "And how's that?"
"Smears? Very common."
"And you think that's what I want?"
Another shrug from Khalil.
"I want the truth," Teddy says.
"Naturally."
They stare at each other.
"All right," Teddy says, with an expression of disgust.
"Where do we do this?"
Morrie says, "You go into the bathroom. Take off all your
clothes. Then hand them out. I check them over. Then come in
and I check you over."
"Jesus!"
"Up to you."
"I said, all right. Let's get it over with."
"You are *willing* to do this?"
Huge sigh from Teddy. "Yes, that's what I said, let's do it."
"Then forget it."
"Whaddya mean?"
"If you're willing to do it, why waste the time."
Teddy laughs with relief. "You pulling my chain?"
"A simple test."
"I'm getting to like you," Teddy says.
"Let's get back to the money."
"I told you about the money."
"Did you, now?"
"You don't recall?"
"I do. That is the problem." Khalil sits back. "The night

Mr. Riles was shot," he says, "the car wasn't there for him. You know why?"

"Of course, I was going to ask you that."

"And I know what you want me to say. You want people to believe that Mr. Althus had something to do with the car not showing up. And maybe Miss Elena. Maybe the both of them together."

Teddy blinks twice. "Who are you?"

"So how much would that be worth? Testimony like that?"

"If it's truthful, possibly a lot."

"I'd like you to mention a number."

"I mentioned fifty thousand."

Morrie laughs derisively. "I remember numbers. Even ones that small."

Teddy says, "Then I'll have to get back to you on this."

"Yes, get back to me. But I'll give you my number. My number is nine hundred ninety thousand dollars. You get back to me on that."

A cloud descends on Teddy's face. "Then I really need to know what you'll say."

"Not really, you don't. Not the words. Not now. I'll give you this. I know Miss Elena talks with Mr. Althus. I know, based on what Mr. Althus said on the phone and directly to me, why the car wasn't there for Mr. Riles. So, a bank check for the figure I gave you, you get everything. All the words you need. When the numbers are right, my memory for words can be easily refreshed. For the person making good on the numbers."

TWENTY-FOUR

Elena turns over on Horatio's hard office sofa. "This gonna take all night?"

"Go to sleep."

Tom's still typing at Josephina's laptop, which he's moved to Horatio's desk.

"Who can sleep with that light on?"

"I got another couple of hours," Tom says, consulting one of the books he's spread out all around him, his fingers never leaving the keyboard.

Elena sits up. "I thought you were supposed to be smart and fast."

"Never said fast. Careful. Good. But fast isn't the way one goes on this point. It's tricky."

"Whatever. Try to move it along, will ya?"

He stops typing. "You're not helping."

"You haven't given me anything to do."

"Yes I have."

"Well, I can't do that with the light on."

"Then take a walk. Find us something to eat."

"We're in nowheresville, Tom. In Nowheresville, fucking Kentucky, USA."

"That restaurant said it was open all night."

"It did?"

"Yeah," Tom says. "There was a sign. Said 24/7."

"I didn't see it."

"It was there. I promise you."

"All right. Better than thrashing around on this sofa."

She looks for her shoes.

"Wait a minute," he says.

"Why?"

"I'll go with you."

"I thought the whole purpose was to leave you alone to finish."

"Yeah, well, I could use a break."

"Really?" she says disbelievingly.

"Yes."

"You didn't look like you needed a break two minutes ago. You were flailing away."

"That was then."

"What aren't you telling me?"

"Nothing. Let's go."

Standing with both shoes in her hands, she gives him a skeptical look. "You're worried about something specific."

"I just think we should just be careful," Tom says. "You especially."

"Careful about what?"

"Patrolling police, who knows?"

She shakes her head with irritation. "This isn't about the cops," she says. "We're about to live here openly. As a married couple no less."

"Forget it, let's just go."

"You're worried about the kidnappers?"

Tom shrugs.

"The kidnappers had us," she says. "They left us a fucking rake. In a shed with a breakable wall. It's obvious they *wanted* us to escape. Wanted us on the run. Makes us look guilty."

"Obviously."

"So what are you worried about—apart from the fact that now we look guilty as hell, having been caught fleeing in Pennsylvania, having broken out of jail."

"Exactly."

Her face darkens with dawning comprehension.

"Think about it," he says. "Now, from the standpoint of whoever's framing us, what, happening to us, would be the best of all possible worlds?"

"Oh, shit," she says.

"I think you got it."

"Yeah, I got it."

"So let's get something to eat."

TWENTY-FIVE

Marcel Fryman sits upright in a red leather Chesterfield chair. His posture, his bow tie, his fountain pen poised over the notebook on his lap are very old school, as is the recumbent position of his patient on a horsehair chaise longue. The situation is comfortable for Marcel, since he, aged ninety-five—though looking and acting at least twenty years younger—is the sole surviving student of Sigmund Freud.

Marcel has kept pace with all modern methods. But he differs from younger practitioners in that he still practices the "talking cure," which is now almost exclusively the province of psychologists.

He says to his patient, a lithe young blonde in spike heels and tubular black pants, "And by what name am I calling you today?"

"Oh," she says, looking up at his molded ceiling, "does it really matter?"

"It might. As a reflection of how you're feeling."

"I doubt that my name choice would shed light on anything. It's entirely random."

"All the more indicative."

She sits up, though with her back still to him. "Are you not understanding me? When I say random, I mean when I need a name, I might be looking at something, anything, and the name will pop out."

"Such as Birdie."

"Yes. Such as that."

"Well, you chose Birdie over Robin."

"And that tells you something?"

"The general over the specific? I should say, yes."

"It was a sparrow, actually. One never sees robins anymore."

"And are you still Birdie?"

"Sometimes. When it suits me."

"In other words, when the man you're with happens to believe it's your real name. Because that's what you've told him."

"Yes."

"This is an actual example?"

"It is."

"Do you like this man?"

"I do."

"And you aren't worried that he might discover your real name?"

"Not in the least. I myself can barely remember it. But I won't be seeing him forever."

"Are you planning to kill him?"

"Not him, no."

"I see."

She cranes her neck around to see him. "You being judgmental again? Isn't that counterproductive? To what we're trying to do here?"

"What do you think we're trying to do?"

"Answering questions with questions, now that's more your usual style."

"I can't answer your question until you answer mine."

"I've told you why I'm here."

"You're quite changeable."

"I'm depressed."

"All right, then," he says. "Do you see a connection between that condition and what you do for a living?"

"I do. But it goes counter to your expectation. Doing what I do *lifts* the depression, it doesn't add to it."

"For how long?"

"A while."

"Hmm. And then?"

"It returns, of course."

"More strongly?"

She hesitates. "Yes."

"Hmm."

She falls back into a reclining position. "I hate all of your 'hmms.'"

"I'll try to limit them. And yes, I am being judgmental, because apart from the mayhem you're visiting on others, which almost anyone would consider morally reprehensible, you're doing serious harm to yourself. I mean present harm. Not simply the future likelihood of life imprisonment or worse."

"And why is that?"

"You know why."

"I feel no guilt," she says. "It's a job. I'm good at it. There are people who slaughter hundreds of animals a day."

"So you're justifying."

"I don't need justification."

"All right," he says. "How do you feel about planning to do … what you do?"

"I feel calm," she says. "I've told you."

"And during the act itself?"

"Exhilarated."

"Then the depression."

"It *is* anticlimactic," she says.

"That's your diagnosis?"

"If I trusted my diagnosis, I wouldn't be here."

"Why don't you just stop?"

"One doesn't. Just stop. Not this sort of thing."

"I could give you drugs," he says.

"I thought you didn't."

"I generally don't."

"I heard never."

"There are exceptions."

"I can't take drugs," she says. "One doesn't in my line of work."

"Then I can't deal with your depression. Unless you discontinue … your line of work."

"You're absolutely convinced of the connection?"

"It's obvious," he says.

"How do you explain the exhilaration?" she asks.

"In addictive behavior? Highs, lows, classic. The difficulty in your case is not to understand it, but to treat it."

"I think you're simplifying."

"Oh yes?"

"There's the whole childhood thing," she says.

"I'm not forgetting it."

"Abused people abuse."

"Now who's simplifying?" he says.

She gives that some thought, apparently agreeing. "Well, I won't need you for a while," she says.

"Oh?"

"I'm about to reenter the exhilaration stage."

TWENTY-SIX

Horatio and Jo arrive at the reception area of their office as Tom collects pages from the printer on Jo's desk.

"That the brief?" asks Horatio.

"It is," Tom says.

"Then give it here," says Horatio, grabbing it and heading to his own office inside.

"One second," Tom says.

Horatio stops. "What?"

Jo says, "Your wife's asleep on the sofa in there?"

"Right," says Tom.

"Well get her outta there," Horatio says.

Tom goes inside and kneels beside the sofa where Elena lies fast asleep. "Hey," he says in her ear while gently rocking a shoulder.

Startled, she thrashes. "Hey!"

"Good morning, they're here."

She looks around, shakes her head. "You finish?"

"Yeah."

She nods. "I gotta get outta these clothes."

"I'd wait till you get new ones."

"Duh!"

Horatio's in the doorway. "Everyone decent?"

"Come in," Tom says, as Elena swings her legs to the floor.

"Thank you," says Horatio. "You're returning my office, thank you."

"No problem," Tom says.

"Great. Now get out of here while I read this brief."

They troupe out, Elena going to the restroom as Horatio disappears behind the closed door.

There's a slatted bench under the large window of the front room. Tom takes that—Elena too when she returns—while Jo is busy at her desk.

"So you kids probably want some breakfast." She reaches into her handbag. "You have any money left over from last night?"

"We'll wait," Tom says, "but thank you."

"What if he doesn't like the brief?" Jo says.

"He'll like it." Tom gives a tired smile.

"That's pretty smug," says Elena.

"Not really."

"A brief is a bunch of arguments, right? You have no idea how people argue here. What passes for smart on Wall Street, or the Yale Law School," Elena says deprecatingly, "might be absolutely the worst way of arguing in Ashaway, Kentucky."

"That's always possible," Tom says.

"I hate that."

"What?"

"That tone of condescension."

"Maybe you do need some breakfast."

"I can offer you coffee," Jo says.

They look at her as a savior. She makes a "sit tight" gesture and, taking off for a back room, says, "Won't be a minute."

"Why'd you have to start up like that?" says Elena under her breath.

"Me?"

"Of course, you."

"You really are too much."

They hear a loud "Ha!" coming through Horatio's door. Then silence. Presently, Jo emerges with three coffees on a tray with a few social tea crackers. "Not much," she says, placing the tray on her desk and beckoning to it, "but a little tide-me-over while we wait for the great man to pronounce."

They thank her, devour the crackers, drink the coffee, and wait some more.

Five minutes later, Horatio opens his door. "You two will need a car to get around in. I've called Charlie. He'll be here in a minute with a loaner. Won't be much. An old Chevy, I'm told, but it'll run. Get you to the house and back."

"What house?" Elena says.

"The one you're going to live in, young lady. That's not much either, but it's snug, furnished—it'll keep the elements off your back."

"And Charlie?" Tom asks.

"A client. Owns the Chevy dealership here. And the house. He'll bring the key, show you where it is."

Tom says, "So the brief's okay?"

Horatio shrugs. "You can file it."

"We'll need a small advance. Walking-around money."

"I've set up a small account at the bank."

"Not in my name," says Tom.

"Of course not. It's in my name. But you can draw on it."

"Using what name?"

"Pick anything you like," Horatio says.

Tom thinks. "You're Downs; I'll be up. Upton. Tom Upton."

"Has a ring to it."

"Let's hope not," Tom says.

As they start to the door, Horatio says, "One more thing. Charlie's also the town sheriff."

He lets it hang there, reading their expressions.

Tom says, "Like our first trip to the diner."

"Little riskier," Horatio says, "but yeah, same principle."

"And," says Elena, "you couldn't possibly be accused of harboring, if you put us right in the sheriff's hands."

"Oh, she's good," Horatio says approvingly.

———

Mike Skillan himself places a call to Harrison Stith and gets his secretary. She knows exactly who Skillan is, however, and puts him through directly to her boss.

"Mike?"

"How are you, Harry?"

"You mean after twenty years?"

"Been that long?"

"Gotta be," Harry says. "I see you landed on your feet."

"In a wobbly sort of way."

"Not what I hear. You're doing great. What's up?"

"Your associate."

"Weldon? You calling about him?"

"Yeah," Mike says. "Heard from him?"

"I'd be the last."

"Oh. Why's that?"

"Firm stuff. Look, Mike …." Stith thinks how best to put this. "I've no idea where the kid is. But there may be people here who do. At least one guy Weldon did get along with. You can try him. I'll have him call you."

"Rather call him myself, if that's all right. Who is it?"

"It's Perry Rauschenberg."

"Perry? Weldon was doing criminal work?"

"Briefly. The sort we do here. White collar."

"And you're thinking he may have called him for advice?"

"It's possible."

"Thanks, Harry."

"It's nothing. See you in twenty years."

Mike laughs. "Hey, we oughta have lunch."

"Love to. Send me some dates."

"I will," Mike says. "Oh, and one more thing. You think Weldon did it?"

"Christ. I would never have thought. But who the hell knows about people?"

Mike, hanging up, immediately calls Stith's partner. Perry Rauschenberg's secretary, having two calls on her lines at once, gives her boss the choice of which to take.

"Mike?" says Rauschenberg, picking up on Skillan.

"Hey, Perry, how you been?"

"Since I took your A team down in the *Bakeries* case?"

"Hardly the A team," Mike says.

"Right," Perry says. "I forgot, you're the A team. So, you still trying cases?"

"You kidding?"

"Yes. I'm kidding. So, what can I do for you, Mike?"

"Tom Weldon."

"What about him?"

"You heard from him?"

"If I had," Rauschenberg says, "you know I couldn't talk about it."

"Don't know that, actually. There are lots of things you could tell me that a privilege wouldn't cover."

Perry says nothing. Mike allows a second of dead air.

"So how should we handle this?" he says.

"You ask, I'll answer, if I've no choice."

"No need to get formal?"

"Waste of time."

"Love dealing with smart people," Mike says.

"Is that the end of the bullshit?"

"Very end," Mike says. "You representing him?"

"Yes."

"Have you gotten any emails from him?"

"Yes."

"How many?"

"One."

"Do you have any other documents relating to him?"

"How do you define documents?"

"Come on, Perry! Take out the last document demand you slapped on some poor bastard, and use that definition. I doubt there's anything broader."

"All right. There's another email. Not from him."

"From whom?"

"Looks like a truck driver."

"A what?"

"You heard me."

"So it's not privileged."

"That's right."

"Guess what," Mike says.

"I read you."

"And are we gonna have to go formal *now*?"

"I'll forward it when I get a moment," Perry says.

"How 'bout while I hold on?"

"Another call pending. But you've made the list, buddy. And I'm working my way toward you."

—◦◦◦—

Harry Stith calls in his secretary, Mariah. She's one of the old-timers, one of the few left at the firm.

"You should tell what's-her-name, Rauschenberg's secretary—I think she's new—you get a call from a partner and an outsider at the same time, you put the partner on first."

"Right," says Mariah, but she's barely listening. "I didn't know you knew the DA."

"We were classmates at law school."

"Ah, the network," Mariah says.

"You being snippy with me?"

An innocent look forms on her face.

"Just call the girl," Harry says.

"You think I haven't? You think I haven't told her exactly what you just said?"

"And?"

"The choice was Mr. Rauschenberg's. She told him you were on."

"Ah."

"He must have been in your class too, Mr. Rauschenberg."

"You know he was."

"Three was always a tricky number," Mariah says.

She exits with a smirk, leaving Harry wondering, for the thousandth time, why he continued to allow put-downs from his secretary.

—⁓—

Charlie drives Tom and Elena in a cop car to the rented house after swinging by the shopping strip to point out the local food market and clothing stores. He's a cheerful man with a small round head and sizable belly. The old red Chevy he's renting them is parked in the driveway. There's no garage. The house is a slender two stories, white wood frame, with a front porch. The first floor has a front sitting room, with a loveseat and wood chairs, and a kitchen in back. Upstairs, there's a tiny bathroom and closet, both off the one bedroom, which features wallpaper of faded florals, door and window frames of dark varnished wood, and a huge double bed with four posts but no canopy. Charlie is running the tour; Tom and Elena are staring at the bed.

"Great piece of furniture, don't you think?" Charlie says. "Best thing in the house."

"Very luxurious," Tom says.

"Wish I was your age," says Charlie. "Make good use of it!" He roars at his own humor.

Tom smiles. "Get your point," he says. "As it were."

"As it were!" Charlie repeats. "You bet! Love it!" He wipes perspiration from his face. "Well, gotta get on. You two enjoy yourselves here." He heads off with a sly glance at the bed.

Tom and Elena don't move as they listen to Charlie making his way out.

"You see the difference?" Tom asks.

"Between this house and where we've been sleeping?"

"Between the sheriff here and Seaversville."

"Charlie hasn't a clue," Elena says. "And why would he, you're saying, not having been tipped."

"Which reinforces the tipping theory, yes."

"Also showing they don't know where we are. So we should be good here." She gives that more thought. "For a while."

"For … a while," he says.

"They're still tracking us."

He says nothing.

"Whatever it is they wanted," she says, "they've killed at least once already to get it. And the best way to keep it at only the one is if we disappear. Permanently."

"We have to be very careful," he says.

"No one can be that careful."

Tom shrugs, returning his glance to the bed. "We have a more immediate problem."

"What problem?" she says. "You get to sleep downstairs on the sofa."

"You mean that loveseat? The one that fits you and not me?"

"You're not suggesting *I* sleep on a loveseat?" she says in a tone of great umbrage.

"This is a very big bed."

"Which you sure as hell ain't getting into."

"You ever hear of a bundling board?"

"Forget it."

"We could stack pillows in the middle of the mattress. Use separate blankets."

"I should trust you to stay on one side?"

"We were in a potting shed together all night, Elena."

"You were unconscious."

"All right," Tom says, laughing, "let's table it. We have things to do."

"I need a bath." She reflects. "*You* need a bath."

"You needn't be so vehement."

"Believe me. Vehemence, on this subject, is not misplaced."

TWENTY-SEVEN

By reputation among those in a position to know, Hamad bin Abdul Saeed is one of the richest and most influential men in the UAE. No doubt *the* richest and most influential among the very small number who eschew the trappings of wealth and power. His Dubai office is relatively small, though with a panoramic view of the harbor. Yasim studies the sight as he waits for his host to get off the phone.

It's a vista now known throughout the world: man-made finger fjords like the giant hands of the looming glass towers. Yasim thinks of it as Disneyland meets Century City. On such matters, Yasim is conservative. In Manhattan, he appreciates urban architecture and the parks. In his homeland, he likes the desert.

"My apologies," Hamad says presently, hanging up. "One of those calls. Sheikh Ramin bin Zayed. You understand."

"Of course."

"So, Yassy, you do not wish to come home."

"It helps no one, my coming home."

"That would be the obvious conclusion."

"So?"

"Decisions here are seldom made for the obvious reasons."

"What am I missing?"

"Well ... you were right to come to me first."

"You know?"

"Not entirely," Hamad says.

"What do you know?"

"You are very blunt."

"With you," Yasim says. "I am blunt with you, because I trust you."

Hamad laughs. "Well then, take my advice. Go back. Pay calls of respect while you're here, but don't raise the subject."

"And let Rashid railroad me out of my job?"

"I didn't say that. But you won't win here. You can win—if at all—only there."

"How?"

"Find out his plan and thwart it."

"You don't know his plan?"

"I don't," Hamad admits.

"I'm not sure he has a plan. Other than to get me sent home so he can take over."

"Too simple. That's not Rashid."

"I'm in the middle of the GT&M takeover."

"The middle?" Hamad says. "It's barely started."

"With all respect, it's quite advanced, the groundwork, the players. It's very complicated. He knows nothing about it."

"I think you'll find that's not the case. No matter how you regard him personally, he's very resourceful."

"He's been studying the project?" Yasim asks. "You know this? There's a limit to what he can find out."

"You may be underestimating again. For example, you mentioned other players."

"He's talking to them? Behind my back?"

"I don't know that," Hamad says.

"You know him better than I do."

"I know him ... as well as he can be known."

"So how do I get rid of him?"

"As I said, do it from there."

"Do what?" says Yasim. "The Istithmar are here, and it's with them the man is plugged in. I should be speaking to them directly, explaining the situation."

"You think *you* should?"

"Who else?" Yasim says, and immediately sees on Hamad's face the clarity of what he's been missing. "Ah. They won't take it from me."

"Too true."

"They'll have to hear it from our partners in this venture. And if Rashid has been talking to them…."

"I've not said a thing."

"For which I thank you."

Hamad nods, rises, goes to a small cabinet in the corner, and brings out a tray of finely wrapped chocolates. "Would you like one?"

"Thank you, yes," Yasim says. It would have been impolite to refuse.

After handing him the tray, Hamad unwraps one slowly for himself. "Robertson Riles was shot, I understand. Shot dead in the street."

"Yes," Yasim says, wondering at the sudden introduction of this subject.

"Some here did not mourn him."

"I can understand why."

"Yes. And you also understand, I'm sure, that people operate primarily on self-interest. Rewarding only those who serve it."

It takes Yasim but a moment. "Rashid was involved in that act?"

"I know nothing about it."

Now many thoughts come tumbling into place. "And again, I thank you," Yasim says.

"I've done nothing, Yassy. I've simply held up a mirror."

"No one else has such a mirror, my friend. It was worth traveling five thousand miles to look into it."

—◈—

Six p.m. DA's office, One Hogan Place. Joe Cunningham is filling in Mike Skillan on the latest, since receiving a copy of the email forwarded to them by Perry Rauschenberger. "The guy who wrote it, name of Ray Poundstone—he's with an independent trucking firm, headquartered in Fort Lee. They'll go pretty much anywhere, but have regular routes to and from Cincinnati, Ohio. Poundstone is one of their drivers, a twelve-year employee. He's out on a run right now."

Sammy Riegert walks in, having caught the end of Joe's sentence. "Actually," Sammy says, "he's on the phone. Been trying to get through, he says, couple of days now. Transfer him up here?"

"Do it," Mike says.

Sammy dials his secretary. They sit there waiting for her signal. It comes.

Mike picks up. "This Ray?"

"Yeah. Who's this?"

"Mike Skillan, Ray. New York District Attorney."

"Oh, right." Belligerence seeps out of Ray's voice.

"Hear you've been wanting to talk to me, Ray. Sorry for all the red tape."

"Hey, no problemo."

"So you picked up that couple we're looking for, Elena Riles and Tom Weldon?"

"I didn't know who they were. At first, I mean. Thought they were just two kids needing a lift. Then they wrote this crazy email to a lawyer in New York, accusing *me*—"

"Of course. We understand. What we'd like to know, Ray, is where you dropped them, what they said about where they were going, you know. So we can find 'em."

"Sure, sure. You understand, as soon as I realized I had two killers in my car, I stopped and told them to get out."

"What anyone would do," Mike says. "So where was that?"

"Middle of nowhere."

"Could you be a little more specific?"

"'Bout fifty miles south of Columbus."

"Columbus, Ohio?"

"That's right."

"They say where they were heading?"

"They said Cincinnati, but I don't think so."

"Why's that, Ray?"

"Instinct. I could tell they were lying. I'm pretty good at that."

"Bet you are," Mike says soothingly. "And you probably know this. Any bus stops near where you left 'em? Any train stations? Train tracks?"

"Some tracks, yeah. A branch line."

"Freight trains? Going where, exactly?"

"Jesus, anywhere. Look at a map. Freights going through there can branch anywhere. I mean, They take the food right off my table."

"I see what you mean. Okay, Ray, you've been very helpful. We've got this number—what you're calling from—you use any others?"

"No, this is it."

"Hold on a couple, then, will you? Gonna turn you back to Sammy."

Mike presses "hold" as Sammy heads back to his office.

"Gotta map here somewhere," Mike mutters, searching his bookshelves.

Joe says, "Computer, Mike. Google maps."

"Eah!" Mike says, disparaging anything that high tech. Finding an AAA book of road maps by state, he spreads out Ohio and gapes at it. Cunningham comes around, and they both study it for a few moments.

"So we get out an alert?" Joe says.

"Ohio and all surrounding states—West Virginia, Illinois, Indiana, Kentucky, Tennessee, maybe Arkansas."

"Why not farther?"

"Well, no harm, sure," Mike says, still studying the map. "But concentrate on those states. If Riles and Weldon hopped a freight, my guess is they got off pretty fast."

"Why you guessing a train?"

Mike looks up. "Why you think this guy called?"

"Covering his ass? From a charge of extortion?"

"An extortion that didn't work, Joe. So where do you think he left them? On a highway?"

"See the point."

"He buried them. Back road for sure. No cars going anywhere useful. A train was the only way out."

———

There's a coffee shop on Tenth Avenue that draws a bit of a lunch crowd, construction workers and cops, but has little traffic off-hours. Birdie sits in a booth with a cup of tea, a map, and two men: Jacob Wozniacki, a hulk with bristling black hair, a black scowl, and a flaming red scar on his cheek; and Piet Dvoon, lumpy and expressionless. It's mid-afternoon, and they're the only customers.

"Town by town," she says, finger moving across the map. "Along this line."

"And what?" Jacob says. "Just ride in and start asking everyone to look at photos?"

"I think you're smarter than that, Jacob. I think you know where to go—"

"Coffee shops, small restaurants."

"And what to ask."

"New people in town."

"You will need a cover, however. Let's say, you're thinking of buying some property and you're looking for a lawyer. Maybe you've heard most of the good ones in town are understaffed."

"You're thinking this guy's got a job as a lawyer?"

"Not unlikely. He is a lawyer."

"Okay," Jacob says. "Why the southern part of Kentucky? They could be anywhere."

Birdie puts down her cup. "How long have you been working for me?"

"You want me to say, your sources are amazing, your analysis is brilliant, and you're never wrong."

"My intel is making you poor?"

"I think we were underpaid for the last job," Jacob says.

"Do you?" Birdie says, with a whiff of surprise. "Why do you think that?"

"The man was a multi-billionaire."

"And you should be compensated by a percentage of his net worth?"

"No. A percentage of your fee."

"And so you were."

"Right," he says, as if tiring of the game. "I had in mind a significant percentage. With full disclosure of the numbers we're talking about."

"Anyone can kill people, Jacob. To be paid for it—that takes talent. And resourcefulness. Contacts, connections, the ability to plan, gather information, the whole package. Which you don't have. So you get a flat fee. An appropriate flat fee. Okay? You good with that?"

He returns a sour expression.

"Look," Birdie says. "I know who picked them up, where he drove them, where he dropped them off. You have that information? You even know how to get such information? And would you know what to do with it, if you even stumbled upon it?"

Blank faces.

"I'll give you a hint," she says, stabbing a finger at a point on the map. "Here! They were dropped right here. This is something my network gave me, and you wouldn't learn on your own in a million years." She points to another spot. "And here's a railroad line. It's a pretty big branch. Trains on that branch might end up thousands of miles away. Right next to it is a local spur line. See it?" They nod, but show nothing. "So how we know they're in southern Kentucky?"

"You know the train they got on?" Jacob suggests.

"No."

Jacob waves his arms in impatience.

"Research, Jacob. Local trains, for the spur, go slow enough to hop. The others don't. You see what I'm saying. I have my role, you have yours. With different pay grades."

"Suppose we don't find 'em? This is a fucking wild-goose chase."

"This time, you get a flat fee for looking, and a bonus for finding," she counters.

"And what's that gonna be?"

"Thousand apiece for the search, with expenses. Five thousand apiece for the find."

"What about the kill?"

"You call me. I do the kill."

"You don't trust us?"

"I do. To help get rid of the bodies."

"We killed the old man."

"Who wasn't expecting it. In the middle of the street. In the middle of the night. In a city where no one gives a damn."

"So what's your fee for the kill?"

"Jacob," she says, "none of your fucking business. You want in on this or not?"

With a tightening of his lips, he nods sullenly.

"And you, Gabby?" she says to Piet.

"Me?" he says with a grin. "You had me at hello."

—◦◦◦—

Mike Skillan calls Perry Rauschenberg, who picks up his own phone.

"Still in the office?" Mike says. "And no night secretary."

"Economy measures. All over the place. What's up?"

"If you've got any way to reach your clients…."

"I don't."

"Well, then, if they reach you—"

"Tell 'em to come in?" Perry says, with a mordant twist. "Tell them I'm far from persuaded they did this, that they have an open field with me."

"Despite the evidence?"

"Because of it," Mike says. "It's too much, and it's too neat."

"You know, I believe you. I believe you, because this whole thing reeks of a frame, and you're not so dumb that you'd miss it."

"So you'll tell 'em?"

"I haven't the foggiest notion where they are," Perry says, "absolutely no idea how to reach them, and no clue as to whether they'll ever contact me."

"But if they do?"

"I'll tell them."

"Thanks," Mike says. "And, by the way, what was your class standing?"

Perry laughs. "Stung by 'dumb,' were you?"

"Pretty sure I ranked you."

"Everyone ranked me, pal. I never went to class. And would you think two grown men would still give a shit?"

TWENTY-EIGHT

At a cavernous J. C. Penney, brimming with affordable clothes, Tom selects a pair of gray summer-weight trousers and two button-down shirts; Elena picks one nightgown and two cotton- print dresses, and they both scoop up running shoes, socks, and underwear. Nothing is tried on; their transaction is fast; they're the only shoppers in the store.

The locus of social activity in Ashaway, Kentucky, is the big Stop and Shop that Charlie pointed out on the drive-by. Tom takes control of the cart, which makes Elena very uncomfortable. Her discomfort mounts when he gathers in packages of sliced ham and cheese.

"That's processed food," she says, as if pointing out something he might not have noticed.

"Unhealthy, you're saying."

"Ordinarily, I wouldn't care what you ate, but we're living off a limited budget."

"You can buy all the organic substances you like," he says.

"Not if you exhaust all our money on junk food."

"If you want to shop efficiently, this stuff lasts a lot longer. Look around you. Couple of hundred people here. What do you think's in all those carts circling these twenty-eight aisles? Food processed to stay edible practically forever."

"Not in my cart," she says grabbing it away from him. Barreling down the same aisle they'd come from, she tosses his packages back on the shelf.

Catching up he says, "This is so stereotypical. It's smug, and it's uninformed."

"I don't think so," she says placidly.

"Organic food's the biggest scam going."

"Look, there," she says pointing. "Fresh food, off the farms. Fruits, vegetables, grains—delicious and healthy."

"Which you're undertaking to cook? From scratch?"

"Sure."

"When have you?"

"We'll get a cookbook."

"So the answer is never."

"Of course I have," she says. "But I just steam stuff. You'd probably want something fancier."

"It just so happens that I know plenty of recipes."

"Like what?"

"I can do amazing things with pasta sauces."

"From a jar, probably."

"Well, some from a jar. There's nothing wrong with jars."

"It's what they put in the jars, dumbbell."

"All right, fine," he says. "You make the sauce, and I'll make the pasta."

"Gluten free."

"You've got to be kidding. Are you allergic to wheat?"

"No," she admits. "Gluten free's just healthier. It doesn't turn to sugar and poison you."

"Bullshit."

"Have you ever tasted gluten free?"

"I'll say. Tastes like straw. Bad straw. Unfit for horses. Discriminating horses."

"Well, I don't eat processed food," she says. "You want to spend all our money on that, go ahead. I'll just starve."

"You ate what's his name's—Seymour's—ham and cheese."

"That's pretty low."

"How 'bout fish?" he asks.

"This is a landlocked state, genius."

"There are rivers here."

"The fresh catch of which you'd expect to find at a super-market," she says sarcastically.

"Let's ask." He grabs the cart and wheels it toward the fish counter, Elena straggling behind. Another customer, a tall woman in an ill-fitting dress, is chatting up the carrot-haired, pimply young man behind the counter.

"Enough for five," she says. "But don't slice it too thick."

"Got you, Mrs. Roles," says the fishmonger, slicing and wrapping professionally.

"Good day to you, Jimmy," she says, taking the package and nodding to Tom and Elena.

"And to you, ma'am," carrottop sings after her. Then to Tom, "What can I do you?"

"Fresh fish?"

"It's all fresh."

"Caught today?"

"That'd be the river trout. Just came in."

"Ah," Tom says, observing the tray behind the glass right in front of him. He turns back to Elena with raised eyebrows. She shrugs.

"How do you cook this?" Tom asks.

"Take a pan," the man says, looking directly at Elena. "Put some oil in it. Throw the fish on. Three minutes a side. That's it."

Elena says, "My husband does the cooking."

"Yes ma'am," says the clerk, shifting a pitying glance to Tom.

—⁓—

The big shingled house on Pine Bluff Avenue has been occupied by Downs families for more than 150 years. There are spacious rooms throughout the first floor, including a large dining room, but Horatio and Jo normally eat on an oak table in the kitchen. Tonight they are about to feast on fresh trout from the Shop and Stop. Horatio is hopeless in the kitchen, but Jo's a good cook, and they enjoy reviewing the day while she practices her art.

She removes the fish from the fridge. "Are you in a grilled mood tonight, Mr. Downs, or shall it be broiled?"

But Horatio, at the moment, is attending more to the situation than the fish. "Doesn't this depress you a bit, this scene we present, this Norman Rockwell scene of Americana contentment?"

"I like Norman Rockwell."

"I know you do. So do I."

"Then what are you talking about, Mr. Downs?"

"I'm talking about us. In contrast to that young couple who just came here."

"Are they a couple?" she asks.

"I think so," he says. "Although what stage they're at, realizing it—well, that's the question, isn't it? I think he does, and she ... maybe not yet. He's very bright. That brief he gave me was ... quite a nice piece of work. Maybe a little too classy for our judge here."

"I think she, Elena, knows ... everything."

"Really?"

"Yes," Jo says. "Quite sure."

"Are they killers?"

"What do you think?"

"Not a chance."

"You're sure of that, are you?"

"Absolutely," he says.

"I agree with you."

He watches her toss the salad.

She says, "So what is there about them to which we compare unfavorably?"

"I didn't say unfavorably, Jo. Don't put words in my mouth."

"You were depressed by the contrast," she rejoins.

"They're young, just falling in love, in danger, on an adventure—"

"We've had an adventure," she says.

"Very true."

"Which you're saying is over?"

"Of course not!"

Jo laughs. "Don't be so defensive."

"I'm not. I'm simply saying—"

"I know what you're saying. And believe me. You like things just as they are. You wouldn't change a jot of it."

He breathes deeply. "You think so?"

"I know you."

"You're probably right."

"So, what's it to be?"

"The rest of our lives?"

"The fish, Mr. Downs. Grilled or broiled?"

———

Elena, from a kitchen chair, watches Tom wash the dishes. "I can't move. How can you move?"

"You mean, given the fact that you actually slept last night and I didn't?"

"Yes. That's what I meant."

"I'm used to it."

"All-nighters."

"Right," he says. "What lawyers do."

"How many *can* you do?"

"In a row?"

"Of course in a row."

"I don't know, but I don't want to find out." He puts the last dish in the strainer. "There's one bathroom in this house. It's upstairs. Do you need assistance?"

"You're letting me go first?"

"Yes."

"How gentlemanly."

"That's me." He holds out his hands to help her up.

"You cooked the fish very nicely."

"Thank you. It's called grilling, and it wasn't very difficult." She lifts herself out of the chair. "See," she says. "Did it in one."

"Excellent. Now the stairs."

"Oh, the stairs."

He looks at her inquiringly.

"I can do that," she says, and starts moving. At the foot of the stairs, she turns. "You're sleeping down here, right?"

"Where would you suggest?"

"The sofa. I already said."

"We *have* been through this. What you insist on calling a sofa is a loveseat that fits about half of me, which leaves the rest of me dangling on the floor. In any event, when you're done with the bathroom, it's my turn, which means I'm also going upstairs, and we can finish this conversation then."

"Hmm," she says and starts climbing, with a lot of mumbling to herself.

She slips into the bathroom. He can hear the click of the lock on the door. After about ten minutes, having finished the dishes, he climbs the stairs and calls out. "Elena, have you fallen asleep in there?"

"No," she calls back in a huffy tone.

"Then why don't you come out?" he says, opening both windows as wide as they will go.

"Because I'm not dressed. Can you find my nightgown, please? I thought I brought it in with me, but, obviously, I haven't."

He looks. The package with all their new clothes is on the dresser. He fishes out the new nightgown and raps on the bathroom door. "Found it."

The lock snaps; the door cracks open. "Will you stand away, please, and just hand it in?"

"Arm extended, you mean. So I can't possibly see anything."

"Don't play with me, man. Just do what I say."

Laughing, he does it. She snatches the gown and slams the door. In a moment, the light goes out in the bathroom.

She calls from inside, "I want you to turn around until I get into bed."

"Are you always this modest?"

"This nightgown is diaphanous."

"You bought a diaphanous nightgown?"

"I couldn't tell that when it was in the package, obviously."

"I don't believe it. They don't sell that stuff at Penney's."

"It's a thin cotton nightgown, Tom. I'm not an exhibitionist. Turn around!"

"Okay," he says, still laughing, and does it.

"You promise?"

"Elena, for Christ's sake, get the hell out of the bathroom!"

The door opens; she darts to the bed and under the covers. "I'm in!"

"Glory be."

He takes less than half the time she did, and comes out in his skivvies into a dark room. "Shove over," he says. "Your body is safe from me. Even if I were irresistibly attracted to you, I'm far too tired to be a threat. Besides, I'll sleep on top of the covers. It's warm enough in here."

"You didn't buy pajamas," she says resignedly.

"That's right," he says, rolling onto his back.

"You're planning to sleep in your underwear?"

"If that offends you, you have the option to not take notice."

"How could I not notice?" she says. "This room is six feet wide."

"Elena, grow up! It's the twenty-first century. You cannot possibly be scandalized by seeing me in boxer shorts."

Silence between them. Which allows other sounds to creep in. Crickets predominantly. Then the distant sound of a train horn.

Elena tosses onto her side.

Crickets, breathing.

"Tom?"

"Christ, Elena! Will you just go to sleep, please? I'm way too tired for pillow talk."

"I just realized—"

"What?" he says crossly.

"Where'd you grow up?"

"*Now* you want to know this?"

"Yeah."

"Westerly, Rhode Island."

"Is that near Newport?" she asks.

"That's what you know, Newport? Where all the rich people go?"

"Is it? Near?"

"Everything in Rhode Island is near everything else in Rhode Island, and I'll bet you know why."

"Okay, and are your parents still there?"

"No," he says. "Spain. Retired schoolteachers, living their dream. Okay?"

"Hey, that's great. Wow. Glad I asked."

"Now can you sleep?"

"Yeah, I can."

And she does in two minutes.

He asks, "What in the world do you find so restful about my parents?" But, being totally unconscious, she gives no response.

Overtired, Tom lies, most of the night, listening to her breathing over the chirping of crickets and the moaning of trains.

TWENTY-NINE

A Rolls-Royce is conspicuous on any road, at any hour. Lowell Jockery's, at six-thirty in the morning, heading to the private jetport at Teterboro, draws every eye on the crowded highway. Jockery himself is indifferent to such attention, shrouded in the back seat by tinted windows. Nor can his conversation be overheard, even by the chauffeur. A glass panel divides them. Not to be eavesdropped or spied upon is of course preferred by LJ, but particularly so when in the company of Teddy Stamos. "What's your guess," Lowell asks, "as to what he'd say? On the stand? The man's testimony?"

"Without coaching?"

"Unadulterated, yes."

"Best case—that he was driving Althus when Riles's daughter, Elena, called the car. And that it was apparently on her instructions that Althus then told Khalil that Riles wouldn't be needing him that night."

"Hmm," says Jockery. "Implicates her, possibly. Not him. And that's what we'd get without payment?"

"I think so," Teddy says, "but frankly, sir, Kahlil is hard to read. It's entirely possible that Riles himself had released the car, and neither Althus nor the daughter had anything to do with it. Khalil may just be trying to play us. The man is cagey."

"Persuasive and persuadable," Jockery muses. "Interesting combination."

"Yes."

"Suppose we do ... *refresh* his recollection, as he's suggesting. Would it be plausible? Any history of a relationship between Elena and Julian Althus?"

"Well, Althus worked for Riles for many years. And she knew her father trusted him."

"More than I do," Lowell says.

"Ah," Teddy remarks, not really understanding that statement.

They drive in silence for another few moments.

Jockery then says, "So the man wants ... a million dollars, was it? That's fairly steep."

"It's ridiculous," Teddy says. "He'll take less than half that, and be glad of it."

"What's his bank?"

"He wants it wire transferred to a bank in Zurich. The Bank Starhofen Von Rolle."

"Really!"

"You know it?"

"I own it," says Lowell. "Changes things a bit."

"I see that it would, yes."

Jockery rubs the top of his forehead with one palm, which creases his satiny scalp into ridges. "Tell you what. Let's sit on this for a while. If we need his testimony—and there's a good chance we'll be able to use it—offer quarter of a mil, half deposited immediately after we work out the whole story, and the rest after he testifies, provided we're satisfied."

"And if we're not? That initial wire transfer—"

"Might evaporate."

"Without a trail?"

"Look at me, Teddy. If I want something—or someone—to evaporate, is there likely to be a trail?"

"Of course not, LJ," says Teddy, squeezing his buttocks hard in the seat.

—◦◦◦—

Tom comes out of the bathroom in the morning wrapped in a towel. Elena says sleepily, "You're ripped."

"I work out," he says.

"I thought you didn't have time."

"Work and workouts. That's about all I do have time for. What I haven't had time for is a life."

Sitting on the bed in her nightgown, she frowns. "This is too fucking intimate."

"We have a choice?" he says.

She gets up. "Go ahead! Look!"

He laughs and turns away. "I obviously have to get to Downs's office. Which means taking the car. You have *this* choice. You can drive me and come back, or go wherever, or stay here."

"I thought I was to go to Downs's place too."

"Why's that?"

"We made a package deal," she says. "I'm to be the receptionist."

"Well, that was a bit ambiguous."

"I think we should find out, don't you?"

"Yes, you're probably right," he says. "But hurry. I'll fix breakfast. You want eggs?"

"Christ, I'm drowning in it."

"What?"

"The fucking intimacy," she says. "Yes, eggs. Scrambled. Toast. You can do this?"

"Can and will. If you make the bed."

"Drowning in it!" she says.

—◦◦◦—

Yasim prepares himself mentally for another plane ride, watching from the jet's window as Jockery takes leave of someone in the darkened rear of his Rolls-Royce. The billionaire, coming aboard, promptly belts himself into the facing seat, which, for a plane, is lavishly upholstered.

"Just get here?" Lowell asks.

"Two minutes before you. I've barely touched ground in three days."

"Well, this is a short flight."

"Oh yes, where we going?"

"St. Barts," says LJ, as if mentioning a cab ride uptown.

"That's four hours."

"Relatively short."

A blond supermodel in a flight attendant's uniform takes their drink orders. "We'll be taxiing in two minutes, gentlemen, taking off in five." *Her voice has an edge*, Yasim thinks, *a bit sardonic. Was this aimed at LJ?*

"You like her?" Jockery asks as the young woman leaves.

"She's lovely," Yasim says.

"For a weekend, quite splendid, but you'd have to win her."

"I have a girlfriend."

"Do you indeed?" Jockery says, interested. "Why didn't you bring her?"

"I actually suggested that to her."

"And, what? Not persuasive? You?"

"It was a matter of the right clothes, I think. Since I'd no idea where we were going."

"Did you tell her with *whom* you were going?"

"I didn't. I said only a very powerful man who doesn't like to reveal his travel plans beforehand."

"In the right circles, that might have given me away," Lowell says with a broad grin.

"My friend doesn't travel in those circles."

"You never know, Yassy. People surprise you. Even those you think you know best."

The plane, a Lear jet, pulls out onto the runway, and the

captain's voice is heard. "We're already cleared for takeoff, Mr. Jockery. Should be airborne in a matter of minutes."

As the jet taxis, Jockery leans toward his guest. "So how are things in the UAE, my friend?"

"Everyone's fine and wishes us well."

"You felt the need to go back?"

"Frankly, I did."

"You detected what?" LJ asks. "Some uneasiness about our transaction? Our transaction is cast in cement."

"They love the deal," Yasim asserts. "But they're thinking of having someone else here close it."

As Jockery begins to react, the engines rev for takeoff and, moments later, the plane surges into flight.

"That's not acceptable," Jockery retorts over the clamor of the engines.

"Thank you, Lowell. I'm so pleased you feel that way."

"Whom do they think they're replacing you with?"

"A man named Rashid al-Calif. Do you know him?"

Jockery hesitates for only an instant. "By reputation," he says. "We'll have to turn that around. It's too late for changes. The matter is entirely too sensitive."

"That's why I wanted to see you."

"Consider it done."

"What about the extra two billion?" Yasim asks.

"We won't need it. Worry not, Yassy. All's in hand."

They sit in silence for some moments. Jockery smoothes his shiny pate.

"Funny," LJ says. "I have a girlfriend too. And she also declined this trip. Nothing about clothes. She keeps plenty of clothes at the house there. She's an actress. Auditioning for some stupid part. Won't let me help her."

"Independent."

"Too much so."

"Would we be interested if they weren't?"

"Probably not," Lowell says with a laugh. "Probably not."
Yasim laughs too, then says, "This man Rashid—"
"I told you, I'll deal with that."
"He's not to be trusted."
"Who is, Yassy? Who is?"
"Apart from our girlfriends, of course."
"Of course," says Jockery, with an enveloping laugh. "They are to be trusted implicitly."

THIRTY

After lunch at Gene's Restaurant, Tom and Elena take a bench in the small park at the center of the Ashaway town square. Tom's assignment that morning had been to sit in the back of the town court, observe arguments before the judge, and just see how things were done there. Useful assignment. The judge, a small dour lank man in a black robe, sat on an elevated chair at a tiny square table in the corner of what might once have been a grocery store. Opposing lawyers argued motions standing catty-corner at the same table, pretty much in each other's faces, and the judge's. It stopped them from raising their voices, so the courtroom was quieter than most. The cases, and the arguments, were pretty basic, and the rulings swift. Papers were submitted, but rarely looked at. The judge obviously preferred receiving information in oral bursts.

At the lunch recess, Tom bought a cell phone, and he and Elena now sit in the park studying it in Tom's lap.

"I think I should call him," Tom says.

"You think you can trust him?"

"Yeah. More than most."

"Not sure that's a ringing endorsement," she says.

"He is a lawyer, subject to an oath and all that."

"Oh, well! A lawyer! Took an oath, did he? That just fills me with confidence."

"I worked for him nearly two years."

"Okay. That's something."

"Never saw him breach a client's confidence."

"So we'd be clients."

"Yes. That's the point. Why? You know someone you would trust more?"

"Me?" she says. "Trust someone?"

"What about me?"

She thinks about that. "Up to a point."

"Where's the point?"

"Don't push. It's expanding. Slowly."

"A point is expanding?"

"Well, the line is," she says. "Let's not get mired in geometry."

He laughs. "So what do you say? Call? Not? You do have a vote."

"All right, call him. I definitely don't want to stay here the rest of my life."

"What's wrong with Ashaway, Kentucky?"

"You're kidding, right?"

"No," he says. "Seriously."

"Apart from the fact there's nothing to do here? Almost no one to talk to?"

"Who do you talk to in New York? You have friends?"

"Of course I have friends," she says.

"Close friends? People you confide in? People you *trust*?"

"What are you now, my shrink?"

"That's what I thought, no real friends."

"I have friends!"

"Right," he says, obviously not believing her. "Look. I have no friends, no close friends, because I work too hard. You have no friends, because you can't trust anyone, and because you're a pain in the ass."

She sits in silence for a moment. "Why are you doing this?"

"Have I hurt your feelings?"

"Yes."

"Okay. That's progress. Now you're confiding. I'm sorry. I don't want to hurt your feelings. I like you."

"Though I'm a pain in the ass?" she says.

"Yes. Despite that. See? I'm confiding now too."

"Well, I don't like you."

"Nonsense," he says. "I wouldn't have gotten close to your bed last night, let alone in it, if you didn't like me."

"Involuntary propinquity is what that was."

"You're saying you're stuck with me."

"For the time being," she says. "So call your lawyer friend. Let's get unstuck."

With a shrug, he opens the phone and dials. Two rings, an operator comes on, and Tom says, "Perry Rauschenberg, please."

Another moment, it's Rauschenberg's secretary. "Who shall I say is calling?"

"Just tell him, Tom. He'll know."

"Mr. Weldon? Is that you?"

"Yes, Sally. Put Perry on."

Another moment, it's her boss. "Tom?"

"It is. And best not to ask me where I'm calling from."

"Understood. But I'm glad you called. Wherever it is you are, you may well want to return to New York. I got a call. Mike Skillan. He says he doesn't believe you and Riles's daughter are murderers. He thinks you're being framed."

"Skillan called you? Just called to say that?"

"We were at law school together. He knew you worked here."

"He happen to mention how he reached his conclusion? About Elena and me?"

"The evidence looks rigged to him," Rauschenberg says. "Too much of it. Exactly what he should be thinking, right?"

"Yeah. If he's genuine."

"I think he is."

Silence for a moment, until Rauschenberg says, "It's not a trick, Tom." He pauses a moment, as if deciding how to proceed. "He wants you to come in, and he wants me to persuade you, but Skillan is a blunt, honest guy. When he says he's inclined to believe you're being framed, I'm inclined to believe him."

"We'll think about it."

"You're still with the girl, Elena Riles?"

"Yes. Who also wants you to represent her."

"That might be a conflict."

"There isn't one," Tom says, "believe me. We're both being framed by the same person or persons."

"She should know, if a conflict were to develop, I'd have to drop one of you."

"I'll tell her, but it won't happen."

"There's something else you should know. Skillan's probably talked by now to that truck driver who tried to blackmail you. What's his name, Roy?"

"How the hell did Skillan get his name?"

"I had to give him Roy's email."

"Roy sent you an email?"

"Furiously denying yours. Threatening me with various and graphic forms of castration."

"Shit."

"It wasn't a privileged communication."

"Obviously," Tom says.

"So Skillan's probably figured out roughly the area you're in."

"Yeah, I get it. But *his* finding us is the least of our problems right now."

"You're worried about whoever's framing you. Damn right. Which is another reason to come in."

"I doubt the ones who are framing us talked to Roy."

"They may have less chance of finding you, but you're still safer here."

"You're *vouching* for Skillan?" Tom says.

"I trust him."

"And you want me to trust you? With my life and Elena's? Because it could come to that."

"Either way, Tom. I think you're more at risk staying out."

"Maybe."

"So what do you say?"

"We'll sleep on it."

Tom hangs up and turns to Elena. "So you heard?"

"Got the gist, yeah."

"Reaction?"

"You're right," she says. "We should sleep on it."

"Together?"

She regards him with impatience. "Another reason for leaving Kentucky."

He laughs. "You know what we should be thinking about."

"You think I haven't been."

"Easy enough to understand why whoever killed your dad is now after us. But who killed your dad?"

"Too many people with motives."

"You're thinking corporate types?" he says.

"Domestic and foreign."

"Businessmen? Typically not the type. Not their kind of risk."

"So who's your candidate?"

"Don't have one," he says. "Not enough facts. Which is maybe the best reason for heading back to New York."

"Oh, really? We go back to solve the crime? You and me, Sherlock?"

"We can help, El. You know lots of things they don't."

She blinks.

"What?" he says.

"You've never called me El before."

He laughs. "People do, don't they?"

"No," she says. "They don't."

"Would you rather I didn't?"

"No, it's okay," she says, blushing slightly. "You can."

—◦◦◦—

Jacob and Piet park their rented Honda on the diagonal in the middle of a small town and sit for several minutes observing the twilight scene. Jacob says, "This search, town by town, could go on forever."

"Not literally forever," Piet says.

"There's no more reason to believe they're in Kentucky than in Saudi Arabia."

"There's some reason," says Piet. "The intel."

"Intel?" says Jacob. "What, are you reading spy novels now?"

"That's what she called it."

With a grunt, Jacob gets out of the car, looks around. "Shit. I'm hungry. You hungry?"

Piet climbs out of the vehicle and stretches. "We've already eaten in six restaurants in six different towns."

"Shitty meals."

"There's a place, looks pretty good. Across the square."

Jacob reads the sign. "Gene's. Looks like a dump."

"Then why's it crowded?"

"Only restaurant in town?" Jacob says.

"All's the more reason to go in, then, doncha think?"

A group vacates a booth as Jacob and Piet walk in. The waitress, Nancy, signals them to take it, then comes over to clean up the table. "Back in a jiff," she says, leaving them menus.

Every other table is occupied, and the place is lively. Civil servants, lawyers, truck drivers, agricultural workers, shop assistants, bank tellers—all dressed in the garb of their trades, all talking loudly. Nancy yells orders, a hash slinger yells back, music blares from an old-fashioned jukebox, and the aroma of meat loaf scents the air.

"What'll you have?" Nancy looms over them with her pad.

"Two eggs over easy with bacon," Jacob says.

"You?"

Piet gives deep thought. "Whaddya recommend?"

"Stew's good. Meat loaf, mashed potatoes with gravy. Most anything."

"I'll have the stew," Piet says.

She swirls and is off.

Looking around at those still waiting to be fed, Jacob says, "This'll take a while."

"Easy," says Piet. "I have a feeling about this place."

"Oh yeah? Why's that?"

"'Cause it's the last town on the spur?"

The meal, when it finally comes, is devoured by both and declared to be excellent. They're ready to order dessert.

"Pie," Nancy says.

"What kinda pie?" asks Jacob.

"I'll see what's left."

She's gone again but back in five seconds. "You're in luck. Two slices of coconut cream. Best we have."

"Suits me," Jacob says.

"Me too," says Piet. "Decaf coffee?"

"Two?"

"Regular for me," Jacob says. "And one more thing. You're so good at recommending pie. Can you recommend a lawyer?"

"Why, you in trouble?"

"No, no, nothing like that," he says cooly. "We're going into some big transaction near here. Need a lawyer, that's all. Who's the best?"

"That would be Horatio."

"And Mr. Horatio, he's not too busy? I mean, he's got other lawyers working for him?"

She looks at him suspiciously. "Now what kind of question is that?"

Piet jumps in. "We'd simply like to assure ourselves he's adequately staffed to take on our matter."

"Well, why don't you ask him yourself?" Nancy says, and takes flight once more.

—◦◦◦—

Elena is already in bed, on the far side, when Tom comes out of the bathroom. Her eyes are on his thin frame.

"You might as well get used to it," he says.

"I am used to it," she retorts.

"I don't buy pajamas, because I sleep in my shorts."

"There are all levels," she says.

"Of what, civilization?"

"Yes! Civilization!"

"Which you equate with pajamas?"

"And other things," she says pointedly.

He spreads his hands on the open side of the mattress and leans toward her. "I'm getting into bed now."

"So turn out the light," she says.

Surprised, he flips off the bed lamp and lies down on his side. "I'm to be trusted, am I?"

"Night at a time."

"Sounds so provisional," he says.

"No accident there."

They lie in silence for some moments.

"Bit of a problem," Tom says.

"Oh?"

"It's a chilly night, and you have both of the blankets."

"You're cold?" she asks innocently. She lifts the edge of the top blanket and tosses it in his direction.

He says, "There are two blankets."

Without a word, she hands him an edge of the other.

"Thank you," he says, covering himself.

"You're welcome."

"You do realize," he says slowly, "there's no barrier between us now."

"Go to sleep, Tom."

"I'm not as tired as I was last night."

She sits up abruptly. "I'm not having sex with you."

"Okay," he says, sitting up too. "Clears the air."

"You think the air needed clearing? That I've been somehow *un*clear on this subject?"

"Hardly convincing, El. We're quite obviously attracted to each other."

She thrusts herself down again on the pillow.

He says, "You're not denying it."

"Are you going to force me to sleep downstairs?"

"No," he says. "I'm going to shut up and let you lie there. Let us both lie—in mutual, and pointless, frustration."

"Speak for yourself."

"Really?" he says.

"What did you say last night about pillow talk?"

"Y'know, El … I don't believe you. I think *you* don't believe you. But you're lucky. I know—eventually—you're coming out of that pit you've dug. So I'm going to wait."

"Dream on," she says.

"What both of us will have to do, now, won't we?"

THIRTY-ONE

On a stretch of downhill road between undulating white fences, Jacob stands, cell phone to his ear, trying to explain the situation to Birdie.

"We're wasting our time," he says, all the green and white beauty of stables and fields lost on him.

"Where are you?" she asks.

"Outside of Lexington."

"Wait, I've a map here. Lexington. That's in the north."

"Yeah, so?"

"What are you doing in the north? I told you to stay south. To stay on that southerly spur."

"Well, we did that," he says. "Then the spur ran out."

"Where?"

"A town called Ashaway."

"And?"

"And nothing. We were there. They aren't."

"Why you so sure?"

"We asked around, like you said. I mean, who the fuck knows? There are a million towns. They could be anywhere."

"And what's in Lexington?"

"It's a city. We've been in the towns, thought we'd try a city next."

"Right. I know where that's going." She's silent for a moment. "All right. Stay there. I'll let you know when I want you."

"What are you thinking?"

"I'm going to Ashaway."

"Why? We were just there."

"Because it's the last town on the spur, stupid."

The line goes dead. Jacob looks in the car, sees it's empty, turns around. There's Piet behind him, sitting on a fence. "What the fuck you doing?"

"Taking in the scenery," Piet says, "breathing the air, luxuriating in life."

"Get your ass in the car, we're going to Lexington."

"Why not just stay here?"

"And what?" Jacob asks. "Get a job shoveling horseshit?"

"You think that's worse than what we're doing?"

"Then why're you doing it?"

"For the company," Piet says.

Jacob looks flummoxed, and Piet laughs. "Come on, big chief. Let's go to Lexington."

—∿∿—

Yasim is not unaccustomed to displays of fabulous wealth, including the appropriation by the rich of nature's great settings. LJ's Atlantic expanse in St. Barts, however, is a triple-terraced, French-windowed pile perched on rocks overlooking white beaches on two sides of the estate. It exceeds anything in his personal experience. He and Lowell lunch on local fish chowder, caviar omelets, and mango soufflé. Their table is set on the pool terrace, which affords close views of the main beach and its sunbathing guests, most of whom are attractive women who absorb the rays in the French style, which is to say, topless.

All is good for Yasim but the news.

"It was a lengthy conversation," Jockery says, "and not entirely satisfactory." He pauses to sip his coffee. "Several conversations, in fact. They want Rashid here, and I'm still not sure why. The obvious answer would be that they don't trust you, my friend. At least insofar as the GT&M deal is concerned.

However—and I can't overstate this—they emphasized repeatedly that's not the case. In fact, they put it on the opposite ground, that they want you back to help them there. They're using terms like "put out the home fires," confusing me with the Brits, I think. Your people often do that."

"To whom did you speak?"

"To the Emir, of course. Eventually. I'm not to be fobbed off with lesser authority. Your friend, Rashid, seems well regarded."

"Strange. He wasn't when I left. Not by the Emir."

"He's found a way."

"So it would appear."

"Well, the news isn't all bad," Jockery says. "I did manage to get you a stay of execution. Six weeks, which should give us time to achieve the takeover."

"With Rashid part of it?"

"I'm afraid so."

"Something's happening I don't understand."

"Perhaps you should ask Rashid?" Jockery asks.

—◦◦◦—

Lunch for Tom and Elena consists of soup, salad, and coffee in their now "own" booth at Gene's. "Pie?" suggests Tom over the din of conversation.

Elena gives him a look.

"You can afford it," he says.

"You talking money?"

"I'm talking figure," he says.

"Then you haven't been looking."

"Oh, I've been looking."

"Hmm," Elena says.

They both sip their coffees, each looking elsewhere in the crowded room.

Tom says, "Want to talk about last night?"

She lowers her cup slowly. "Are you going to be a pain in

the ass on this subject?"

"No. If you really don't want to talk about it, I'll admit I was mistaken, and the matter is closed."

"Hmm," she says.

"We could do a capella," he suggests.

She looks upward at the tin ceiling and heaves a sigh. "You weren't ... entirely mistaken."

"Ah."

"Look ... before I start sleeping with a guy—I mean, sleeping with him in the biblical sense—I'm gonna want to be very sure of him."

"And you need more time," Tom says. "We haven't already been through enough together."

As Elena looks pained, Nancy comes over. "Gimme room," she says, easing in next to Elena. "Yesterday, two guys were here, funny-looking guys, asking questions that didn't quite sit right. They seemed to be poking around for information. They pretended to be involved in some big transaction—which I didn't believe for a second—and asked about lawyers in town. They were interested in Horatio and his ... staffing, as they put it."

"Oh shit," Elena says.

"Don't know why," Nancy says, "but the first thing I thought of, these guys are nosing around about you guys."

"Where'd they go?" Tom asks.

"Dunno. But it looked like they may have left town. They weren't here this morning."

"Thanks, Nancy."

"It's nothing." She pulls out of the booth. "Just thought you should know."

Watching her go, Elena says, trying to sound calm, "That's pretty scary."

"I agree."

"So what do we do?"

"Sit tight," he says, "or run to New York."

"Staying here is an option?" she says, surprised.

"Probably safe for the time being. They came; they didn't find us; why should they come back?"

"Reinforcements?"

"For us?" he says. "We're that dangerous?"

"Only to each other."

"There is that."

"But your feeling is we should stay put," she says.

"I think so," he says, upbeat. "For the moment. We have jobs. A house. The men looking for us have come and gone with no reason to return that we know of."

"Yesterday you were saying we'd be better off taking the DA up on his offer."

"Still true," he says. "In due course. I'll tell Rauschenberg to make a proffer."

"What's that?"

"He sets out our version of the facts. Normally, it's done as a nonbinding admission of guilt, to get a deal on sentencing, but here we could use it as an assertion of innocence, and as a way to present evidence, so we can negotiate the terms on which we come back. In any event, the negotiations will take time, and I suggest we stay here while that happens instead of roaming around the countryside."

"Yeah," she says, musing aloud. "Just what I thought. You like the sleeping arrangements."

"Oh, really?" he says.

She looks away.

"Elena?"

"You were the one who said how easy it would be. Remember? Mr. Bundling Board?"

"I was wrong," he says, then puts some money on the table. Then suddenly rises. "Let's get out of here."

On the green, Tom leads, to their now "own" bench, with

Elena a reluctant follower. "Let's be honest," he says. "We're heading that way. It's gonna happen. If you don't screw it up."

"If *I* don't screw it up?" she scoffs.

"Well, I'm not going to."

THIRTY-TWO

Julian Althus, as acting chairman, presides over a meeting of the Riles Whitney board. Ten other board members are attending, plus Harrison Stith, the company's outside attorney. The boardroom commands a corner of the top floor of the Riles Building, thereby providing a view of the Hudson River as well as downtown Manhattan. It's connected by private dining rooms and secretarial suites to Robertson Riles's old office, on the opposite corner of the building now occupied by Althus. His continued occupancy depends on the report about to be made by the nominating committee, and the board's action on that report, but neither outcome is much in doubt.

Torrence Stearns, the chairman of the committee, is now asked by Julian whether there are nominations to be made. "I have the great pleasure," Stearns says, "to announce our unanimous proposal that you, Julian, shall be the president, chief executive officer, and chairman of this company." To confirm his pleasure, Stearns beams it from a full round face.

"Thank you, Torry," says Julian. "I should now excuse myself, to give the board the opportunity to discuss the matter and vote on it."

"I doubt that's really necessary," Stearns says, with a cheerful lilt to his voice.

Julian glances about until his eyes stop on Frank Buckmaster, CEO of Addison Paper, and Robertson Riles's oldest friend. "Might be better if you did, Julian," Frank opines.

"Oh?" Julian says.

"Come on, Frank," says Torrence. "We're all grownups here. If what has to be said can't be said to his face, it's not worth saying."

Frank says, "Your call, Julian."

"Actually … I think Torry's right."

"Very well." Buckmaster has a weathered countenance, which he rubs thoughtfully with a lean, freckled hand. "As much as I respect you, Julian, I feel we shouldn't act on the succession until the largest individual shareholder of the company has been heard from."

"You mean Elena," Julian says.

"Of course, Elena."

"Her sisters have been heard from, and their husbands."

All look to Lawton Sergeant, husband of the oldest sister, who gives a nod of approval.

"Quite right," continues Julian. "And of course Elena's now a fugitive, wanted on a charge of murdering her father."

"Do you believe such a charge?"

"I wouldn't have, no," Julian says. "But I also wouldn't have believed the evidence they seem to have found against her."

"So you think we should try her here?" Frank says. "Right now? On the basis of what we read in the newspapers?"

"I'm not saying that."

"If we proceed on the succession without hearing from Elena, we'd be doing precisely that. Surely, if she were here, we'd want her views."

"Naturally. I above all. But she's not here. Quite possibly by no fault of her own, though her flight with that Weldon fellow is not helping her case. But the company must be run. Run strongly and effectively. By a chief executive who is not merely 'acting.' Clients, competitors, the world must know that that person is totally in charge and will be so for the foreseeable future. For the good of the company and all its shareholders. Isn't that so, gentlemen?"

Around the table, from powerful men, there issues a general murmur of approval.

"Moreover," Althus says, "we're on the brink of war to take over one of the most important corporations in the United States. We cannot go to battle with an *acting* general."

"So you favor that acquisition?" Buckmaster says.

"Absolutely," Julian says.

Torrence says, "Is there a motion?"

Five men at once move and second the nominating committee's proposal. As Harry Stith rises to take the vote, the motion is carried by acclamation.

—◈—

Teddy Stamos reaches Jockery on his cell phone at the airport in St. Barts. "You've heard, LJ?"

"About Julian's election? Of course."

"About his support for Riles's takeover plan?"

After a long silence, Stamos says, "LJ?"

"How good's your source on that, Teddy?"

"Impeccable."

"Mine didn't mention it."

"'S'why you pay me the big bucks, LJ."

"What exactly did he say?"

"That Althus totally favored pursuing Riles's plan to take over GT&M."

"Althus announced this to the board?"

"Very warmly, I'm told."

"Who is he, your source?"

"It won't help you to know that."

"It will help me to evaluate what he's telling you," says Jockery, with irritation.

"I've evaluated it, LJ. It's solid. Because the source is solid. And if I name him … or her, he … or she won't be."

"It's a woman?"

"I haven't said that."

"You think what?" says Jockery, with increased umbrage. "I'm not to be trusted?"

"Of course I'm not saying that, LJ. But the person is skittish. You look at him, or her, a certain way—you probably wouldn't even know you're doing it—"

"All right, Teddy," Lowell, gazing at the hilltops of St. Barts, says calmly. "Bring in Khalil."

—◆◆◆—

The light is off when Tom emerges from the bathroom. Momentarily he can't see, then makes out Elena's form on the far side of the bed. *We already have sides*, he thinks. *Have we established anything else?*

He slips into "his" side. Not a stirring from hers. He'll just lean over a bit, take a look. She turns, her face under his.

"Ye-es?" she says.

Taking that as an invitation, he kisses her on the lips. She tastes like toothpaste.

She kiss back? A little ambiguous. Try again?

"Elena?" he tries.

"Shut up," she says and pulls him to her, like pulling breath from the air.

Then pulls away.

Surprised, he can think of nothing to say.

Finally, she says, "I like you. More than I thought I would. I'm not in love with you."

"Too early for that," he says.

"Way too. Infatuation, maybe."

"It was a pretty serious kiss. That last one."

"Okay," she says. "Maybe definitely infatuation."

"Maybe definitely?"

"Whatever," she says. "It's unstable. Might be gone tomorrow."

He sits up. "We just kissed each other and meant it. And now you want to go back to cool?"

He waits for an answer, but gets only her turning away from him.

"You always do this?" he asks.

"There's no 'always' with me, Tom."

"No prior relationships?"

She sits up too. "That's not what I meant."

"But have there been? Prior relationships?"

"Nothing you'd likely call one."

"You're inexperienced," he says. "It happens."

"I know enough."

"Yeah?" he says. "So what do you think? About us? As clearly as you can see it."

"On this subject you want clarity?" she says, as if the idea were ridiculous.

"I worship at its shrine."

"I just said, I don't know. That's honest, that's something, and it's as clear as I can get."

"I'll take it, it's progress."

"Good," she says.

"People have slept together with less reason than that."

"We are sleeping together," she says, sliding over to her side of the bed, leaving much space between them.

"You're tough," he says.

"You'd like easy?"

"No, El. I'd like you. And I've no confusion about that at all."

THIRTY-THREE

Cincinnati to Ashaway, partly on bad roads, is a two-hour drive, even on a Saturday morning. Worse for Birdie was New York to Cincinnati on a six a.m. flight. Losing sleep blackens her mood, which becomes pitch waiting for her luggage. She was forced to check it. It contains her guns. In unrecognizable pieces, of course. But the need to check ordnance always makes travel doubly infuriating.

Easily enough, however, she finds the Ashaway town square, parks her rented Dodge in one of the diagonal spaces, buys a newspaper, and gets a table at Gene's Restaurant for lunch. Within minutes, Tom and Elena walk in. *This,* Birdie thinks, *is looking too easy.*

She orders a salad, coffee, and a bottle of water from a woman whose manner seems more suited to stand-up than waitressing. The pie looks great, and Birdie is tempted, but gauges even one slice to exceed her daily calories. Ostensibly studying the real estate ads in the newspaper, she watches the waitress scoot over to Elena and Tom. They carry on a conversation that's a bit more than ordering. Birdie strains unsuccessfully to pick up what they say.

She finishes early, pays first, then lingers over a second cup. When they leave, she leaves, and, at a cautious distance, follows them out of town onto a narrow two-laner. They stop at their house; Birdie keeps going. Now she knows where they live. A mile away, she pulls off the road onto a dirt trail between

two cornfields. She gets out, takes some sun in her face and
stretches. A simple plan forms in her head. Take a nap in the
back seat; assemble the rifle; "do" both those kids in their own
house; drive back to Cincinnati. *A walk in the park.*
    Is it? she thinks, drifting off.

—⁓—

Birdie awakes just after eight p.m., only partly refreshed and
with a great urge to pee. She wanders out onto one of the cornfields, finds a spot, lowers her panties, and irrigates some stalks.
Walking back to the car, she realizes she's thirsty, and gulps
down the bottle of water she'd bought at Gene's. Next she pulls
the rifle sections from the car and assembles the weapon on
her lap. It's a job she's done often, for practice and for real,
so it takes no more than four minutes. She's done it in three,
but doesn't feel that kind of urgency now. Having put the gun
together and loaded it, she's ready to go. But doesn't. Not right
away. Something's giving her pause. Something about those
two she's preparing to turn into corpses.
    Her reflex is to flip the visor so she can look in the mirror,
check her appearance, check out her hair. Despite the nap, she
feels tired. *Is it those kids,* she wonders, *or just me? Getting tired
of this job? Burned out?*
    It doesn't detain her for long, however, whatever it was.
In the cornfield, as the sun drops under the horizon, she piv-
ots as if on parade, turning away from the fire streaks in the
sky. *There's the job; do it; leave town.* That's her *modus.* Without
dwelling further on doubts, she's back in the car, on the road,
heading for the mission.
    There's the house: downstairs light on; their car in the
driveway. Birdie parks on the road, gets out with her rifle,
heads toward the field to the right of the house. Slowly, noise-
lessly, she makes her way onto the front porch. A board creaks
slightly under her weight. *Shouldn't alert them; it could have*

been anything. But she allows minutes to pass. Her next step is silent. Then she tries the front door. It's locked.

No problem. The pick in her pocket makes short work of locked doors. This one: only a low click when opening, and Birdie's in the front hall. Which is quiet. *They must be upstairs, maybe even in bed.* Then Birdie thinks she recognizes the source of her hesitation. *Not me,* she thinks. *I'm okay. It was those two in the coffee shop, feelings on display. Even more, their wish to hide them. A shame, really.*

Birdie stops, shoulders drooping. Silently she laughs at herself. *What's this? Sentimental? Me? Ridiculous!*

She takes the stairs slowly but two at a time. They're solid, no creak at all. At every instant she's ready to fire. The rifle has a silencer; it's her own design. She bursts into the bedroom and opens fire, thumping four shots into a mattress populated by pillows.

—⁓—

In the back of a bus, Tom talks to Charlie by cell phone, and Elena wants to know what's happening.

"He's sorry he didn't believe us," says Tom, turning away from the phone.

"She actually went to the house?" Elena says.

"Let me talk to the man," Tom says to her; then to Charlie, "So what did you see?"

"The bed's shot to hell," Charlie says. "I'm looking right at it."

"She shot up the bed, thinking we were in it?"

"Apparently," says Charlie. "Or she was just pissed off you weren't. I've put out a five-stater. Might pick her up. Doubt it though. So tell me. Nice kids like you, what you involved in? Paid killer coming after you, shooting up my bed?"

"I tried to tell you from the bus earlier."

"Now I'm listening."

"We're being framed, Charlie, for something we didn't do, and whoever's framing us is trying to make sure we don't get out of it."

"I'll be damned!" says Charlie.

"Imagine how we feel."

"So where you going? Houston or New Orleans?"

"Can't tell you that."

"Why the hell not?"

"Not out of the frame yet," Tom says. "Or free of that killer."

"You think I'm gonna tell her?"

"You'll tell someone who might tell her. How'd the hell she find us in Ashaway?"

"Why not just come back?" Charlie says. "We'll work something out."

"Oh, yes? You going to protect us?"

Long silence.

"See your point," Charlie says.

"You'll tell Horatio?"

"Yeah, will."

"See ya, Charlie," Tom says. "Thanks for everything."

Tom hangs up and turns to Elena in the next seat. "We're having an adventure," he says.

She's not amused. "They're not going to stop looking for us."

"So we're going to have to go in. Soon. I'll call Rauschenberg, make the best deal we can, then back to New York."

"How long will that take, Rauschenberg, a deal?"

"Can't take that long," Tom says, knowing it's unpredictable whether any deal could be made at all.

"They can figure out we're headed to New Orleans," she says. "Only so many buses out of Ashaway in that time slot."

"New Orleans is a big city. Lots of places to hide."

"With money, yeah. We don't have any."

"We have a little." He puts his arm around her, and she doesn't squirm away.

She says, "We should get a ticket to another city. As soon as we arrive."

"We can't afford that," he says. "Not right away. I'll get Rauschenberg to wire us some money."

"I can get money."

"Yeah? From someone you can trust?"

She blows her cheeks out in frustration.

He says, "This will end well, you know. Someone tried to kill us. Goes a long way to showing we're the framees here. And more than that. Killing us would have worked only if they could have hidden the bodies, made it look like we just went underground, vanished. After an attempted shooting that fails, the whole thing loses its point for them. Shooting us doesn't put the blame on us, so why bother?"

"Let's not play it out."

"Okay," he says. "Where's the hole?"

"You know damn well. They have my phone."

"Frankly, I forgot that."

They ride in silence.

"You're too damn smart," he says. "But we're better off in New Orleans for a while anyway."

THIRTY-FOUR

Jockery's apartment in Time-Warner Plaza has its own gymnasium in which LJ works out every morning. It's a good place for private meetings as well. With people whom Jockery employs. Those who won't be offended by sweat. Or who won't matter, if they are.

Downstairs, Teddy Stamos is shown to the back elevator, which, on the top floor of the building, opens on LJ's exertions. Teddy blinks at the light streaming through the extra-large windows, glinting off the shiny machines. He's greeted by a shout from a whirring XTERRA. "Bungled, Teddy! Flat out bungled, fucked up!"

"Yes," Stamos agrees. "Someone tipped them. What's worse, we don't know what gave her away."

Lowell comes off the machine. "Her. Right. Who the hell is she? I thought you'd employed two men."

"I employed a firm. Two men and a woman, the woman's the boss. They're all first rate. But we thought it best, at this juncture, to send the woman, and it's well that we did."

"Oh?" says Jockery, mopping himself with a towel.

"Had we sent the men, there'd be no fix to the thing, you see."

"I'm listening."

"Now we have a scenario that's more elegant, though a bit more expensive. The police here were told by our eyewitness, the janitor, that Riles was shot by a woman."

"Yes, and?"

"I have Elena's BlackBerry. Very simple password, as it turns out. It will now be evident to anyone who finds the device that she sent an email to this professional assassin just two days ago, laying out a devious scheme."

"Ah."

"We had alternative plans from the start, LJ. Plan A was a simple frame. Problem is the DA doesn't seem to be buying it. So we go to Plan B. Elena, as devious as her dad, sets up a story to make it look like someone is trying to frame her."

"She frames herself?"

"In a sense," Teddy says. "Making it appear someone else is doing it."

"And her message to the hired assassin?"

"'Come shoot up the place,' is what she said in the email, meaning the place in Kentucky. 'When we disappear, everyone will think we were killed by people framing us, will stop looking for us; even more, will stop blaming us, and we'll be free.' And, LJ, to make this airtight, we'll have a bank record showing Elena cashing out fifty million dollars on the same date she wrote that email. Presumably, it's the money she and her boyfriend will live on."

"Is this plausible? The story is she killed her father for money. Billions. Now she's supposed to have settled for fifty million?"

"In our scenario B, the fifty million may have been the original motivation. It's in a trust fund. She couldn't get it until Robbie Riles died. And in any event, she realizes that coming back now for the billions is too risky. She faces prison or even capital punishment. And how much does anyone really need, anyway? Fifty million, tax-free—that's a hundred mil in ten years at least. Pretty good life."

"What bank?" Jockery asks.

"It's a small bank. In the Cayman Islands. You wouldn't have heard of it."

"Who owns it?"

"I do, LJ. Though that's absolutely not traceable."

Jockery laughs and tosses his trowel in a bin. "So you're a banker too."

"Not on your scale, LJ."

"And the cashing in of the trust account?"

"Also not traceable. Until, of course, we want it to be."

Jockery takes a moment ingesting it. "This is all quite brilliant, Teddy."

"A little contingency planning, LJ, in case things didn't work out on this round."

"You'll move the BlackBerry—"

"To their last known address, yes."

"And the woman?"

"In pursuit. To New Orleans, where they're headed. The BlackBerry has been overnighted to her there."

"There is a problem, Teddy."

"What's that, LJ?"

"Our eyewitness. Told the cops he saw Elena herself shoot her father."

"They showed him a photo. He said he *thought* it was her. But far more plausible that he couldn't be certain, from thirty feet away. And also more plausible that she'd hire someone than do it herself. It really all fits together this way much better, LJ."

"Not for the woman, however. She's wanted by the police."

"Not a problem for her," Teddy says soothingly. "And she's very well paid."

"Really?"

"By her standards, yes."

"What I admire, Mr. Stamos, is your bullshit."

"Thank you, LJ."

"It's not a compliment. Your plan B might work, but only if Elena and her boyfriend disappear—quickly and forever. You understand that?"

"Of course, LJ."

"Does your woman understand that?"

"Absolutely."

"She just better not fuck this up any more, Teddy."

"She's a closer, believe me. Hasn't failed me yet. Ultimately."

Jockery says, "Where do we stand on the chauffeur situation?"

"In the works, LJ."

"What the fuck does that mean?"

"Well…" Teddy licks his lips. "Means I'm on it. Khalil and his wife have gone on a holiday, it would appear. To Disneyland, we believe. Soon to be back though. I'm tracking them."

Lowell reaches down to grip the little man's shoulder. "I want *you* to understand something more. Failure in this matter would be extremely hurtful. I mean physically hurtful. Not to me, Teddy. *You read?* Not to me."

———

Birdie's first stop is the bus terminal. She parks a block away, uses the Ladies in the station, strides out again into the street, communes with the atmosphere of the place, gets a sense. She's good at this. A human compass. She just fills her mind with *I need somewhere to stay, I need somewhere to stay*—and lets her instinct guide her to the most likely establishment.

In this case, however, it leads indiscriminately to the French Quarter. Hotels, B&Bs, flophouses abound. They could be in any of these. Or, of course, in another district entirely. The girl might even know people in New Orleans. So might he. Or they might have traveled to a different city. In which event, Birdie wouldn't have a clue where to look. *Might as well stay in the Quarter then. If they're here, they'll have to come out on the streets at some time. Need a little luck.* She picks a touristy bar with a good view of Bourbon Street and takes a table at the window.

———

Elena stands at the one large window of a third-floor room in the back of a B&B walk-up. Her view is of a small courtyard. She sees patches of grass and weeds and a little forlorn tree that might have once borne apples.

"This is an awful place," she says, going from the window to a side table to inspect a layer of dust. She runs her finger through it. "See?"

"Fits our budget," he says. "Barely."

"We have a budget?"

"Get to spend next to nothing every day."

"Sounds great. Do we have anything in there for food?"

"Doesn't matter," he says.

"We're fasting now?"

"We can't go out."

"We're in the goddamn French Quarter, Tom. There are a million fucking tourists out there."

"And?"

"We'd blend," she says.

"No" he says humorlessly. "We wouldn't."

Elena scans the room again: spindly furniture on worn carpets; cramped space; faded walls. "She can't be on every street at once, for heaven's sake."

"There are only two main streets," he points out.

"Right. So we'll go on a side street."

"No."

"Who made you boss?" she asks.

"I'm just giving you advice, El. You're free to not take it."

"Then you'll get pissed off and sulky."

"No, but if you leave, you'll force me to go with you."

She sits hard on the one chair. "I'm starving, Tom."

"You think I'm not?"

"Then let's risk it."

He leans down to grasp her shoulders. "We could wait until dark. And in the meantime, distract our minds from food."

She diverts her eyes. "I'm not going near that bed. There are live things in the mattress."

"Have you looked under the covers?"

"Of the two fears I have right now—going out on the streets and lifting those covers—I'd rather take to the streets."

—⁓—

Murphy's Law! Damn rule is inviolable. Birdie nursed drinks nearly two hours before ordering a steak. It arrives at the same time as her quarry.

She throws some cash on the table and bursts out onto the street. There! Still in view, through the stream of tourists, a block away. They dip down a side street, then into a grocery. From an adjacent storefront, Birdie waits. She thinks, *I have the advantage. They've little idea, if any, what I look like.* Presently, they come out. Walk by her without noticing as she inspects the dresses displayed on a rack in front of the store. She gives them a block, then follows. Not far. Their B&B is only two blocks away in a residential section of the Quarter.

From the corner, Birdie watches the light go on in a back bedroom on the third floor. *They keep making this too easy,* she thinks. *Yet they're slippery.* Then: *Don't overthink this,* she admonishes herself.

Two businessmen approach, a Mutt and Jeff in suits. They seem to be looking for the sort of woman who palely loiters on such a corner. The signal sent by Birdie, however—bared teeth—conflicts jarringly with their expectations, and they hasten away. She walks away herself, in the direction from which she had come, looking back intermittently at the lighted third-floor window. Then stops at another storefront, browsing for several minutes. Finally, she strolls past the house and comes back. *Showtime,* she thinks.

A fence would block her entrance to the backyard, were it locked, but it isn't. The back door would impede her progress to the back stairway, but it readily yields to her pick. Before entering the house, she looks about. No particular reason. Pure impulse. She sees the backs of French Quarter houses, two neat rows of them, with their scruffy yards and pitiable fruit trees, all pulling shadows from a full moon and street-lights. Spices and a whiff of pot fill the air. Oddly, the image of the couple floods again into her mind. *Oh well,* she thinks, *no one lives forever.*

Two flights of stairs mean nothing to Birdie; she's in great shape. The stifling air inside is more of a problem, and she's sweating slightly when she reaches the landing. No sounds from either room on the floor. It takes but a moment to fig-ure out which one is the couple's. The other one looked dark from the street and is probably empty. Birdie gently tries the door handle. Locked. Out comes her trusty lock pick. Tricky. No silencer for the pick. One has to be extremely careful. She removes a handgun with a silencer from her capacious hand-bag, places it in her left hand. With her right, she works the lock gingerly. Click.

Swinging the door open, Birdie storms into the room, gun held in firing position.

Brightly lit, shocked silence; no one there. Still cautious, Birdie scouts the bathroom, the closet, and under the bed. No one. But on the top of the bedspread is a handwritten note. It says, "How can you stand yourself?" Birdie laughs, stuffs the note in her pocket, and drops a BlackBerry where the note had been.

THIRTY-FIVE

Elena wakes in the back of a bus, surprised to find herself using Tom's lap as a pillow. "Are we living on buses now, or does it just feel that way?"

"We're living on buses," he says.

"For how long?"

"Until we get to Atlanta."

"Will she know that's where we're going?"

"Probably."

"She's like a tar baby."

"At least we now know what she looks like."

"Do you?"

"Not clearly," he admits. "A glimpse in the coffee shop. Now another from a block away."

Elena sits up. "So how, again, are you so sure it was her?"

"Believe me, I know."

"You mean we just ran from a pretty good hiding spot on your hunch?"

"You hated that room."

"It was safe!"

"Not once she saw us and followed us there," he notes.

"Did she? Follow? You saw that?"

"I did."

"Why didn't you tell me that right away?"

"I thought I'd let you drag it out of me."

She blinks. "You actually mean that, don't you?"

He shrugs.

"You bastard!" she says, punching him, until the others in the bus turn around. "We're just kidding," she informs them.

"Oh, yes," says a woman three rows ahead. She wears what might be a fright wig and throws an arm around an older man half her size. "We do that all the time."

Elena smiles wanly. Then to Tom under her breath. "Next stop, we have to get off this bus."

"Can't," he says. "There's money waiting for us in Atlanta."

"Whose money?"

"Mine, ultimately. On loan from Rauschenberg."

"He's financing our flight?"

"Back to New York, he is, yeah. That's the deal."

"What deal? You made a deal for me?"

"You were asleep. Besides, at this stage, we've run out of good options."

She says, as if trying to be patient, "New York is the one place that crazy tar baby will probably be trying to find us and kill us."

"As a place for us to be, it's still the least undesirable alternative."

"Who's gonna protect us in New York?"

"We are," he says. "She's almost certainly under contract. We make killing us undesirable, at least for the people who are paying her. How well do you know Julian Althus?"

"He's not the guy," Elena says.

"You're sure?"

"Sure? Well, very unlikely."

"Okay," he says. "Who else has a motive to want you dead?"

"Just me, you're saying? You're not part of this?"

"Of course I am. Now."

She looks out on the moving roadside of generic foliage and signs. "Classic wrong-place-wrong-time guy."

"Depends how you look at it," he says.

"You're having fun?" she asks incredulously.

"Has its moments."

She straightens up in the seat. "Okay, so how do we turn this around?"

"I'm working on it," he says.

———✺———

Mike Skillan has, maybe, ten minutes a day to be alone in his office. Typically there's a brief spell late morning, and another late afternoon. He enjoys those moments. Kick back, think. Clear his head, maybe close his eyes. Especially welcome now, since he has a summer cold. He really hates interruptions.

Intercom buzzer. His secretary. "You said to tell you if Perry Rauschenberg called."

"He's on?"

"Line one," she says.

He picks up. "Perry?"

"Hi Mike. So here's the deal. They're willing to head back, see you in person."

"When?"

"As early as this evening."

"Bring 'em over."

"No, that's the thing. They want to see you alone. Here. In my office."

"That's bullshit. Who the fuck they think they are? These two are wanted for murder."

"I know, Mike. But neither you nor I think they did it. In fact, we both think they're being framed. And they have information on the framer, which should help you. So the reality is, you can see them tonight, judge firsthand for yourself, and get some information immediately, or you can stand on ceremony regarding the venue of this meeting and then spend a large part of your budget trying to track them down in God knows what part of this country."

Mike puts the phone down for a few seconds, sneezes, and blows hard into a Kleenex. "I don't like it."

"They're not being arbitrary, Mike. They have good reasons for wanting to see you alone here."

"Oh, yeah? What reasons?"

"They'll tell you tonight?"

"How 'bout you telling me now?"

"I can't, but I'll tell you this. When they do tell you, you'll agree these conditions make sense."

"I should just accept that?"

"Yes," says Perry. "Because I'm giving you my word."

——*∿∿*——

Atlanta airport; shuttle train between terminals; Elena and Tom, holding onto the same pole, moving smoothly through the tunnel, listen to a recorded announcement of the oncoming station.

"That's Hal," Elena says. "From the movie."

"Thought I recognized that voice,'" Tom says.

They hear Hal confirming their stop.

"Is this really wise?" she says.

"Using Hal in the airport?"

"Our staying in the airport, jerko. Traveling together. Undisguised. I mean—what was it, ten minutes ago?—your buddy Rauschenberg says the DA lifts the alert on us, and we're supposed to think they already know that in Atlanta, a thousand miles away? Assuming it actually happened. And that there won't be ten cops waiting for us at the gate to the New York flight?"

"Have some trust."

"Really?" she says. "Why's that? Why not just wait a day and be sure?"

"And give that killer woman another crack at us tonight in Atlanta?"

"If she can track us to Atlanta, she can follow us to New York. She probably lives in New York."

"That's probably right," he says.

"So why're you being so fucking calm about this?"

"Because now I have a plan," he says.

"Which now you're planning to share?"

"Not here."

"And what? I'm supposed to just rely on that?"

"Wish you would," he says.

Her look says, *that's not something I do*, but then changes to something like wonder—at the way her body seems to relax into trust.

THIRTY-SIX

Mike Skillan, on his way to the elevator, is waylaid in the hall by Foster Donachetti. "You gotta see this. Just came in." He hands Mike a hard copy of an email from the Atlanta police.

Mike reads a note apparently from Elena to a code-name addressee. "What's this?"

"It's off a BlackBerry belonging to the Riles girl. They found it in a B&B in New Orleans."

"How'd they find the room?"

Foster looks confused. "Don't know, come to think of it. Think I heard cops there checked on some disturbance."

"Who's it to, the email?"

"Presumably to the woman who shot up the bedroom in Ashaway, Kentucky."

"How we know it's a woman?"

"You're right. We don't. Riles told the local sheriff—the guy she was renting the house from—that it was a woman."

"Which might have been misdirection."

"Might've been."

"And so could this BlackBerry message."

"Well, this one's against interest."

"True." Mike studies it again. "Okay, thanks. Got a meeting. See you in the morning."

The elevator arrives, and he takes it. On the way down he thinks, *I'm getting to see a very small piece of this.*

—◦◦◦—

Perry Rauschenberg works in a six-window corner office. Even at large firms there are relatively few of these to go around. In some, it's allotted by seniority, but that's rare. More commonly they're a bargained-for perk. Occasionally—and this was true in Rauschenberg's case—the perk is dispensed by consensus to a rainmaking star.

Tom and Elena are with him, straight from the airport. No one is seated: Perry, six feet tall, dark acne-scarred skin, black crinkly hair, is standing behind his desk, slitting mail with a letter opener while he talks. Tom looks out the window, parting the blinds with his fingers. Elena paces as if she were caged.

"And if he doesn't believe us?" Tom asks.

"There's nothing stopping him from arresting you on the spot."

"We might run."

"He might have cops downstairs, right outside the building."

"There was no agreement as to downstairs?"

Perry looks up. "He's limited only as to this office."

Elena says, "Probably a set up."

"I think he'll give you a fair hearing."

"He's not the judge," she says.

"In reality," Perry says, "at this stage, he is."

The buzzer. On the speaker, Rauschenberg's secretary's voice. "He's at reception."

Perry casts an inquiring look at his clients. Tom nods. "Bring him in," Rauschenberg says.

There are three Corbu leather armchairs arranged in front of Perry's desk. Tom and Elena take two of them.

Mike is led in, shakes hands with his classmate while glancing at the other two who have risen, nods to both when introduced, and settles in the third chair. "So," he says. "At long last. The desperados."

"You think it's funny?" Elena says.

"No," Mike says. "I don't."

"Desperate fits," Elena says. "Grabbed, kidnapped, orphaned, hounded. Falsely accused!"

"Really?" Mike says. "You probably know the evidence against you. It's been on the news for days. Your lawyer says you've been framed. Why should I believe that?"

"You already do," Tom says.

"Or I wouldn't be here?" Mike loudly blows his nose. "You have something to tell me, or am I wasting my time?"

Tom says, "A woman, probably a contract assassin, has tried to kill us twice. In Kentucky, we put pillows under the blankets, and she shot up the beds in a dark room. She tracked us to New Orleans and stalked us outside our B&B. Whoever's framing us wants us missing, apparently in flight, so the frame sticks. No one else has the motive to kill us."

"How do I know you didn't shoot up the bed yourself?"

"You talk to Charlie, the Ashaway sheriff?"

"He didn't see her."

"The waitress did."

"Yeah, I got that. But nothing connecting her to the shooting—or to New Orleans—but your saying it. So there's another scenario." Mike hands Perry the copy of the email, supposedly from Elena to the purported assassin.

Perry studies it, and frowns. He hands it to Tom, who reads, shakes his head in denial, hands it to Elena, who shouts, "I didn't write this!"

"It was on your BlackBerry."

"Which they stole from me when they kidnapped us."

Tom asks, "Where'd you get this?"

"New Orleans police. They found the phone in your B&B."

"That right?" Tom says. "And how the hell they know to look there?"

"Presumably they were tipped."

"I'll bet they were."

"Maybe by you," Mike says.

"Why the hell would we do that?"

"So you could put on the show you're now giving me?"

"And according to that email," Tom says, "our plan was to get lost in America. Yet here we are. Whaddya know!"

"Part of the show."

"I don't think you believe that."

"Frankly," Mike says, "I don't know what to believe. What I know is that there's a lot of money at stake. People have been known to do a lot more for a lot less."

"I'll tell you the question to ask," Tom says, "which will tell you what's really happening. How the hell did that woman know we were in Ashaway, Kentucky, or anywhere close? From out of town somewhere, some woman no one's ever seen makes a beeline trip to some no-account greasy spoon in the middle of nowhere, USA, where we happen to eat every day."

"Traveling saleswoman?"

"You can check that. She did nothing in that town but follow us to our house and then shoot up our bed."

"We'll check it."

"Yeah," Tom says, "but I don't think you're really getting the point."

"That you're being framed? Yeah I get that's your assertion."

"What I said, you're not getting it. Whoever's framing us has a mole in your office. Because the only people who knew we were in Kentucky were the guy who dropped us close, the truck driver, and whomever he talked to in your office. I assume you talked to him. So who knew in your office? And what are they getting out of this?"

Mike's reflex, when hit with the unexpected, is to show nothing but a smile. "Let me talk to your lawyer. Alone."

Lawyer and clients exchange looks; Perry nods and beckons

Mike out of the room. They walk to an open conference room a few steps down the hall.

"This is what I'll do," Mike says. "For their own protection, if they're telling the truth, or for mine, if they're not. They stay in a room, or an apartment, in this city, under guard. And no one knows, except the people I need for security."

"For how long?"

"Indefinitely."

"Jesus, Mike."

"Until we can make some sense of this."

"They *are* telling the truth."

"Maybe."

"Come on, Mike. You would have arrested them by now if you didn't believe them. And they wouldn't have come back if they weren't innocent."

"That young woman is set to inherit about five billion dollars. Pretty good motivation to return."

"What you're suggesting—requiring—is totally off the books, Mike."

"Call it informal sequester. You can do anything by consent, Perry. And that's what I need. Otherwise they go to the lockup. And we fight bail. Which we'll win, and you know it."

⸺◦⁓◦⸺

Strolling from his office to his co-op on UN Plaza, pleasuring in a gentle breeze off the river, Yasim notices the light on in his apartment on the sixteenth floor. He's given the key to only one other person. He did this reluctantly, and with interdictions about using it except in emergencies. In the light of that light, Yasim rearranges his plans for the rest of the evening. Visualizing her upstairs generates a delicious concoction of desire and rage.

"I was so hoping you'd be here tonight," Birdie says, holding the covers up to her chin, as Yasim enters the bedroom. Her voice is given a coquettish lilt by the question of whether she's wearing anything under the sheet.

"Did you get my messages?" he asks. Though his anger is dissipating, it chills his voice.

"Yes, my love, but of what use are messages? They told me you missed me, but not when you were returning."

"To get in here, you used the key I gave you?"

"Of course I used the key."

"And what did I tell you about the use of the key?"

"But this *is* an emergency, darling."

"Really?" he says in a tone mocking the thought.

"Have I done wrong?" she says. "Do I need to be spanked?"

She lowers the covers, answering the question of her attire—or lack thereof—in a manner that scatters his thoughts.

THIRTY-SEVEN

At breakfast in their West Side apartment, Dottie asks Mike, "Do you think they did it?"

"Not sure," he says. He allows himself one fried egg a day, and he devours the last of this one. "Talking to them, you'd think it's impossible, but it's conceivable they're great actors. Biggest problem is there's not a single piece of exculpatory evidence. Clean evidence. Almost the best thing they have going for them is that there's too much going the other way."

"Difficult position" she says.

"For them?"

"For you," she says. "Most of the evidence has leaked. The media's convicted them. There's an actual eyewitness, prints on the gun—which she bought illegally just before the murder—now this email message. My God, what will you say? If you release them? How will you explain that?"

"You're the PR genius."

"It's beyond me, darling. Or anyone. It's not spinnable."

He takes a bite of his toast, glances at the news droning from the countertop TV. A financial analyst is excitedly reporting the launch of competing hostile takeover bids by two Manhattan-based companies for a third, General Technology & Media. Mike puts his toast down and listens. When Dottie interrupts, he hushes her.

"What?" she says.

"GT&M's in play. Didn't you represent them?"

"Not the company. I did some work for Sofi Harding, who owns a great deal of it. Controls it, as a practical matter."

"One of the bidders is Riles Whitney."

"How interesting," she says.

"Indeed." He drinks some coffee.

"What are you thinking, Mike?"

"I'll let you know when I finish thinking it."

———

In a sitting room off the lower gallery of a Fifth Avenue triplex, Rashid al-Calif waits to be told he's deemed admittable upstairs. It's not unlike being seated in an antechamber in Versailles. "Would you care for tea, sir?" asks a theatrical young man in livery.

"Down here?" Rashid says.

The young man shifts his eyes upward.

Rashid says, "That's the option? I'll wait, then, until...." He lifts his own eyes toward the ceiling. "But thank you."

"Won't be long, sir." The young man departs, as if yanked away by a string, leaving Rashid to make further study of his surroundings.

He gets up, goes to a small window offering a view of the park south of the museum. From the tenth floor, he can see treetops and meadows, a system of ponds and paths, and, at Seventy-Second Street, a convergence of park drives and transverses. His own apartment also faces the park, but on Central Park West; on a much higher floor, in a new building. On balance, he prefers Mrs. Harding's location and thinks he might change his own. It's not only the view. He's beginning to think of himself as more of an Upper East Side person.

The young man reenters. "Madame is ready for you, sir."

They climb a straight, rather plain staircase into a high-ceilinged, forty-foot-long gallery lit by three ancient glass chandeliers. The gallery walls are papered in chinoiserie. On a pedestal in each corner stands a Teng horse, the four of them appearing to leap across centuries. The parquetry is covered in carpets woven by artists known only to experts, such as Rashid. The most conspicuous feature, however, is an ornate spiral staircase to the third floor, where, Rashid imagines, bedrooms abound of equally rarified furnishings and views.

He is led into an immense living room whose windows offer such sweeping park vistas he has the feeling he's flying over them. Mrs. Sofi Harding greets him without rising from her sofa seat in the embrasure of the middle window. She wears a dress of teal blue silk, a bit shocking against the pale yellow of the draperies. Rashid takes not the opposite seat tendered, which would have blinded him with glare, but a side chair that forces Mrs. Harding to swivel toward him.

"So, Mr. al-Calif," she says, "you wish to retire me from the fray? You and Lowell? All that new money and Arab money. Oil money, do I have that right?"

"Not entirely oil money," Rashid says, admiring how young this woman looks, despite her white hair and reported sixty-four years. "And there are frays and frays."

"Indeed," she says with a bit of an edge. "Tea? I've only the English kind. It's all I drink."

"Literally?"

"Oh, you mean, do I drink booze? I do drink booze. Not excessively, of course. I don't swill it. Do you?"

"Swill?" He laughs at the absurdity.

"Drink at all, I mean."

"Oh yes," Rashid says. "On occasion."

"Good." She wafts her small hand upward, apparently delivering their tea orders to some unseen minion, perhaps the young man. "I dislike dealing with fundamentalists."

"I'm a man of my faith," he says, smiling, "but my faith can be as sophisticated as the next one. For example, I believe that you, Mrs. Harding, are Catholic. Yet you are also an intellectual and a member of the various boards that run the Church's business affairs in this city. As a result, you are permitted to read indexed books, which would be a great sin for people of a different class."

"And you're permitted whiskey."

"On occasion."

"What else are you permitted?"

"I can read anything I like."

"Such as the financials of my company."

"Naturally."

"Which you've of course done," she says.

"I hope diligently."

"And what have you concluded, Mr. al-Calif?"

"Would it trouble you to call me Rashid?"

"Not in the least," she says with a laugh, but without sign of reciprocating.

"I've concluded," Rashid says, "that your company could be making more money than it does."

"And why would I wish it to do that?" she asks.

"For the benefit of your stockholders. And it's the way business is done."

"Not my business," she says. "Which my stockholders know. Or should have when they bought into it."

"Perhaps they bought … to retire you from the fray."

"Like you and Lowell?"

"Actually," he says "we thought you might like to stay on in some capacity."

"Be a figurehead, you mean."

"Chairman of the board, is what we were thinking."

"Chair*man*?"

"A figure of speech," he says. "But surely not a figurehead position. You could help guide the corporate mission."

"Oh, I love words like that. Mission! So *now*, so fashionable, so corporate hip."

"I said something wrong?"

"You slip rather easily," she says, "into the institutional version of the politically correct. Next you'll be telling me about 'community' and 'diversity.'"

"We would be achieving that."

"Your folks all being Arabs."

"Not necessarily. And not Lowell's, in all probability."

"Look, Mr. al-Calif. I can well understand why you and doubtless others have chosen to put my company in play. But it won't be an easy conquest. I do own a controlling interest."

"Not, however, a majority interest," he points out. "The funds and institutions—who do converse in the language you find objectionable—may, nonetheless, be more inclined to maximize profits than to do good."

"And I'm perceived as a do-gooder?"

Rashid bows his head.

"Any good that I do," says Mrs. Harding, "is entirely accidental. I have a much simpler 'mission.' To have fun. And turning the company over to you boys would doubtless get in the way of that. Do you know, I co-founded this company with my husband."

"We are prepared to pay you very handsomely for your shares. Twenty-five points over market, which is already inflated by our recent purchases of stock."

"He ran it," she says, ostensibly ignoring the offer, "but consulting with me at every step. Meaningfully consulting. And so when he died—"

"Thirty points over market?"

"Do you have any idea who I am?"

"Forty-eight points. Our limit. Which comes to twelve point three billion dollars."

"I've asked you a non-rhetorical question."

"The thirteenth-richest woman in the world? It is not a lucky number. We would be delighted to move you into seventh place."

"And you think I care?" she says. "Tell me something … *Rashid*. Lowell and you … or whomever the UAE wants to send here to run things—how in the world do you plan to coexist, much less co-manage?"

"Why would you think we'd have to?" he asks.

She tries to read his impassive face. "I see. You now have a deal about that? One of you is really the banker and will step aside after the takeover?"

"All things are possible," he says.

"Like Lowell doesn't know he's to move aside? You're just planning to screw him?"

He looks horrified. "Sell out a partner? How would I do that?"

"If the end doesn't trouble you, Rashid, I'm sure you'll have no problem figuring out the means."

—◦◦◦—

In Elena's tiny one-bedroom apartment, Tom, in his customary shorts, plunks down on the living room sofa. Elena, in the kitchenette, near the front door, inspects the dubious contents of containers she's just retrieved from the fridge. Tom says, "You live pretty frugally for a rich kid."

Looking up, Elena says, "You might put some clothes on."

"I might, despite the condition they're in. And in time, which we seem to have lots of." Rising, he plucks the shirt he wore the day before off a nearby side chair and takes a cautionary whiff. "Ugh," he says.

"You must have some clothes someplace."

"Of course. In the apartment I was living in before"—he spreads his hands out—"*you*."

"Is it empty?"

"I doubt it. The rent was paid."

"By you?"

"Naturally. She's an actress."

"You're saying she's likely to be there, sponging?"

"Sponging, well ..." he says, "... rent having been paid, she's on her own, I'm not showing up ...."

"But if you did, she'd leave?"

"What are you thinking? You want me out of here?"

"You couldn't possibly be comfortable sleeping on that sofa again," Elena says.

Tom glances down at this piece of furniture—still sagging forlornly with his impression, colors fading in the morning sun—then up to her.

"Don't look at me that way," she says.

He continues to do so.

"With blaming eyes," she says.

"Not my idea last night, that sofa."

"We should split up," she says.

"We made a deal with the DA," Tom says. "We stay in one apartment."

"Because he thinks we're a couple. We should disabuse him of that, renegotiate the deal."

"We could try. Probably wouldn't work, though. Takes fewer of their men to keep watch over one apartment."

She slumps dejectedly onto the sofa. The room, twelve by fifteen, looks like it might have been decorated during a half-hour spree at Pottery Barn, or even less time on the retailer's website. Her one remarkable possession is an Egon Schiele print, which looks real, hanging in isolation on the opposite wall. The apartment is on the sixth floor of an old building, with a large window overlooking Broadway and Eighty-First Street. Elena is dressed in jeans and a polo shirt. Tom is still standing there in his shorts.

"They've got the door padlocked," she says, sounding disheartened.

"And," he adds, "they've taken an empty apartment right below this one. I saw them moving in this morning. They've gone to a lot of trouble."

"Shit."

He says, "Do you really want me to leave?"

"Yes," she says. "I don't like the pressure."

"What ... pressure?"

"Don't be dense."

He stares at her; she looks away.

"The pressure," he says, "is self-imposed."

"Forget it. We have bigger problems. There's nothing to eat."

"Absolutely nothing left in the fridge?"

"We ate it all last night," she says. "The food that's not spoiled, I mean."

"The deal is, we call, and they'll go shopping for us. Or pick up takeout."

"I can't believe this," she says. "We're total prisoners? We can't even go shopping?"

He sits next to her on the sofa. "I noticed a fire escape out your bedroom window. Goes down to an alley that leads into the street, which you can see from here."

She turns to face him. "You game for that?"

He shrugs. "Starts the manhunt again."

"Where would we go?"

He thinks. "New Jersey?"

"Shit."

"We barely have enough money to get there."

"Dammit, Tom, I'm starving again! Since I met you, I've constantly been hungry."

"Let's give them a shopping list," he says. "Just for now."

"I don't want to wait. I want to climb down that fire escape." She jumps off the sofa and darts by him to the large window. He watches her peer out, then return with a disconsolate face. "They're in a car out there."

"How can you tell?"

"You don't believe me? Look for yourself."

He does look. Black car, two men, drinking coffee.

"All right," he says. "Let me get some clothes on."

"You have another plan?"

"We go down the fire escape."

"Great," she says. "And then what?"

"I'll think of something on the way down."

A knock on the front door startles both of them.

"You expecting visitors?" Tom says.

Then the sound of someone opening a lock.

She jumps up to peer through the peephole. "It's that guy we met with last night. The DA. Skillan."

"He can hear you, El," Tom says, getting into his pants. "Just open the door."

She does with a shrug, confronts Skillan and says, "You didn't put enough food in the fridge."

"You won't be needing it," Mike says.

"Going to hang us right now, are you?" she says.

"Why don't the both of you sit down?"

Tom says, "May we offer you some hospitality? The water here's terrific."

"Just sit the fuck down, Weldon. I've something to tell you."

Elena says, "I'll tell you where we'll sit down. There's a coffee shop on Eighty-Second. We'll sit there. Eating breakfast."

"Great," says Mike. "That's exactly what I had in mind."

THIRTY-EIGHT

In a half-empty diner, the breakfast crowd mostly gone, Elena attacks an egg white omelet with spinach; Tom, two fried eggs and bacon. Mike, sipping coffee, does the talking. "I'm indicting you," he says, "because I have no choice. On the one hand, the evidence against you is overwhelming. On the other hand, it's the only way I can let you go free."

Tom says, "Those sound like contradictory propositions."

"I know." He eyes Tom's fried eggs enviously.

"So, in effect, you're saying you won't oppose our bail application?"

"Token opposition. The judges know the difference."

"But not the newspapers," Tom says.

"Probably right."

"So you're covered with the press."

Mike shrugs.

Elena says, with a mouth full of omelet, "But you do believe we're innocent."

"I haven't said that. What I believe is that there are two possibilities. Either you're much better con artists than I'm inclined to give you credit for, or someone's doing an excellent job of fabricating evidence against you."

"In other words," Tom says, "you're *inclined* to believe we're innocent."

"I do not know, Weldon. That's the blunt fact. But I'm likely to learn more by setting you free than I am by putting you in jail. And I risk very little. If you run again, you're guilty. And it probably wouldn't take too much digging this time to root you out."

"How 'bout if we're killed?"

"Then we'll know you're innocent."

"Great," Tom says. "But not if we disappear."

"We'll try to prevent that." The voice is soothing; the assurance is not.

"Tell me this," Tom says. "I've heard on the news that you have telephone company records of my having called Elena. Those records *are* phony—I'd never met Elena before in my life, nor had I any idea of her existence—but that's not my point. The DA's office does not voluntarily release evidence of that kind before trial, much less before an indictment."

"Very true."

"So there's a leak. Probably same guy who's feeding info, as I said last night."

"I agree with that," Mike says.

"And you're doing something about it?"

"What do you think?"

Elena looks up from her now empty plate. "Why did you change your mind from last night? About us? About letting us go free?"

A waitress refills Mike's coffee, and he empties a packet of sugar substitute into the brew. "You've been following the news about Riles Whitney getting into a hostile takeover war?"

"I saw it this morning, yeah," Elena says.

"As I understand it," Mike says, "you now own a controlling interest in your dad's company."

"And?" says Elena. "What? That makes me no longer a suspect?"

"You're still a suspect, but now you're useful. Well, possibly useful."

Tom says, "You've finally figured out that the murder was

motivated by some element of corporate greed, such as this takeover battle."

"Possibly motivated," Mike says. "Unfortunately, many businessmen here and abroad had many motives for...." He spreads his hands apologetically.

"Killing my dad," Elena says, keeping her face calm.

"Sorry," Mike says, "but yes."

Tom says, "I doubt if it's that simple."

"Oh?" Mike asks with a raised eyebrow. "You've got a theory?"

"Working on it. But if it is another corporate raider or such, what you're looking for is the borderline psychotic. The pathologically narcissistic. The guy who thinks whatever he does is right simply because he does it."

"Not sure that narrows the field much, but great," Mike says. "Let's find him."

"You want Elena to spy for you?" Tom says.

"Both of you, actually. You come in as her lawyer. No one has a bigger stake in this takeover than she. So no one has more right to the facts. And no one in my office has better legal training than you to understand what's happening. So to be honest, you're a good team for us. Also, very highly motivated."

Tom thinks about this while Elena steals a slice of his toast and butters it. They eat for a moment in silence.

Mike says to Elena, "How well do you know Julian Althus?"

Tom says, "He's a suspect?"

"You know him too?" Mike asks.

"Done some work for him, yeah. He had a motive, of course, but—"

"It's not him," Elena says quickly.

"Why you so sure?"

She shakes her head emphatically.

"Not the type?" Mike says ironically, not really trusting such judgments.

"Why do you suspect him?" Tom says. "Apart from the motive?"

"Tip. From an anonymous source."

"And you trust *him*?"

"I don't even know him. Call came into one of my team, just saying, 'While you're watching, watch him.'"

—⁓⁓—

They're on the street, on Broadway, after Skillan leaves them to themselves. Traffic is grinding. A siren blares blocks away. People rush by, different ages and races. They know where they're going and anxious to get there. Unlike Elena and Tom. She says, "What do we do now?" The sudden freedom is as bewildering as the sun's glare in their eyes.

"We?" he asks, as if that were the important question.

"You heard him, right? You're my lawyer. We poke around at Riles Whitney. It's in our interest."

"I heard one thing loud and clear," he says. "We disappear, we're guilty. Alive or dead. That's how they'll read it." The implications sink in, which creates a pocket of silence.

"So we're targets again," she says. "It's in the best interests of whoever to kill us."

"I should think," he says. "Even more, now."

"He obviously sees that, Skillan … but he didn't offer us protection. You think he doesn't care whether we get killed?"

"I don't know," Tom says. "Might make his job easier. Another crime, more clues. Or an easier solution. Just go with the flow, pin it on us. And since he will have opposed our bail applications…."

"We have to hide," she says quickly. "In the city. Be seen during the day, in public, maybe at Riles Whitney—so it's obvious we haven't run—but otherwise stay hidden."

"I've got a better idea," he says. "We split up. You get your own protection. A security firm. There are good ones.

Twenty-four hours a day."

"Leaving you out there."

"They don't want me."

"Why not?" she says. "Takes them off the hook for murder. You disappear, you're the one who did it. And if they can blame it on you, that implicates me."

"So what are you saying?"

"I've already said it," she says.

"We stay together?"

She looks up at him impatiently.

"Half hour ago," he says, "you were trying to get rid of me."

"Facts have changed."

"No they haven't," he says.

"Don't badger me on this!"

"Okay," he says. "What are the arrangements?"

"What do you mean?"

"Me on the sofa?"

Her look turns fierce.

"I'm not sleeping on the sofa," he says.

"Jesus!" she says. "This *again*?"

"What's the 'this'?"

"The 'this' is this goddamn negotiation! This pressure! About our having sex is the fucking 'this'!"

"Making love, you mean?"

"Christ, Tom! We're on fucking Broadway!"

"Am I on the fucking sofa or in the bed?"

"There are people here!"

"Am I on the—"

"You're in the bed, okay!"

"Okay," he says.

"Damn," she says.

"Wasn't so hard."

"You're impossible," she says.

"You think you're a bargain?"

THIRTY-NINE

In the maple-paneled boardroom of Riles Whitney & Co., Julian Althus and the company's attorney, Harrison Stith, explain the situation, as they know it, to Robertson Riles's two oldest daughters and their husbands. All sit at the boardroom table, except Stith, who, having said his piece, has helped himself to coffee at the credenza and now peers at a glinting cityscape through the windows on the forty-ninth floor.

Both girls are tall, slender, long-faced, and mean. They might have been models, had they need of employment, which of course they do not. Their mother was a model—plucked right off the runway by the then–bon vivant, Robbie. He later divorced her and married a young woman who had an entry-level job at Sotheby's. They met at the York Avenue gallery over a new consignment of post-impressionist paintings and parted thereafter as little as possible. She and their daughter, Elena, were the loves of Robbie's truncated life.

The problem facing the unloved daughters is not that they were disinherited. Each had already been endowed with considerable fortunes and would be additionally, and handsomely, provided for at the probate of Robbie's will. It's that they were given no stock in the company, which left them without any real power. They would have charity boards, and the balls that went with them, but not credentials for the people running things, the people who mattered—certainly to the sisters, Constance and Patricia, and their respective spouses, Lawton Sergeant and Jasper Kane.

Lawton does most of the questioning. He'd been to law school for one semester, ten years ago, which he believes qualifies him to lead the discussion. "Surely," he says, "these unusual circumstances would warrant some equitable relief."

"The circumstances being our takeover bid?" says Julian.

"That and … what Elena's obviously done. You can't inherit from someone you've … whose life you've taken. Given what's at stake, power should be exercised by the presumptive heirs, Connie and Patty."

Stith says, "You're presuming Elena's guilty and will lose her inheritance."

"Of course," pipes in Jasper. "Of course she's guilty."

"Yes, well," Harry says, "in this country—"

"Don't lecture us on the presumption of innocence," says Lawton. "That's for the criminal courts. Our application would be to a court of equity."

Stith eyes the young man with disapproval. "And you would like this application to say precisely what? That the equity court should now try Elena for murder—or maybe just read the newspapers and find her guilty—and then let your wife and sister-in-law vote the stock?"

"I'm sure," Lawton says, "a good lawyer can find a more persuasive way to put our position."

"A good lawyer," Stith says, "would not put such a position. For, if he were to do so, sir, he would never be heard to put any other position, at least before that particular judge."

"Can't we at least stop Elena from voting the stock?" Connie says. "She's wanted for murder and in flight from the law."

Julian says, "I'm afraid you may have missed the news. Just came over the wires. Elena's back and under indictment."

"Even better," Jasper says.

"I don't really think so," Julian says.

"I agree," says Harry, returning to his seat at the table.

"Nonetheless, Connie, I think we can get some relief for you along the lines *you* just suggested. Harder case, now that she's returned, but not impossible, if played right."

Althus's secretary puts her head in the door. "May I speak with you, sir?"

Glancing at them briefly, Julian steps out, then almost immediately returns. "They're here," he says. "Elena and Tom Weldon."

Connie and Patty, both standing now, looming over their husbands, say, almost in unison, "We don't want to see her."

"Of course," says Julian. "You stay here. Harry and I will meet with them in my office, while you depart. And I'll report to...?"

"Me," Connie says. "You report to me."

———

They're all standing: Stith, Althus, Elena, and Tom.

"The thing is," says Tom, "we need to be filled in on your GT&M takeover bid. If you'd just direct your principal M&A people to spare us some time...."

"We?" Harry says. "Us?" He clucks at Weldon. "You're a couple now, you two?"

"You know, Harry," says Tom, "that's none of your business."

Julian says, "I've no problem with the request. Indeed, I'm happy to fill you in myself. But it would seem you two had something more important to worry about right now."

"The indictment?" Elena says offhandedly.

"You think it trifling?"

"We're dealing with it," Tom says.

"How?" Harry asks, then sees Tom smile. "Perry? Are you being represented by Perry Rauschenberg?" He looks offended, as if the victim of a trick.

Tom says, "Can we get back to the takeover?"

"Your interest is what?" says Stith. "Casual? Just like to keep informed?"

"Of course not, Harry. We want to determine whether it's in the best interests of the shareholders."

"*You* want to determine that?"

"Elena does. And she's asked me to advise her."

"I have, yes," Elena says.

"And if you think it's not? In the company's best interest?"

"We'll cross that bridge when we come to it," Tom says. "Okay?"

"You and?"

"Elena, of course."

"Who, at the moment—before probate—has yet to inherit the stock of this company, if she ever does so."

"Until probate," Tom says, "the stock is voted by the executor of the estate. And have you read the will?"

"She hasn't been approved yet," Harry states. "And her sisters will oppose the appointment."

"You know where that leads, Harry," Tom says. "The probate judge won't appoint the sisters. He'll appoint some party hack to serve as interim executor until the criminal matter is cleared up. And the hack will be responsive to the highest bidder. You want that? Another bidding war, this one under the table? That Jockery might win? Or you want to do what we asked when we came in here? Fill us in. We might well end up on your side. We might even be able to help you."

Julian says, "Makes sense to me, Harry."

They're in Julian's office, which used to be Elena's father's office, and is therefore an awkward place for Julian to be receiving her. Particularly since all Riles's artwork and artifacts have been replaced with Althus's own art and memorabilia. He covers his embarrassment with a show of affability. "Fairly straightforward, this GT&M matter. There were three bidders; now it appears it's just us and the A-rabs, the UAE to be more precise. The key to the outcome is, of course, Sofi Harding, who owns at least thirty percent of the company. Her vote can determine whether the company invokes its poison pill, which as you probably know would make any takeover difficult, if not impossible."

"Do you know her?" Elena asks.

"I've met her, of course."

"But you aren't friends?"

They've all been standing, but at this point, Julian sits behind his desk, and Tom and Elena in front of it. Stith doesn't move. He says, "There are circles, and then there are circles."

Tom, glancing at Julian, says, "And hers is ... above yours?"

"Considerably."

"Until now," Elena says. "Now that my dad has died and you've taken over."

"We'll see," Julian says.

"Did you know she was friendly with my dad?"

"Their circles coincided. And that would probably explain why your father appeared to be confident about this acquisition. Invariably, before a takeover battle, one hires an investment banking firm. At an enormous fee, I might add. He didn't do that, at least not for the strategizing. Said he'd handle this one with just the lawyers. Their fees are a fraction of the bankers.'"

"And now?" Elena asks. "How would you rate our chances?"

"I retained a banking firm."

"So you're not so confident."

"The UAE could outbid us. They certainly have the greater resources, so it's a matter of how much they're willing to spend. Or Ms. Harding—who, I gather, does not now want to sell—could block us. Either of those possibilities is probably greater than our succeeding."

Tom asks, "Would it be a good fit? And is the value there?"

"I think so. Would of course diversify us tremendously. But, naturally, it depends on the price. Our latest offer was two-twenty a share, which was nearly fifteen points over market. We think the Arabs will go to at least two-forty."

"And you?"

"The bankers advise a limit of two-forty-seven." Julian says.

"Before you bring it to the board," Tom says, "Elena should be consulted."

"I'm advised by counsel—"

"Stith, you mean."

"Harry, yes—that until probate—"

Stith breaks in. "I think we've gone far enough with this."

Tom says, "Whom do you represent, Harry? The company or the other daughters?"

"I see no conflict."

Tom laughs. "Really? No conflict? My, my."

Julian, looking surprised, says, "If you're acting for the other daughters, Harry, even I see a conflict."

Harry harrumphs. "I'll take this under advisement."

Tom says, "You do that. And when you arrive at the obvious conclusion, do call. The company's largest shareholder, for whom I'm acting, would like to know whether your representation is divided. Before the end of the day would be fine. Because if you're not acting for the corporation, then it's you from whom further information will be withheld."

FORTY

Skillan's brain trust on the Riles case has assembled itself in a rebellious arc facing the Acting DA's desk. Chief Deputy DA Joe Cunningham says, "No one here agrees with this, Mike," and gains nods from Foster Donachetti and his principal aide, Sammy Riegert.

"Not surprising," Mike says.

"You're saying you think they're innocent?"

"People keep putting those words in my mouth. I'm saying I don't know. And if I don't know, a jury won't know, in which case they'll acquit."

"But you're also saying," says Sammy, "you want me to blow the bail application."

"Yes," Mike says in a tone of solicitude.

"That's hard on me, Mike. Fucks me up."

"Right. Bad, I know."

"Shitload of press there."

"So get a junior guy to do it."

Foster says, "That'll look bad on you."

Mike shrugs. "Someone's gotta take the hit."

"Fuck it," says Sammy. "I'll do it. Probably I can talk to the clerk. Put on a show, but get your result anyway."

"Thanks, Sammy. And then we can watch them. Watch the whole group. Their interactions. Which reminds me. Where do we stand with that guy, what's his name? The new CEO?"

"Althus," Joe says. "Julian Althus."

"Yeah, Sammy, weren't you supposed to interview him?"

"Next one up."

"You're suggesting," Foster says, "the Riles girl might be acting with him?"

"I'm suggesting we do our jobs. We had a list. Althus is on it."

"There's someone else," Foster says. "The chauffeur. A man named Morrie Khalil."

"You haven't seen him yet?" Mike says.

"He's been out of state. Back now."

"Bring him in. Maybe frighten him a little."

—⁂—

On a park bench in Brooklyn, Teddy Stamos watches Morrie Khalil lose a chess game to a seventeen-year-old kid.

Khalil gets up, walks off. Teddy follows.

"You distracted me," Morrie says.

"It's showtime, Morrie. Chess is the distraction. We're going to need all your concentration now. Big time."

—⁂—

"Will you tell me again," Elena says over the roar of the subway, "why're we going to Red Hook?"

"Just beginning to gentrify," Tom says.

"That's a good thing?"

"The district is, for two reasons. One, whoever's hunting us may think outer boroughs, but probably not as far out. Two, it's in an early stage of gentrification. There're likely to be plenty of places newly renovated by overextended owners who'd love a short-term rental for cash."

"You ever been there?"

"Once."

"And you saw such places?"

"No, it was years ago."

"So how do you know this?"

"I just said. Gentrifying neighborhood. Gotta be. And there's a third reason. Which you just reminded me of. Right on the water there's a factory."

"You want to live near a factory?"

"This one I do," he says.

"Okay, what do they make?"

"Bake, actually. Key lime pie. Any great restaurant in the city offers Key lime pie, it comes from this factory. Fantastic dessert."

"We're moving to Brooklyn so you can eat pie?"

"We. You'll love it. Best in the world."

"I don't like Key lime pie."

"Neither do I, ordinarily. This is special. You'll see."

Out of the subway, onto the streets, they see the signs of gentrification they're looking for: women's boutiques, a Turkish-blend coffee shop, restaurants with blackboard menus out front, antiques shops, and several renovation sites. But no "For-Rent" signs on any of them.

Elena says, "Maybe there's a local newspaper?"

"So you're willing to live here?"

"I've seen worse."

"Let's just keep walking. Something'll turn up."

They turn a corner, toward the water, and it does. A sign, offering apartments for rent. On a building of three stories, clad in brown plastic shingles. It has new windows, a five-step stoop, and a flat roof. Elena says wryly, "House of my dreams."

A handsome black man in work clothes opens the door.

Tom says, "We saw your sign."

"One left," says the apparent owner, who puts down an electric saw. "It's a third-floor walkup. Wanna look?"

"How many rooms?" Elena asks.

"Just the one. But it's large. And furnished." Then proudly, "my model apartment." Then brightly, "has a terrace."

"Let's see it," Tom says.

"One room, you crazy?" says Elena.

The owner looks from one to the other. "Maybe I let you go up alone. Here's the key."

They ascend a new staircase, still encased in white sheetrock. On the top landing, they open a new unpainted wooden door, enter and look: bright floral spread on a king-size bed, high ceiling, wall-to-wall carpet, big windows, new love seat and chairs. And inspect: newly equipped kitchenette, newly tiled bathroom, fresh linen and blankets in a linen closet, plates in the cabinets, cutlery in the drawers. They go out on the deck, which is almost as large as the room. It's two blocks from the bay, and over the roofs of low buildings, they can see piers and the water.

Tom says, "This place is perfect."

"Perfect? One room?"

"That guy—he's gone for broke on the furnishings. Wall-to-wall carpet in Red Hook! And there's the terrace."

"What terrace?" she says. "We're standing on tar paper. It's the roof to the second-story apartment."

He laughs. "Look, we're going to be here two, three weeks at most."

"In one room? Without driving each other crazy?"

"There is that," he acknowledges. "So let's take it week at a time. Use it like a hotel room, while we look for something else. Big advantage not to have to shop for all the stuff he's put in."

She thinks about it while gazing at the harbor view. "Let's see what he's asking," Elena says.

Pleased, Tom follows her down the stairs. Small sofa, big bed, and not a word about either.

—⁓—

At a neighborhood sidewalk café, sipping Greek coffee, Teddy says, "I'm willing to trust you. We go back to your house. First thing, I deposit a hundred thousand dollars into your account. Then you tell me your whole story, and once I've vetted it, you call the DA's office and give that story to anyone who will record it. In the same conversation, you make a date to see that person ASAP."

"You want all this for one hundred thousand?" Morrie Khalil asks.

"Well, after you testify—tell the same story on the stand—you get the rest of the money."

"The full nine hundred ninety-nine?"

"No. The full two hundred."

"Two hundred thousand? For testimony that's probably worth a billion?" Morrie laughs. "I'm not simpleminded. Maybe you are."

"All right, Morrie. Quarter of a million. Half now, half later. That's it. That's all I got. You want more, I have to go back to my client. I do that, the extreme probability is, he says fuck you, and finds another witness."

"Not with what I have."

"Well you see, that's a problem. I don't know what you have. I'm negotiating in the blind."

"Okay," Morrie says. "Tell you what. Hundred thousand now. I tell you the full story. You like it, it's another two hundred thou for the call and the visit, and two hundred thou more for the testimony."

"I'll call my client."

"You do that," Morrie says. "Because now I'm at the end of *my* limit. You understand, I've got a good job. You're asking me to throw it away. I'm not doing that for peanuts."

"Suppose I offered you another job?"

"With who? Your client? Who I don't even know."

"With me." Teddy says. "And not as a driver."

"Hmm," Morrie says. "Doesn't lower my terms. But might make me happier about offering them."

FORTY-ONE

Tom and Elena are in bed.

It's been a busy day. They subwayed back to Manhattan; she packed some clothes and toiletries; he bought some; they each ATM'd some cash; and returned separately by subway to Red Hook. There they found a bodega, provisioned their fridge, had dinner in a neighborhood café, retired to their studio apartment, changed into their sleeping attire, switched off the lights, and slipped one by one under the covers.

After a minute, Elena says, "So, I suppose now you'll want to have sex."

"How romantic," Tom says.

"It's true, isn't it? That's what you expect."

"I know you're nervous, El."

"Aren't you?" she says.

"Of course."

"So it's better to talk about it, right?" she says.

"Absolutely the opposite."

"You just turn off the lights and go to it?"

"Generally, yes."

"Generally? You have a process? You do this so often?"

"No," he says. "I don't."

Silence ensues.

"Okay then," she says.

"Can't now," he says. "You've broken the mood."

"What mood?" she says. "We had a mood?"

"Close."

"I didn't feel it. And you want to know the truth? I never have with anyone. Not really."

"Done it?"

"Felt it, stupid."

"There's an obvious reason for that."

"You're going to say, because it hasn't been the right guy."

"Don't you think?"

She says nothing. Neither does he. They lie there listening: to a distant shout, a nearby laugh, a boat horn, a passing car, someone's television turned up, then down.

He says, "We're going to have to take your pajamas off."

"Found the mood, have you?"

"What I suggested would help."

"With all that light streaming in from the windows?"

"The better to see you," he says.

"Why do you have to see me?"

"I'll assume you're kidding."

"Not entirely."

"Elena!"

"Yours first," she says.

"I'm not wearing pajamas."

"All the more reason. Your … skivvies."

"Then you'll take your pajamas off?" he asks hopefully.

"Then I'll think about it."

"All right," he says, laughing. He slides out of bed and shuts the blinds.

She sits up and says, "They close more tightly."

"They don't seem to, no."

"There's light still coming in. Don't you see it?"

He reopens the blinds, then snaps them shut.

"Doesn't help," she says.

"No one out there can see into here."

"It's not anyone from out there I'm worried about."

"You're modest with me?" He jumps back into bed and thrusts off his T-shirt.

"That's it?" she says.

"That was me going first."

"You call that going first? Classic."

"What is this," he says, "high school?"

Without a word, she gets up on her knees and, in two sudden motions, swoops off her top and yanks down her pajama pants. "Okay? Me! Anatomically correct. Usual parts in all the right places. Happy?"

"You're beautiful," he says.

"No, I'm not beautiful. I'm flawed. Like a human. For one thing, my boobs are small. Pointy and small."

He rushes to hold her. "No, really. You're beautiful."

"And you?"

He flops on his back, lowers his shorts, and kicks them onto the floor.

She says, "You're pretty big."

"I'm just aroused," he says.

"Really?"

He pulls her down to him, and she curls to his side. He says, "Of course, first times are shambles."

"Are they?" she says weakly.

"So we'll take it slowly," he says.

"Good idea."

He pulls her closer and lays his hand on the back of her leg, grazing her bare bottom. Then he kisses her on the mouth. It's a deep, long kiss with lots of yearning from each of them.

"Oh, my," she says.

"What?"

"It seems to be working."

Teddy Stamos rings the Khalils' front door, jabbing repeatedly. It's opened by Anna Khalil, Morrie's wife, who's dressed in a terry-cloth bathrobe, with the big "D" for Disney embroidered on its front.

"Sorry," Teddy says, "but it's urgent, and will be very rewarding to you if you let me in."

"I'll get him," she says, but Morrie is already descending the stairs, also in a white bathrobe identically embroidered.

"You've got your deal," Teddy says. "But we must act on it immediately."

Khalil puts on an act of geniality. "Come in, come in." He ushers Teddy into the living room, and deposits him into a chair. The Khalils take the sofa. "So, Morrie says. "My deal, meaning, specifically…."

Teddy pulls out his iPhone. "Look at this page. It's your new account at the bank you specified. You will note your account balance. One hundred thousand dollars. Full story please."

Morrie glances at the screen, then hands it to Anna. "You'd like a drink?" he asks.

"No, Morrie. Thank you. No drinks, all business, big rush. I want your story. Then I'll want you to call a man named Sammy Riegert at the DA's office and tell it to him."

"It's past ten."

"He's there."

"How could you know this?"

"Morrie, I know many things most people don't know. It's my stock-in-trade, my inventory, as it were. Now. Story please. For the moment, net, net."

"Okay." Morrie looks at his wife, who nods. "Very simple. On the night Mr. Riles was killed, I got a call from Mr. Althus. He said Mr. Riles would not be needing the car that night, so I should drive for him, Mr. Althus. I asked him how he knew this, that Mr. Riles wouldn't need the car, and he seemed to get very offended. Not like him at all. In an angry voice, he told

me to pick him up at his apartment at seven and be prepared
to stay with him until late that night."

"That was it? End of conversation?"

"With him, yes. But two minutes later, Mr. Riles's daughter
called. Elena. She said to do what Mr. Althus had told me and
not go near the office any time that night."

Teddy took his phone back from Anna, dialed a number
and handed it to Morrie. "Remember, the guy you want is
Sammy Riegert. Same story. Go."

"Doesn't it look funny, I ask for someone by name?"

"Of course."

"I mean, how do I explain how I know this."

"You don't. You ask for the guy heading up the team on
the Riles murder. You keep insisting on that guy, and you'll get
Sammy Riegert. Just tell 'em who you are. They want to talk
to you."

—⦚∾⦚—

Lowell Jockery returns to his penthouse apartment to find
Birdie in his bed. The smile of pleasure vanishes from his face
when he sees her bring from under the covers a Glock 27 with
silencer. She shoots him twice in the head before his dead body
hits the carpet.

FORTY-TWO

At approximately ten-thirty in the morning, at One Hogan Place, Tom Weldon works his way through two separate security stations before being shown into Mike Skillan's office. He says, without sitting down, "I did not shoot Lowell Jockery."

"Good morning, Tom," Mike says without getting up. "Thanks for coming in."

"I was in Brooklyn last night."

"I know," Mike says. "Red Hook."

"You had me followed?"

"Elena, actually. From when she picked up that suitcase. Followed you guys to dinner and back."

"We didn't notice."

"No."

"One guy?"

"Two, as it happens."

"They're good."

"Sometimes," Mike says. "But some other things happened last night too, which started me thinking." He squints at Tom. "Why don't you sit down?"

"I'm okay," Tom says, pushing the heel of his hand against the back of a chair.

"All right," Mike says. "We got a call last night. Robbie Riles's chauffeur. Said he was told not to pick up his boss on the night he was shot. Called off by ... Elena."

"And?"

"Well, the implications are fairly obvious."

"Are they? Like his just telling you this now?"

"Not so unnatural," Mike says, "his sitting on this for a while."

"And you're telling me because …? You want to see how I react?"

"That's right."

"For one thing," Tom says, "I've no idea if it's true. For another, if it were true, there'd be an innocent explanation. Because if you actually think Elena killed her father, you're out of your fucking mind."

"Well, another reason I invited you here may lead you faster to that conclusion. You're out of a job right now, right?"

"And what? You want to offer me one?"

"That's right."

Tom laughs out loud, then starts thinking Skillan might mean it. "That's ridiculous," he says.

"Maybe amusing, but unintentionally so."

"Or is this just more of what you were asking us to do?"

"No. This is an official job."

"I'm under indictment, for murder. And you want me to be an ADA?"

"I had cause to indict you," Mike says.

"And now you don't?"

"Well, you see, that's another thing that happened last night."

"Finally dawned, did it?" Tom says.

"More like additional evidence. From Verizon. Their detective work may be better than ours. At least when given a proper incentive—which you can thank me for. They've now figured out their records were tampered with. They haven't yet identified who did that, but they're reporting no calls were made from your line to Elena's, or from hers to yours."

"Really!" Tom says and sits on the chair he'd been tilting.

"It's a fact."

"And evidence of the frame."

"One might say."

"So you're lifting the indictment off both of us."

"Off you," Mike says. "Not her … quite yet. The only thing linking you to her prior to the murder was Verizon. That gone, you're out. There's still a lot of evidence incriminating her."

"All of which is now tainted."

"Called into question."

"It's a criminal case," Tom notes. "If the evidence is questionable, it's insufficient."

"At this stage, if it raises a question, the question must be answered."

"Great," Tom says. "I'll answer it. I was there. I saw what happened. Two thugs jumped out of the cab they were driving, shot Elena's father, and kidnapped the both of us."

"You saw Riles being shot?"

Tom hesitates. "No. I saw him being grabbed. The other guy knocked me out before they shot him."

"Your testimony's probably not worth much anyway."

"Because I'm biased in her favor?"

"Aren't you?"

"Of course I am. But I just told you the truth when I could have lied."

"Duly noted," Mike says. "And I do trust you. One of the reasons I want you to work here."

Tom's having trouble fully believing Mike to be serious. "As an assistant district attorney? An ADA?"

"That's right."

"Would I be assigned to this case?"

"Yes."

"How's that going to look?"

"Almost no one will know it," Mike says. "You and Elena will continue doing exactly what I asked. All anyone need know is that you're helping your girlfriend figure out how to deal with getting ownership of a company in the middle of a takeover battle."

Tom starts shaking his head, while Mike gets up and begins to pace. "Listen to me, Tom. This seemingly bizarre offer makes sense from both of our standpoints. From mine, editors-in-chief of the Yale Law Journal don't normally walk in here, much less apply for a job. A few have, in the past, and have done very well. But it's rare. Besides that, it gives you a chance to help break a case, for which you've gotta be super motivated. And on top of it all, you have unique qualifications for a special task we both want done urgently. If your assignment to the case is kept quiet."

Tom looks at him skeptically.

"The mole, Tom. Remember? Your suggestion we have a mole here?"

"And I'm best qualified to find him?"

"No one better. I don't have to trust some additional person with the fact you already know, and no one else here does. I'm not running the risk that the guy I'm trusting is himself the culprit. And you'd be the least likely guy I could put on this job to be suspected of having it."

"You obviously have some idea how to do this."

"I do," Mike says. "Pretty basic. We'll start with one staffer. Someone who knew what was later leaked. After my public announcement—that I'm not only dropping the indictment against you, but hiring you for this office—you'll be assigned to some other cases. In fact, I'll say in the press release that you won't be working on the Riles murder case for obvious reasons. At some point in casual conversation, maybe over lunch, you'll tell this guy in confidence that I wanted you working sub rosa on the case, and that was the real reason you were hired."

"And you'll expect him to leak it."

"If it's the guy I think it is, it would make both of us look bad. Which he wants to do, apparently. Me—probably because he wants my job. You—probably because he's being paid off by whoever's trying to frame you."

Tom says, pretty much knowing the answer, "Why don't you tell him yourself?"

"Works better if you do. When the leak gets published, he'll think, either you won't confess you told him, or, if you do, he can get away with denying it."

"Suppose it's not leaked?"

"Then I'll give you another guy to work on."

"How long is your list?"

"Too long."

"I don't know, Mike."

"What's your problem?"

"I don't see myself as a spy," he says. "Or, for that matter, as a prosecutor."

"You want to protect your girlfriend, don't you?"

"She's not my girlfriend," Tom says. "We've been thrown together, quite literally, and we're still trying to figure everything out."

"But you do want to protect her? And yourself?"

"Because you can't?"

"Kennedy was shot with a hundred security officers around him. You want protection, join up. Nobody shoots an ADA. Because *that* no one gets away with. Ever."

Tom thinks about it.

"And one more thing," Mike says. "Jockery's murder ups the odds they're coming after you. Both of you. And now they don't have to be so careful. They're out of the closet, so to speak. Riles and Jockery, rivals for the same takeover target, have both been shot. Now it's obvious, if it wasn't before, that the killer—at least the guy paying him—is someone somehow involved in that deal. Only if you two disappear might that picture be cloudy enough to prevent a conviction. The best way to beat a murder rap is to be able to point to another possible perp."

"Meaning Elena."

"Against whom the evidence is still pretty strong, and would get stronger if she disappears." Mike sits on his desk, jaw jutting at Weldon.

Tom says, "The first guy I'd question is the chauffeur. Who paid him to make that call?"

"See. You're already thinking like a prosecutor."

"I'll need some time."

"Of course you do. Take the rest of the day."

"One day, you're giving me?"

"You may not live another," Mike says. "You or her. Enough motivation? Oh, and the salary, by the way, is peanuts. But you won't be caring about that now, I suspect."

FORTY-THREE

At the same sidewalk café in Brooklyn where Morrie Khalil had last dictated his terms, he and Teddy Stamos take a table in the shade. There's little traffic, automobile or pedestrian. It has the feel of being on a side street in Rome.

After ordering coffees, Teddy says, "I wouldn't spend that money in your account so fast. Or at all, possibly."

"I already have," Morrie says.

"Oh, my, you are precipitous."

"What's the problem?"

"You saw who was killed last night?" Teddy asks.

"I assume lots of people were killed last night."

"Lowell Jockery is the one of significance to us."

"To you maybe," Morrie says. "He meant nothing to me."

"It's his money you spent."

"Wrong there. Mine. I earned it."

"No doubt," Teddy says. "But you've now committed yourself to the DA's office. They have your name, your information; they'll want you as a witness; and you'll have no choice. But you won't get paid for that part. The man who wanted you to do it doesn't care anymore. He's dead."

Their coffees arrive. Morrie stares at his and says contemplatively, "Jockery, huh?"

"Now deceased."

"I suspect someone else may want that story told. And pay for it."

"I wouldn't count on it," Teddy says.

"Well, I'll give you some time. I won't change it immediately."

"You've already given it. How can you change it?"

"What do you think? I'm an ignorant man? You think I have no subtlety? Can't shade my statements?"

"You told them Julian Althus called you that night. Told you that Riles wouldn't be needing the car."

"Very true," Khalil says, as if there's more to that story. "He did say that."

"And that his daughter, Elena, called you right after to warn you off the Riles Whitney building."

"Ah," Morrie says. "Maybe not quite. Here's where the subtleties might come in."

"How much could you really change that?" Teddy says with a scoffing tone.

"As much as I want."

"Because it didn't happen at all."

Morrie simply smiles.

They drink. A Filipino nanny walks by with her charges: twins in a carriage; another tot holding onto her hand. To a casual observer, like Teddy, they comprise scenery.

Teddy says, "The more I see of you, Morrie, the more I see of you."

"So maybe you'll find another client who will pay." Khalil's smile is filled with knowing.

"Not possible. No one else has reason to want the murder rap pinned on either Althus or Elena."

Khalil laughs. "You're toying with me, Teddy. Or trying to. If you didn't already have another client, why would we even be sitting in this ratty café drinking reheated coffee? The fact is, I'll need another two hundred thousand dollars. Before I go visit the DA tonight."

"You've been given three hundred thousand already!"

"That was for the call to the DA's office and the statement.

This is for not changing it."

Teddy blows out his cheeks. "You're too fucking much."

"Just think, Teddy, how useful I'll be when I'm actually working for you."

———⁓———

Tom and Elena meet for a late lunch at a tiny Italian restaurant on West Fifty-Second Street. Their table is between a wall of exposed brick and another decorated with family photos. To Tom's back is a large mullioned window onto the street; behind Elena, an open kitchen. None of the other five tables is occupied. After serving their meal, the cook and the waiter seem to have abandoned them.

"So you going to do it?" she says, twirling the last of her spaghetti pomodoro around her fork. "Take the job?"

"You see any downside?"

"Where's the plus?"

"To being part of the investigation, not the subjects of it? And increasing the odds on staying alive?"

'Hmm," she acknowledges.

"And we did agree to help."

"Great," she says. "We'll do the cops' job. So where do we start?"

"Your dad's files. Especially those about GT&M."

"Been there," she says. "This morning. While you were being stroked by Mike Skillan. They've already been ransacked. If there was anything there of importance, it's gone."

"See. That's interesting."

"Maybe," she says. "Could mean anything."

"Any other files? That haven't been raked over? What about your dad's apartment?"

"Nothing there. Not even a safe or a locked drawer. If he had private papers, they'd be at his place in Greenwich."

"His place?"

214 IT HAPPENED AT TWO IN THE MORNING

"A house. A *mansion*," she adds defensively. "I grew up there."

"I see."

She looks at him as if to say, *You, in fact, know very little about me.*

"Under his will…?"

"The house is mine," she says.

"You do seem very familiar with the will. I know you're the executor, but—"

"He asked me to read it. Made sure I understood it." Her lips press against the emotion.

Tom says, "You busy this weekend?"

"You'd like to weekend in Greenwich?"

"I'd like to look at his files," Tom says.

She looks down at her empty plate, then back up at him. "Won't you have conflicts?" she says. "As an assistant DA? With me still a suspect?"

"Absolutely not," he says. "The case against you is essentially dead. Skillan would never have offered the job if he thought otherwise."

"But suppose he starts suspecting me again? You'd have to be loyal to Skillan, right?"

He lowers his own fork still laden with pasta. "El, what do you think's going on here?"

"Where?" she says.

"Where do you think? Here! Between you and me."

"Dunno. What's going on?"

He stares at her; she looks down again.

"Jesus!" he says, ostensibly peering at the opposite wall.

She props her elbows on the table. "I should tell you something."

"All ears," he says in a tone implying limited patience.

"I don't like being a rich person. I'm going to give it all away. Almost all of it."

"Excellent idea."

"You think so?"

"Of course," he says. "Having all that money is very limiting. In the kind of friends you can make, for one thing."

"How about you?" she says. "You became my friend, knowing I was a rich kid."

"I'm unusual."

"How's that?"

"Very broad-minded," he says.

"Willing to overlook extreme disadvantages, like filthy wealth?"

"Possibly," he says. "If the girl's sweet."

She says, "I know I'm not sweet."

"You have moments."

"This isn't one of them."

"Isn't, no," he says.

"But you like me anyway?"

"Like?"

"You don't?"

"We're in love, El."

"Love?" she says, looking as if she might faint. "That's what's going on here?"

"It is," he says.

She pushes her dish away. "Whew," she says. "Awful lot to take in so fast."

"Should we slow it down?"

"Is that what you want?" she says.

"What *I* want?"

"Doesn't seem to be what I want," she says, as if surprised by that conclusion.

"My darling unsweet girl—what is it that you *do* want?"

Her lips part, but she says nothing, as if nothing in her vocabulary would seem to fit.

"Question's pending," he says.

"Want?" she says. "Ah, well … *want*—"

"That is the question."

"So happens," she says, a little breathlessly, "a block from here … you know what's there?"

"What's there?"

"A new hotel."

"I've seen it," he says.

"I own it."

"You'd like to inspect it?"

"Just a room," she says.

—*ww*—

"This is not my problem," Rashid asserts vehemently. "I did not want Riles killed. That was entirely you and Jockery."

"Was I paid that large sum for nothing, then?" Teddy Stamos says.

"I never asked you to kill the man."

"*That* man," says Teddy. "Well. Perhaps a matter of interpretation?"

Rashid had reluctantly agreed to a late-day meeting on the East River Esplanade near Carl Schurz Park. He and Stamos are sitting on a bench like any tourists, seemingly watching the boats, feeling the sun lowering on their backs through the tops of the East Side buildings. But for someone priding himself on control, Rashid looks dangerously close to losing it. "Have you just shifted our focus?"

"Most sorry. But Rashid, it's all rather tied together."

"I have absolutely no traceable connection to the death of Lowell Jockery. Not even you, Teddy, could—"

"I wouldn't! Couldn't even, without ruining myself."

"You wouldn't be believed. I and the Emirates have repeatedly made clear that we wanted Jockery to run the combined companies."

"I understand," Teddy says.

"We were discussing Riles, as to whom you misread me."

"Let's simply agree," Teddy purrs, "you wanted him out of the way. His company out of the way."

"There were other methods of achieving that."

"Not really," says Stamos. "Not effectively. And you knew what was happening. You went along."

"Are you threatening me, Teddy?"

"I'm trying to make you see reason," Stamos says. "If the Riles girl disappears, with her boyfriend, Weldon, no one can be convicted of the Riles murder. In all probability, no one could even be prosecuted. Because suspicion of that pair will always cast reasonable doubt on the guilt of anyone else. So whatever blame might otherwise attach to you—poof! Gone! But more than that—from a purely commercial standpoint— how effective can the Riles Whitney opposition be when the ownership of their controlling block of stock is in limbo? Which it will be for years when the sole heir is the likely suspect to a murder and apparently in flight. And when the CEO is himself tainted by suspicion. It's an almost perfect scenario, don't you think?"

Rashid's eyes remain fixed on the river traffic. An enormously elongated barge streams past, bulging with bitumen. Teddy says, "Did you hear what I just said?"

"Since you haven't mentioned Khalil, I assume you're not finished saying it."

"Right," says Teddy, giving a sharp tilt to his head. "Khalil is the key. He adds materially to the evidence against both— has already intensified suspicion of them with his telephone call to Riegert, which his office certainly recorded. But if Khalil recants tonight...." Teddy makes his clucking sound of doom. "Then the finger points right at us! Why is he recanting? Who's paying this guy to do what? But the beauty of the whole thing is we can buy him for a paltry two hundred thousand, when there are billions to be gained."

Rashid says, "Why *wasn't* Riles's car there?"

"Honestly, we don't know. Seems like a happy coincidence. We knew Riles had a date with his daughter; we had a tap on her phone. And we were prepared to deal with the driver, if he showed. But why Riles released the car...." Teddy shrugs. "Dumb luck. And it turns Khalil from victim to accomplice, for a few hundred grand."

Rashid gives a crooked smile. "And you think you can trust this man?"

"I do. If we give him the money, I think he has only one course of action."

Rashid says, "No one should pin any hopes on the word, or acts, of a bribed person."

"So how would you deal with tonight's problem?"

Rashid gives him a look, as if to say, *it's obvious,* and the sky reddens melodramatically, as if on cue.

"No," Teddy says flatly. "Too suspicious. And too much blood. Especially given ... our needs with regard to the daughter and boyfriend. And Rashid—we really are talking about a trivial amount of money, in the larger scheme of things."

"It's not the amount, my friend. It's the efficacy. Regarding tonight. I should think Khalil's likely to see himself in a box. Two people, a lot more important than he, have already been murdered. If he changes his story, he might well join their ranks. But if he sticks with his story—well, that's a real pit of uncertainty. Who knows, he'll think, who's really on the other side and what they'll do to him once they get what they want? Also, will he have to testify at trial or a deposition and risk a perjury indictment? Especially, if Althus refutes his story. So who knows what Khalil'll say tonight, no matter how much money he's given?"

"If he's there," Teddy says calmly.

Rashid looks at the little man and repeats pensively, "If he's there."

"After all," Teddy says, "now that he's already muddied up the case, he's safe to us only if gone—with the motivation and resources to stay gone. As you just explained, with your customary brilliance. No doubt he sees exactly the box he's in and that flight is his only recourse."

After a moment, Rashid says, "You're sure he sees that?"

"I am," Teddy says. "The man is really quite clever."

Rashid closes his eyes, as if sinking into meditation, except that appearance is betrayed by a repeating twitch in his right cheek.

Teddy says, "We're running out of time."

"Hmm," Rashid says.

"So the extra funds?"

Rashid's head leans slightly forward, then back.

Teddy says, "I saw you nod—barely perceptively, but enough for me to go on. So it's two hundred thou for Khalil, another two hundred for my people and their chore—the daughter and her boyfriend; another hundred for—"

Rashid gets up and starts walking away.

"I'm not wearing a wire, Rashid!"

The UAE man doesn't stop.

"You have my address, right?" Teddy calls after him. "For wire transfers?"

FORTY-FOUR

Tom jabs the buzzer of Khalil's two-family in Brooklyn, while Elena waits patiently on the wide stoop. She's always wondered where a man like Khalil would live. The settled aspect of the house, the quietness of the street, the morning sun in her face—indeed, everything!—seems to be pleasing her at the moment. *How uncharacteristic of me*, she thinks. But, after several minutes of fruitless waiting, she presses her nose to the window. "No one home," she announces. "People live here, but they're gone."

She crosses to the other side of the stoop and peers into that window. "This one's empty." She comes away. "Curious," she says. "No To-Let sign."

"So what now?" he says.

"No point standing around here."

"No point," he echoes.

"So let's go see Sofi."

"Sofi Harding?" he says, with surprise.

"She's probably at home. I'll call first."

"You know her?"

"She's practically a relative."

"So this takeover … she and your dad—"

"No question. Gave Dad a huge advantage. Probably bigger than Althus thought. But of course Jockery and the Arabs had been buying for months, and she has her own board to contend with."

"Your dad told you all this?"

She sits again on the stoop. "Well, he tried to." She takes out her phone and dials. "Hello? Is this Clive? Hi. Elena Riles. Is she in?" Elena stands, still holding the phone. "It'll be fine," she says to Tom. "Let's get going."

—∞∞—

"Excellent timing," says Sofi. "I have tea every morning at approximately this hour and usually in this spot. Delightful to have your company, both of you."

A bit dazzled by the elegance of the Harding living room, with its "important" antiques and extraordinary views of the park, Tom has a hard time voicing anything but reciprocal delight.

"I assume you know," Elena says, "I'm suspected of murdering my father."

"And isn't that preposterous!" Sofi exclaims.

"Tom is now working for the office that suspects me."

"Nice for you, darling. Having a friend in court, as it were."

"The blunt question, Mrs. Harding," says Tom, "is whether you have any information that might lead us to the actual killer?"

"Since I intend to address you by your first name, you should call me Sofi. Is that understood?"

"Plainly."

"Very good. And I've lots of reasons, Tom, to suspect many people. Too many. Robbie didn't seem to care very much about how he was regarded. When he trampled over someone, which was a daily occurrence, he didn't pause to sew up their wounds. As for information, there's a great deal of public stuff, most recently about this takeover skirmish. But private information that's relevant? I can't think. I have talked to your office, you know. A very aggressive young man."

"That would be Sammy Riegert. You talked to Mr. Riles about a takeover?"

"Of course," Sofi says. "It was my idea. I learned that that loathsome man, Jockery, was buying stock, and then the Emirates, so I talked Robbie into it. About seventy percent of the company is publicly held. We started buying late, but would have pulled it off if he hadn't been murdered. I don't know Julian Althus well. At all, really. He seems bent on the same outcome, but I'm not nearly as comfortable with him in my company as I would have been with Robbie." She turns to Elena. "Now, if *you* would become involved, my dear, that would change everything."

"I," Elena says, "know absolutely nothing about running a company."

"You were at business school!"

"I rest my case."

"Well, whatever they taught you there," Sofi says, "it couldn't be simpler. You get the best people you can find on opposite sides of any question you're considering, hear them out, then exercise common sense. Much more difficult being lower down. At the top, it's child's play."

She butters some toast. "But you didn't come here for my principles of corporate management, as excellent as they may be."

Tom says, "Did you and Elena's father talk about the Riles Whitney loan to the UAE?"

"We did."

"Was he planning to call it?"

"He was thinking about it," Sofi says. "I suspect Robbie's interest in taking over my company came as a complete surprise to the Arabs and very bad news. They were vulnerable to him; he could have used the loan as leverage. Though I doubt they would have murdered him for that. Too obvious."

"Maybe. But calling that loan, foreclosing on the Emirates's property, bringing the State Department down on your head—Robbie Riles was known to have the nerve for that; not sure how many others are."

Sofi sips her tea, then takes it to the window. "Have you talked to Teddy Stamos?"

"Stamos?" says Tom. "Isn't he a gumshoe?"

"Yes he is."

"And involved, I assume from your tone."

"Up to his elfin ears." Sofi laughs. "Robbie wanted *me* to hire him. I said he was already working for the UAE. 'All the more reason,' said Robbie."

"Conflicts?" says Tom.

"There are no conflicts for Teddy Stamos. Only opportunities. Both sides? No problem. As far as Teddy's concerned, working for one side simply makes him more valuable to the other. And he'll do the approaching. Everyone with any conceivable interest in the matter. I didn't even have to call him. He called me."

"And did you hire him?" Tom asks.

"Absolutely. And he's been worth what I paid him. I knew before anyone that Lowell Jockery was dead. When that news hit, my brokers were poised to buy another huge chunk on the predictable downtick."

Tom says, "When you say he knew it before—"

"Before it was on the broad tape."

"Any idea how?" Elena asks.

Sofi shrugs. "He's more plugged in than J. Edgar Hoover was … and probably more dangerous."

FORTY-FIVE

Mid-afternoon, office of the District Attorney. The acting incumbent, Mike Skillan, is telling his new recruit, Tom Weldon, how pleased he is to have him on staff, when Sammy Riegert breaks in, speaking to Mike, but looking strangely at Tom. "Can we talk?"

Mike nods.

"I mean alone," Sammy says.

"Now's fine, let's hear it."

Sammy continues to look uncomfortable.

"I said—"

"Right," Sammy says. "We've got the chauffeur coming in, then Althus, but now this guy, right off the street, some big Arab mucky-muck, part of the UAE delegation, just shows up. No lawyers, no fanfare, no notice. Says he wants to chat. How 'bout that?"

"What do we know about him?" Mike asks.

"Not much. When I interviewed the guy running the New York office—sub-consulate, whatever they call it—this guy, Rashid al-Calif, was there."

Mike, registering this information, says almost distractedly, "Sammy, this is Tom. Tom Weldon. He's joining our staff. I'll announce tomorrow."

"Recognized him," Sammy says. "From the photo of the guy we recently indicted."

"We're dropping the indictment, Sammy. The proof's been discredited. That will be part of the announcement. We won't put him on the Riles case, of course, but I think he can help us in other areas. Complex frauds, for example."

"Been a day of surprises," Sammy says. "Anyone else here

know about this?"

"Joe and Foster, few minutes ago."

"Should we talk?"

"No need."

"Yeah, well," Sammy says, "you're the boss."

"Where'd you put al-Calif?"

"Room three."

"Let's start with him. You examine. We'll observe."

Sammy looks at Tom.

"Get his feet wet," Mike says.

Usual setup: windowless room; gray walls, vinyl floor; witness, interrogator; two chairs and a metal table; two-way mirror, allowing observers to observe without being observed. Mike leads Tom into the carpeted room on the transparent side of the glass, where they're joined by Joe Cunningham and Foster Donachetti, both of whom look uneasily at the team's new member.

"So," says Sammy, switching on a device, "you have something to tell us?"

"This will be recorded?" Rashid says.

"Do you object to that?"

"On the contrary. I want there to be a record. Will I be given a copy?"

"I'm afraid not."

Rashid retrieves a small device from his pocket. "But you'll have no objection to my making my own recording?"

"I'm afraid I do."

"A bit one-sided, wouldn't you say? Uneven playing field?"

"I don't make the rules," Sammy says.

"You agree it's unfair, though? Were you to make the rules, you would permit mutuality in the matter of recording?"

"I didn't say that."

"Suppose we just take this into your office? Or perhaps a conference room? Invite the others to join us? The ones behind the glass. Then I would know to whom I was talking."

Mike leaves his chair, says to Tom, "Stay here." He beckons Joe and Foster to follow him. The three file into the interrogation room, and Rashid smiles in greeting. "The man who does make the rules," he says.

"I'm Michael Skillan."

"Yes, that's what I meant."

"Joe Cunningham, chief assistant, and Foster Donachetti, head of the trial division. My office is a mess. We're probably more comfortable in here."

Chairs arrived as he spoke, and the three seated themselves, Mike alongside Rashid. "So what have you come to tell us, Mr. al-Calif?"

"Not all that much, really. I'm here because of the murder of Lowell Jockery. When Robbie Riles was shot, it seemed to be a family matter, evidence pointing to the daughter. Jockery's murder may of course put all that in question. Regrettably, however, it also points the finger at me."

"Does it?" Mike says, affecting surprise.

"It's not necessarily public knowledge," Rashid says, "but it soon will be, that Jockery had backing in the UAE for his takeover bid of GT&M. I am in charge of the UAE's interests in this matter."

"Which gave you a motive for killing him?"

"On the contrary. And that's the reality. But on the surface—two competing bidders for the same company are killed. At least that makes me a person of interest. I came here to tell you I am interested. Interested in helping you. Lowell Jockery was a friend. Also a highly valued business partner in a venture of great importance to the Emirates. His death has set us back immeasurably. So I'm here to offer my services. I will help you in any way I can."

They consider this statement for enough time to make Rashid uncomfortable. Then Sammy says, "Riles held a huge loan of yours, didn't he?"

"His company did, yes."

"So—"

"Please, sir. Having a man killed in those circumstances would have been not only immoral but extremely stupid."

Sammy nods and says, "Do you remember me?"

"Of course. You interviewed my associate Yasim Maktoum. I was present."

"And what about Mr. Maktoum?"

"Yes, what about him?" Rashid says. "He had been heading up the Emirates team on GT&M until I arrived to take over."

"Was he happy about that, your taking over?"

"Of course not. But he accepts it."

"How did Mr. Jockery feel about your taking over from Maktoum?"

"He was very much in favor of the move. He may even have engineered it."

"He had influence in the UAE?"

"At the highest level."

"Did Yasim know that?"

"We all knew it. But frankly, gentlemen, if you have suspicions of Yasim, he's too unlikely. Not at all the type."

Mike Skillan asks, "What do you know about Elena Riles?"

"I've never met her."

"But you've collected information on her?"

"Naturally. And paid well for it. But that sort of intelligence is never totally reliable."

"You willing to share, for whatever it's worth?"

"I've no objection. Our sources say she hated her father. He interfered in her life; she always resented it."

"Who are your sources?"

"One of the investigation firms in the city. I didn't hire them."

"Mr. Maktoum did?"

"Either he or Mr. Jockery. Such people—investigators—are only marginally competent."

"Was it Teddy Stamos?" Mike asks.

"I think that's right, yes."

"With Lowell Jockery gone, will his company stay in the fight for GT&M?"

"They're contractually committed. But…."

"Yes?"

"It won't be the same."

"Putting you at a disadvantage?"

"Over Riles Whitney? Well…."

"I understand that the Riles family is solidly behind the takeover."

"Perhaps."

"You sound confident, despite the loss of Jockery."

"There's no question that was a setback. Among other things, we wanted him to run the combined company. But I think I personally have an advantage over the Riles family. I think Mrs. Harding trusts me."

Sammy leans back in his chair. "Let me just suggest, sir, that it would be a good idea for you not to leave the city."

"I've no intention of leaving the city," Rashid says. "It's my favorite place on earth."

—◊◊◊—

With the team reassembled in Skillan's office, Mike asks Sammy, "Why'd he come in, al-Calif?"

"Ballsy move? Thought we'd distrust him less, if he did?"

"Do we?"

"I don't," says Sammy.

Mike nods, waves them toward room number three. Which is empty.

A young ADA arrives. They call him "Little Mike," since he's half Skillan's size and, on the depth chart, ranks close to the bottom. "Khalil's not here. No calls, no word."

Big Mike says, "Track him. Call him, go to the house,

inside, if possible, call me as soon as you get there."

Tom says, "I think he's flown. I was there this morning."

"Were you?" Mike says, surprised. He turns back to Little Mike. "Check it anyway." Then to Sammy as Little Mike leaves, "Althus?"

"Waiting," Sammy says.

Skillan leads all but Riegert into the observation room.

On the other side of the glass, they watch Sammy greet witness and lawyer. He says, his eyes on Harry Stith, "You're not a suspect, Mr. Althus."

"So why pay a lawyer his exorbitant fees to be here?" Julian says. "The fact is, Mr. Riegert, I go few places unaccompanied by counsel, and the DA's office isn't one of them."

"It's fine. I just have a few questions. Been meaning to speak to you earlier. Good of you to come down here."

"Happy to help in any way I can."

"Excellent. One thing you can clear up right away is who told the chauffeur, Morrie Khalil, not to wait for Mr. Riles on the night he was killed?"

"That's simple enough. I did. I may not have been the only one, but I certainly mentioned it to him when he dropped me off at my building."

"Did Mr. Riles himself ask you call off Khalil?"

Julian smiles. "You're thinking that's a rather menial job for the COO of a large company."

"Isn't it?"

"No doubt. But the Hollywood version of how a company like ours operates and the reality are two very different things. Robbie ran an extremely taut ship. We have one executive car and one driver. Robbie had first call, I second. So every day, usually in passing, Robbie said, 'Car's yours tonight, Julian' or 'I'm using it.' Or his secretary told mine."

"And on the night in question?"

"I believe it was Robbie. As I recall it, he had a date that night with Elena. She and her father sometimes met after work, and he liked to walk her home. She lives just twenty blocks or so north of the office."

"So she might have arranged to meet him outside the building that night and called off the car?"

"She might well have arranged to meet him, but I doubt she would have gotten involved with the car."

Sammy stops a moment to digest this. "Do you have any idea where the driver, Khalil, is tonight?"

Julian looks confused. "I thought he was on vacation."

"So you don't know where he is?"

"I, no. If it's important—"

"Who do you think gained from Robbie Riles's death?"

"Certainly not Khalil."

"Who then?"

"I assume you're not asking me for an evaluation of guilt?"

"No. Just who gained financially or any other way?"

"Obviously his heirs, though I believe they were all fond of him. Elena especially."

"Especially fond or especially benefited by his death?"

"Both, I should imagine."

"And others benefited?"

"Of course anyone owing him money might expect his death would provide some easing of the pressure to repay. Time pressure at least. Robbie was notoriously ... shall we say, hard-nosed. And, obviously, our adversaries in the GT&M takeover battle might see themselves as benefiting."

"Lowell Jockery, for one."

"I suppose we can take him off the list?"

"Why's that?" says Sammy in a flat tone that somehow manages to question Julian's acuity.

"Right," Julian says. "I see your point. His being murdered doesn't necessarily mean—"

"Anyone else?"

"There's a rather long list of people who might have conceived a dislike for him."

"Could you supply such a list?"

"I could, yes," Julian says, "but with the explicit understanding I'm not accusing them of anything."

"You got it."

"And," Julian says, "may I ask you something? Does the fact your investigation is continuing mean that the indictments will be—"

"Let me stop you right there, sir."

"I understand."

"We do not talk about suspects in an ongoing investigation."

"To be sure."

"Very good," says Sammy, getting to his feet. "That list. Soon as possible, please. I think you can appreciate time is short on this. Can you get it to us by tomorrow?"

Harrison Stith holds up his hand. "That's a request best addressed to me, sir."

"All right, fine," Sammy says. "To you, then. What's the response?"

"We'll take your request under advisement."

Sammy's heard this before. "You want a court order?"

"Apply for one, if you like, but I have every confidence the advisement will be favorable to your request."

Sammy laughs.

In the adjoining room, Tom turns to Mike. "This is the first time you've questioned Althus?"

"Welcome to government office," Mike says. "We prioritize the obvious. A few hours ago, the evidence overwhelmingly pointed one way."

"At me. And now I work for you. Although I used to work for that asshole purporting to represent Althus."

"Ain't it wonderful?" Mike croons. "Life? Full of surprises. And do you think he's guilty, Althus?"

"I don't, actually," Tom says. "Elena likes him."

"And you trust her instinct."

"I do."

"Also wonderful," Mike says. "True—"

"Don't," Tom warns.

FORTY-SIX

This!" Tom exclaims, pulling into the driveway of an enormous white-shingled house in Old Greenwich. "This pile is yours?" Parked on the pavers are two blue Bentleys, a silver Porsche, and a gray-gold Aston Martin. Tom and Elena step out of their rented Camry. She wanted a Prius, but Tom couldn't fit in.

Elena walks directly to the side lawn, where Tom joins her. Over the ridge, behind the house, there's a view of five rolling acres of gardens and trees and, beyond that, the Long Island Sound.

"This, I assume, you don't tire of."

"I don't," she says.

"And the auto show in the driveway?"

She gives him an expression of distaste.

"What about the memories?" he asks.

"Some good ones," she says. "Not many."

"Older sisters can be bitches."

"Yeah," she says, in a tone implying a level of cruelty he knows nothing about.

———

They walk in on the two sisters and their husbands lounging in the living room amid scattered sections of the *Journal* and *The Times*.

Elena says, "Everyone comfortable?"

"Elena!" says Constance, greatly surprised. "How delightful to see you."

"I'll bet."

"And this must be Tom."

"Hi," says Tom noncommittally.

"You guys living here?" Elena asks in a tone of sweet insincerity.

Patricia says, "Jasper and I are in the guest house."

"And when did this happen?"

"Daddy let us move in," says Patricia defensively.

"And you and Lawton are living here, in the big house?" Elena says to Constance.

"You object to that?"

"It's the first time I've been asked."

"Must we, Elena?" says Connie. "The house was empty. You weren't here, were you? If you and … Tom want to move in, I'm sure we can come to some sort of accommodation."

"You know damn well I won't live here."

"Then what's all the bother about?' Connie says. "Really, Elena."

Lawton, flipping pages as if bored by the whole conversation, says, "You two like some coffee? It's a bit cold, but we could heat it up."

"Lawton," Elena says to him, "look at me." He does with an attitude of withering sufferance.

"Tom and I are here for the weekend. We want the house to ourselves."

"And what?" Connie says, with a harsh laugh. "We should move out?"

"You don't belong here."

"That's not quite settled yet. Tom, you're a lawyer. Surely you understand that. And until it's settled, I'd say possession is nine-tenths of the law."

"Indeed," Lawton says. "In the circumstances, I'd say it was damn white of Connie to invite you to stay at all."

Tom Weldon steps forth. "This may startle you people, but it appears we have a situation here requiring the use of force."

Heads snap, eyes blink.

"What the hell is that supposed to mean?" Lawton says, as if reacting belatedly to an off-color remark.

"Very simple," Tom says. "You've been asked to leave. I suggest you start packing immediately. Because if you don't, I'll lift your pompous ass out of that sofa and deposit it into the street. Or maybe into one of those fancy cars in the driveway."

The sisters and spouses regard him with disbelief.

"The guest house," says Jasper, "where we are, is actually the gate house. It's a hundred yards away."

Elena says to Connie, "You live five blocks from here."

"Oh, that place," Lawton says. "We've listed it for sale."

"Planning on staying here permanently, are you?" Elena asks, uninterested in the answer.

Lawton shrugs. "Suits us quite well, yes."

Tom steps between them. "You seem to think I was joking. I wasn't. You either get the fuck outta here now, or I'll throw you out. One by one. And enjoy it."

Connie smiles condescendingly at her sister. "Fascinating friends you make."

"He means it," Elena says. "I've seen him do worse."

"I'm sure you have. No doubt in your own bedroom." She takes her husband's arm. "Come along, Lawton. We'll fumigate after they leave."

"You can take your clothes with you," Elena snaps.

"Oh, we have lots of clothes," Connie says. "You can pick through them, take whatever you like."

With that, Connie walks to the front door and out of the house, the others dutifully following. Standing alone together in the living room, Tom says, "So you and your sisters get on real well."

"Fuck them," Elena says.

"Yes, that's what I meant."

—⟋⟍⟍—

They stake out Robbie Riles's bedroom for themselves. Second floor, back corner, view through the draperied windows of a significant part of southern Connecticut. Inside it's a high-ceilinged, pastel paradise of old-but-good furniture and antique rugs.

"Does this bother you?" Tom asks.

"It's just a bedroom," Elena says. "I'm sure Connie and Lawton slept here. We change the sheets, should be fine."

There's a staff in attendance. Not workers who hover below stairs; they have a separate wing. And they're happy to change the sheets.

The rest of the day, Elena and Tom go hunting through the entire premises: living room, dining room, study, library, solarium, kitchen, pantry, basement rooms, wine cellar, pool house, four-car garage, and all the bedrooms and parlors upstairs. If her father had stashed documents in this house, his papers are not to be found, upstairs or down, or even in the servants' wing.

Before dinner, they wander to the edge of the property, at the seawall on an inlet to the Sound. They sit on the wall, which is fashioned of fieldstones with a smooth concrete top. There's a Hallmark view of a spectacular sunset, but Elena is still thinking about their arrival. "What would you have done if they hadn't taken your bluff?"

"What makes you think I was bluffing?" he says.

"I can't really see you picking up my sisters and tossing them out on the pavement."

"What about Lawton?"

"I suppose I could see that."

"And if I tossed him," Tom says, "what do you suppose the others would have done?"

"So that was your plan?"

"I didn't need a plan. I knew they'd leave on the threat."

"So you do this often?" she says.

"What do you think?"

"You mean based on the ten days I've known you?"

"How else could you judge?"

"I think you're pretty crazy."

"Yeah?" he says.

"Yeah. I do."

"Turns you off?"

She smiles. "What do *you* think?"

They both gaze at the sky streaking colors in overwrought hues, like a performer overanxious to please.

———

At bedtime, in a darkly lit room, rummaging in the back of a night table drawer, Elena, in PJs, comes upon a handwritten letter addressed affectionately to her father. "Oh, ho!" she exclaims, getting into bed.

"What?"

She reads aloud, "Dearest Robbie. I hate the absences. Even more the silences." Sitting up on crossed legs, she gives Tom a look. "Your S. Not Yours, S. *Your* S. And S is Sofi, I know it." She hands him the letter. "They were lovers!"

"Not surprising," he says.

"You picked up on that?"

"The way she talked about him, yeah."

He's standing at the side of the bed in his shorts, not getting in.

"Tom?" she says, in a tone questioning his reticence.

"Do you realize," he says, "that this will be the first night we've slept together, when we could each have slept in a bedroom alone?"

"You're making a point," she says.

"Significant one, don't you think?"

"How 'bout just getting into bed?"

He laughs, but there's a louder sound downstairs. Like breaking glass.

They freeze, listening for more.

There *is* more. A creaking window. Tom says, instinctively whispering, "Is there an alarm system in this house?"

"I think," she says in a hushed voice.

"Which you didn't activate?"

"Shit," she says.

Steps on the staircase.

"This whole night," she bemoans, "is about to be ruined."

The door slams open. Three armed figures burst in, casting high shadows behind them, like characters on a comic book cover. Black ski hood masks, black gloves, black exercise jumpsuits. One of them, a woman, says, "Do what we say, no one gets hurt." With a scream meant to rouse servants, Tom hurls himself at one of the men, his momentum thrusting them both through the doorway and out the room. The woman pulls Elena, screaming, from the bed and drags her into the hallway by her hair. They and the other man stand over the battle, consisting of two men, untrained for the event, wrestling and punching, trying to kill each other.

As Elena keeps screaming, the woman silences her momentarily with a swipe of the gun barrel into her face. Tom and his adversary tumble near the edge of the staircase, then careen down the stairs, both of them rattling their heads against the banister and landing, slumped and still, on the floor below. Elena, wresting free and now screaming nonstop, runs down after them, her assailants in pursuit. At the foot of the stairs, the woman grabs Elena by the throat. She and the other assailant observe the two lying on the lower step, both bleeding from scalp wounds. "Cuff her and cover her eyes," she directs the tall man beside her.

"We could kill this one," he says, nodding down at Tom, while affixing handcuffs and a hood to a struggling Elena.

Lights flash on in the servants' wing.

"Both or neither," the woman says.

"You'd kill Piet?"

"It's complicated. You wouldn't understand."

"So we leave the both of them just lying here?"

"You think we have time to drag them to the car while we're also dragging the girl?"

"I dunno," he says, now panicked with indecision.

"Just fucking leave," says the woman, yanking Elena again by the hair. "He doesn't know anything."

FORTY-SEVEN

Teddy and Birdie meet at the bar of a Cuban restaurant on Amsterdam Avenue. Neither of them has ever been there before, but Teddy knows of it. About Manhattan, and public places in which one might invisibly confer, Teddy knows most everything.

It's past midnight, but the crowd still lingers over dinner in the next room. At their end of the bar, Teddy and Birdie sit alone, nursing piña coladas. The establishment is old but clean, and everything—the long bar, the high stools, the wall paneling—is made of bamboo darkened with age.

"Another fuckup," Teddy says, "but this one may be irredeemable."

"You'll think of something," Birdie says. "You always do."

"Yes, yes, I already know how to *try* to fix this. But the more ingenious these solutions, the more implausible they become."

"We have the girl."

"And that helps how? Given that you left the boy, who's now an eyewitness that the girl did not flee but was kidnapped. And you left Piet, who's living confirmation of the boy's story."

Birdie has already thought this through. "We could—"

"I know," Teddy says impatiently, "since there's only one play left having even the remotest chance of succeeding."

She nevertheless wants to say it. "Get Piet to say tonight was staged," she urges. "By the boy and Elena. Just like New

Orleans. Whenever Elena feels she's under suspicion, that's her knee-jerk, to stage someone attacking her."

"Obviously. But he'd also have to say his being knocked out was an accident. The boy, Weldon, overdid the playacting."

Birdie's brow furrows. "We need to tell Piet immediately. He won't think of this on his own."

"I'm sure he wouldn't. Or carry out such a plan, without convincing threats to his continued existence."

"Which you will be able to deliver?"

"Future tense?" Teddy says. "Even ten minutes from now would probably be too late."

"So it's been done?"

He gives her a look the equivalent of a sarcastically delivered *Oh please!* "Where do they have him?" she asks.

"In the lockup. Supreme, New York County."

"And you have someone, there," she says, "in the lockup."

"My dear, you should know by now, I have people wherever I might need them. Or people who can get there."

Birdie finishes her drink and takes a deep breath. "Well, I'm afraid you won't have me any longer. I'm quitting."

"Oh, really." He doesn't believe it.

"You're right about tonight. And there've been too many. Fuckups. So the girl's gratis. But I need some time off, and I mean to get lost. New town, maybe a new life. And Teddy," she pauses as she gives him a knowing look. "I would not take kindly to anyone tracking me."

Teddy gives this speech a sour expression. "You just came to this conclusion? All in a rush, tonight?"

"It's been growing on me," she says.

"I want you to finish this job. After that, you can go anywhere you like."

"Jacob can do it."

"I don't know Jacob," he says. "He works for you. You control him."

"No more. And for me, *no mas*. I'm gone, I mean it. Jacob's ready. More than ready. He's no idea who you are, but wants to. He's had it with being a subcontractor. And you'll like him. He's absolutely ruthless."

"Smart?"

"You don't need that smart," she says. "I'm that smart, and I keep screwing this job up."

"Because you don't want to do it, Birdie."

"That's bullshit. I'm just tired."

"Tired?" Teddy repeats, as if he had more of a right to claim that condition.

"That's what I said."

"So now you're a civilian?"

"That's right."

"Just walk away?" Teddy laughs, tosses the umbrella from his drink. "What's happened, Birdie? You've fallen for someone?"

"I'm done, Teddy. That's all you need to know."

Teddy downs the remains of his colada. "Okay, tell you what," he says. "I'll talk to your man. If I like him, you're free to go. But I won't have to come looking for you. Wherever you're going, you won't last six months. You'll be back here looking for me."

FORTY-EIGHT

Shortly past seven a.m., Tom awakes with a migraine. He's in Greenwich Hospital with a bandaged head.

"You have a concussion," says Mike Skillan, a seated figure in the white room.

"Where's El?" Tom says, starting to get out of bed. Someone thoughtful has hung his clothes in the closet.

Mike jumps up to restrain him. "Easy! You're beached for a day more, at least."

"Where the hell is she?" Tom sees himself staggering within two rooms that don't quite coincide.

"They have her," Mike says. "We've no idea where." He looks purposefully at Tom. "Do you?"

"Me?" Tom, still in a hospital gown, sits heavily on the bed. "How the hell would I know? Did anyone see them? See what happened?"

"Some of it," Skillan says, pulling his chair closer to the bed and sitting directly opposite Tom. "We do have a witness. That thug you fought with and apparently threw downstairs."

"He was there when you came?"

"When the Greenwich police arrived, yeah. Still unconscious, like you. He didn't see Elena being grabbed, and he doesn't know what was done with her—is his present story. As is his assertion that the fight and the kidnapping were staged. By you. That you've been part of their team from the outset."

"That I've been *what?*" says Tom, now rising again.

Skillan leans forward and pushes his ADA, still weak, back on the mattress. "Nurse!" he calls out.

"That's ridiculous."

"Maybe."

"What," Tom says, "you believe this shit?"

"At the moment, I'm not in a position to believe or disbelieve it. But he's given us the name—Jacob Wozniacki—and physical description of the other guy you recruited for your plan, the one who got away with her last night."

"*My* plan?"

"That's his story. You're the brains."

"Why the fuck would I do anything that stupid?"

Skillan shrugs. "Money?"

"Oh, Christ!"

"You asked," Mike says.

"And if the fight was staged, why would I knock him out, so the cops could get him?"

"Fight got out of hand, is his version. You took playacting too far. That's why he's pissed and is ratting on you."

"This is so fucking implausible."

"Has its weak points, I agree."

"Right. Like how does the murder of Robbie Riles fit in?"

"According to Piet—that's his name—you shot Riles. Wasn't supposed to happen, as far as Piet knew. In fact, Riles was there only so he could see his daughter being kidnapped and pay up."

"Really, so what's the present plan?"

"Piet doesn't know, but suspects you and Elena have something very clever worked out."

Tom laughs. "This story is falling apart all over the place."

"Maybe," Mike says. "It's a wacky story. But sometimes wacky stories are true."

"Okay, look, believe what you want—"

"I didn't say I *believed* anything."

"The important thing is to find Elena. Get me out of here, and I'll help you do that."

"I can't get you out of here!" Mike says, as if the idea were preposterous.

"Of course you can. You're the goddamn New York District Attorney. You can say you're transferring me to a hospital in the city."

"You're risking your health, man."

"Right. And how does that stack up to our risking Elena's life?"

―∾∾―

In an ambulance on I-95, Tom, dressed but strapped to a gurney, says, "Salient facts. One bidder for GT&M gets killed. His daughter and a bystander get kidnapped; stuck someplace that's easy to escape from; and as soon as there's a record of their fleeing, a contract killer, a woman, is sent to murder them in Ashaway, Kentucky, then New Orleans. A second bidder gets killed. A third races to tell us—unconvincingly—he's innocent and wants to help. And then the first victim's chauffeur lies about who directed him elsewhere on the night of the first murder. The next day he leaves town, apparently in flight. Obviously, someone paid him to lie, and he may be running scared of that person. No doubt the same person who paid the contract killer who stalked Elena and me, and paid whoever shot Jockery and the two thugs who shot Robbie Riles, and whoever now has Elena. Does anything in these facts suggest who that person might be?"

Mike gives him a smirk. "You're missing some salient facts."

"Which? The ones you think incriminate Elena—or just me? You really want to fool with that horseshit now? When she may have hours to live, if she hasn't been killed already?"

They hit a pothole and hold on for dear life.

"Try to stay calm," Mike says.

"I am. Who's the other guy in the UAE consulate that Riegert talked to?"

"A guy named Yasim Maktoum. Why?"

"Let's bring him in," Tom says. "Now. We should talk to him."

"We already have."

"You've brought him in again already?"

"Well, bringing."

"He knows a lot about Rashid al-Calif that we don't, and he hasn't told us."

"I agree," Mike says.

"So who's bringing? Sammy?"

Mike, reflecting for a moment, puts in a call to Riegert, who has news that shocks both of them. Yasim is gone. Run off with the consulate receptionist, an American woman named Birdie O'Shane.

"It's a goddamn exodus," Skillan says.

Tom says, "Tell Sammy to get their files. And tell him to tell Rashid this will test his willingness to cooperate."

"You hear that Sammy?" Mike asks on the phone.

"Got it," Sammy says and hangs up.

"Whatta you expecting to find?" Mike says.

"Another piece of this." Tom smiles grimly. "Or nothing."

"Let's hope it's the former."

"Khalil's in flight; Yasim's in flight; an American in an Arab embassy is with him? Dots in a puzzle, Mike. Something connects them. Something bad."

—◦◦◦—

Just as they arrive at Mike's office, Sammy bursts in. "Look at your emails."

Mike finds one from Sammy and opens the attached PDF. Photographs flash on the screen. He turns to Tom who is also observing.

Tom says, "That's her. The woman sent to kill us in New Orleans. And probably Ashaway. We can confirm that with the waitress at the local restaurant."

Mike looks at him strangely. "You knew this? That the consulate receptionist was a paid assassin?"

"Before seeing this photo? Of course not."

"But you asked for their files. So, what are you, a mystic?"

"Just rational, Mike. To suspect a connection."

"That she'd run off with Yasim Maktoum?"

"Well, that's al-Calif's story."

"So what else is coming to you?"

"Nothing," Tom says. "We're still missing something."

"It's the goddamn Arabs at the bottom of this."

"I don't think so. Looks like somehow they got pulled in, but they didn't start it. Way too risky for them."

"I'm gonna pull Rashid in right now," Mike says. "Of all the suspects—can't think of anyone more likely to know where Elena is."

"I can." Tom slaps his hands together. "Fucking obvious!"

He has their attention.

"Teddy Stamos," Tom says. "He's all over this GT&M thing. He's working for everyone, but probably mostly for himself. Look, a man like Rashid al-Calif doesn't deal directly with contract killers. Neither would someone like Jockery. They'd have an intermediary. Gotta be Stamos. And it's likely to have been Stamos who bought Khalil. And then either paid him to leave or scared him enough to do it."

Mike regards him with new appreciation. "That's pretty fucking inspired. Now what, if anything, does that tell us about where they took Elena?"

"Khalil's house?"

"Where'd that come from?"

"It's possible."

"So is the boat basin."

"I know," Tom says, with a shudder. "I've thought of that too."

"But these brain waves of yours tell you that it's the chauffeur's house?"

"I wouldn't call them brain waves."

"You just feel it? Instinct? Or grasping at straws?"

"I'm going there!"

"Why?"

"I've got to go somewhere. I'm going a bit crazy."

"It's something more!" Mike insists. "What is it?"

"We were just there—it's an empty house. They're likely to know it's empty. They won't want to take her to that same farm place they dumped us in last time. I dunno, I'm just going."

"I'll send some squad cars."

"Great," Tom says. "I'll meet them there. Subway's faster."

"Still, the boat basin—"

"If they went there, Mike, they're now out to sea."

"Right," Skillan says. "I'll send the Coast Guard."

—⟪∿⟫—

"So you're Jacob," says Teddy, as the large man enters the car. It's a black Lexus, but not conspicuously luxurious. They're parked on a side street on the Upper West Side.

"Where's Birdie? What's going on?"

"Right to the point," Teddy says. "That's good. Birdie has retired. And departed. She's left the business to you. Says you're qualified … and hungry. Is that true?"

"You her source? The feeder?"

"That's right."

"So I deal with you now? Directly?"

Teddy turns down the air conditioning. "You haven't answered my question."

"I'm happy to do the work," Jacob says. "But not for the cut I was getting."

"If you're good—and we can test that on this job—I'll pay you what I was paying her, which, I imagine, is several steps above your present pay grade."

"You have money for me now?"

"Some of it."

"And you want me to trust you for the rest?"

"This is how it's done, Jacob. We earn each other's trust. Bit by bit. You should know that by now." Teddy hands him a large envelope filled with hundred-dollar bills.

Jacob counts the money. "Yes, okay. And the rest?"

"Double that. For success."

"Who are you? How do I reach you?"

"I'll reach you."

"More trust?"

"Correct."

"You want her killed, right? And disposed of. I could have done that last night. It's better at night."

"Well, I didn't have clearance last night. From my client. And it will be night again soon. She's secure?"

Jacob laughs. It's an evil sound. "Oh, yes."

—◦◦◦—

Elena is handcuffed to a steam pipe on a bare wooden floor in a windowless room. She can't be sure whether it's basement or attic—she was barely conscious when carried there.

It started with a woman and a large, ugly man. The handcuffs came on right away, as did a hood, while Tom was fighting with another one. They threw her into the trunk of a car and drove for a little less than an hour. The man dragged her out, carried her into some building, and cuffed her to the pipe. Later, the woman left, the hood came off, and the man left. Bad signs. The man would not have let her see him if he meant to keep her alive. And she can't quite imagine what he wants her to see, but some disturbing possibilities do occur to her. She wears her nightgown and nothing else. The room of unplastered wood-framed walls is bare of furniture except for one ladder-backed chair. Numb with terror, she expects two things to happen: the man will come back, and this place will become her torture chamber.

The first prophesy is almost immediately fulfilled. She hears him approach—climbing or descending, she can't be certain, it's too far away—and then enter through a small door in the far wall. She's guessing it's a separate room in the attic. The chair creaks as he sits on it. He's gnawing at a chicken bone, which he then tosses into a KFC bag.

"You want something to eat?" he says.

"No, thank you." Might as well be polite. Keep it civil.

"Okay," he says. "Then let's start. With your free hand, I want you to lift your nightgown up to your neck."

"I'm sorry, I won't do that."

"I think you will. Because the alternative is that I will kill you."

"I think you're planning to kill me anyway," she says.

"Why would I do that?"

"Why did you kidnap me?"

"For the money, of course."

"And if you get some money, you'll let me go?"

"Naturally."

"Then I'll give you money," she says. "Much more than they're paying you."

He laughs and rises from the chair.

Elena says, "I think you killed my father."

"Really? What makes you say that?"

"I was there, but I won't tell anyone."

"I know that."

"So that's like saying you're going to kill me."

Jacob moves toward her. "You're right. But there are many ways to be killed. Some are very painful."

"You let me go," she says, "and I'll make you a rich man. Many multiples of whatever they're paying you. I'm sure you know I can afford it."

"I can't let you go. Then they kill me. Painfully."

"I could offer you protection. A new identity. A life like a king's in another country."

He laughs again. "You know I can't trust you."

"But you can. I really mean it. Listen to me."

"No, you listen to me," he says. "Lift up the nightgown, because I like it sweet. If it has to be bitter, you will not like the pain."

—⁓⁓⁓—

Tom bursts out of the subway and his cell phone rings. "Who's this?" he says running.

"Mike. Slow down. Cops in Brooklyn have already been to the house. No one there. Totally empty. Sorry."

Tom stops. "What do you mean? When?"

"They just left."

"You said you were sending cops from Manhattan."

"Guys in Brooklyn were closer and available."

"And now gone."

"The house is empty, Tom. Come back."

"You find Stamos?"

"Not answering his phone, not in his office."

"Rashid?"

"Same thing."

Tom starts running again. "Bye, Mike. I'll let you know what I find."

—⁓⁓⁓—

The front door is locked, but it's glass, so Tom breaks it. Not so simple. He almost severs his foot. But once smashed open, the door is easy enough to unlock.

The house certainly feels empty. No lights, no sounds. He takes the stairs two at a time. Bedrooms still furnished but devoid of people, photos or clothes. As are all the closets. No towels in the bathroom, or pharmaceutical products, though cardboard boxes and plastic containers are littered about. Khalil and his household have definitely fled.

He inspects the ceiling of every room, and of the upstairs hallway. In the ceiling of the master bedroom closet, there's a square perforation implying an attic door.

He finds a straight-back chair that will support his weight and fit in the closet. In moments he has the ceiling door open and has hoisted himself through. Dark, dusty, open, empty. He's sweating profusely and in near panic.

Tom rattles back down the stairs. *There are radiators in this house, it's got to have a basement. Where's the damn door?* Living room, dining room, kitchen—no cellar door. None in the front hallway. There was nothing in the front of the house, he remembers, so he goes out the back. A small garden. No door there either. Or cellar windows.

What am I missing?

He goes back inside, stands in the hallway, and tries calmly to think. *"Christ!"*

Back in the living room. The rug isn't straight. He pulls it aside with some effort. There's the door. In the floor. The bottom of the rug is Velcroed to it. The door has a pull latch. And stairs leading down. And light coming from around a door to a room past the furnace at the far end of the basement.

Tom opens that door to an awful sight: a gun aimed squarely at his head by a large ugly man also holding a nightgown, and Elena crouching naked in a corner, covering herself with her knees and arms.

Tom, flashing his badge, summons from somewhere miraculous wellsprings of cool. "Evening, Jacob. Jacob Wozniacki, to use your full name."

Which causes Jacob to blink.

"So here's the situation," Tom continues. "In about two, three minutes tops, half the police force of New York City will be in and around this building. They're after you. And they will have the area surrounded. They do that—surround places—so if the culprit, meaning you, takes a hostage, they can shoot him in the back."

"How do you know my name?"

"Well, we have your name, and Piet's name—he's doing a lot of the talking. I know, for example, you both took orders from Birdie O'Shane. But let's focus on your options. Taking hostages, you're a dead man, as I said. Besides, it would slow you down. You have a better chance just running. If you take off immediately, it's conceivable you'll slip through, though frankly that's not what I'd do in your circumstances. See, we've been told it was your shot that killed Robbie Riles. Piet and Birdie both—"

"That's bullshit."

"Ah, really? So you deny their story. Well, you run, the cops spot you, you don't get to tell your side, they'll probably just shoot you on sight. The third option is to stay right here. Turn yourself in when the cops arrive—and I'll make sure they don't shoot you. We'll also cover up Elena and pretend this ugly sexual abuse didn't happen."

"What abuse? I never touched her!"

"Good. Then you'll get to tell your story, with a lawyer representing you, as someone who gave himself up, rather than as a fugitive caught in flight. Much stronger position. And the fact is, they're not really interested in you. They're interested in Teddy Stamos. The mastermind of this whole thing. You, I know, were just taking orders from Birdie who took them from Stamos."

"How ... do you know all this?"

"I've *known* about Stamos for a while. What I need is some direct proof."

"Oh yeah. That's worth a lot, right?"

"It is," Tom says calmly. "To you."

"So what do I get?"

"I just said."

"Not enough."

"I'm an assistant DA, not the DA. I can't guarantee a result. But you need someone inside. And I will argue forcefully against the death penalty. You give me what I need, and you have my word."

"How do I know you're even in the DA's office?"

"You saw my badge."

Jacob laughs. "I could buy one."

"How else would I know your name? Come on, Jacob! You're running out of time."

The man gives a tortured expression of uncertainty.

"You've met him?" Tom prods. "Stamos?"

"Today," Jacob says. "He gave me money to do this."

"Well. Okay. That's great. I think we can deal. And I think you understand. Dealing is by far your best option right now. Just toss that nightgown over to Elena, uncuff her, and drop the gun."

They hear sirens.

Tom says, hiding his great relief, "You see? It's coming to pass, Jacob. Follow my instructions and all will end for you far better than it otherwise might."

Jacob does as he is told. As he hands Elena back her nightgown, she smacks him right in the face.

FORTY-NINE

In the squad car taking them home, Elena says nothing. Upstairs in their tiny Red Hook apartment, she goes to the bathroom, gets dressed in more than a nightgown and a borrowed sweater, gets out her suitcase, and starts packing.

"I've somehow disappointed you?" he asks.

"You saw what that guy did to me?" she says.

"And what he was about to do, yes."

"And you made a deal with him! For evidence! You totally let him get away with humiliating me and killing my father."

"I think maybe you don't understand the deal. He was about to kill both of us with that gun. Or to take us hostage, which very likely would have gotten us killed. The point was to get him to put the gun down. Everything else was meaningless piffle."

"You gave him your word!" she says, grabbing blouses and jeans from the dresser. "That was meaningless?"

"Absolutely. There is no death penalty in the state of New York. But he will go up for life for felony murder. In which case, what's the point of adding twenty years to his sentence?"

"There's a point to me!" she says.

"Okay. I see that. You want to prosecute him? Go ahead. You didn't give your word."

"He took my nightgown off."

"I saw."

"And touched me when he did it," she says.

On each of their faces a suppression of tears.

He says roughly, "Of course I want to kill him. But there was never a chance of that, El."

She slings the clothes into her suitcase. He goes to hold her. "I know you're angry, El."

"It's no consolation that you saved my life."

"I know that too."

"You're too fucking rational for me, Tom."

"Too rational?"

She pulls away. "And now you're patronizing me."

"I do realize nothing I can say at the moment can be right."

"Right," she says and snaps the suitcase shut. "So I'm leaving."

"You've had a trauma. We should deal with it, go to the hospital."

"I don't need a hospital," she says, turning. "I need to get away from you."

"Wait!" he says.

Her tight lips imply he has seconds.

"We could go for some pie," he says. "Y'know, Key lime, the place I mentioned."

"Not funny, Tom! Not fucking funny!"

She's gone, and there's no humor to that either.

———◦∾◦———

Tom wakes up alone, doesn't much like it. He understands the psychology of Elena's departure, but dislikes that too. Comforting each other would have been a better alternative. Of course, he would never have admitted such a need, which is maybe why he's not entirely blameless. Musing about that, he showers and dresses, then grabs some breakfast at the coffee shop on Van Brunt Street, before taking a subway to work. He keeps thinking, *I will fix this.* But he's not sure how.

He goes directly to Mike's office. The boss is there but reading and doesn't look up. "Jacob is talking," Mike says.

"Interesting story. Dovetails exactly with Piet's. Little more detailed, because he says he knows more than Piet does, but there's no inconsistency. For example, Jacob says you came to him; he then recruited Piet."

Tom takes a chair. Shakes his head. Laughs out loud. "Last night he was handing me Stamos."

"You have it recorded?"

"I had a gun on me. But I have a witness."

"Elena?" Mike says, looking up. "Not exactly disinterested, but okay, bring her in."

"She's probably more disinterested than you think. I have to find her."

Mike studies him. "She split? After you saved her life?"

"Probably because of it. Look," Tom says, then stops, thinks, gets up excitedly. "Jacob's telling the same story? The same story Piet told? That's it!"

Mike doesn't get it.

Tom says, "Someone got to him! Because he didn't know it, when I arrived in that basement. What's the trail afterward?"

"He was brought right here. Then the lockup. Probably being arraigned right now. From there, of course, he'll go to Rikers."

"Who questioned him here?"

"Sammy."

"Okay," Tom says, leaning over Mike's desk.

"You're suggesting what? Sammy turned Jacob?"

"I doubt it. But that first assignment you gave me? The day I arrived here? Given what you just told me, I might have the answer by the end of today." He goes to the door, hesitates, and turns. "You're not arresting me, I see."

Mike smiles faintly. "You have the day," he says. Then, "Oh. Pressroom is packed. So you also have a choice. You can be the hero for last night, or you can pass and give it to the force."

"I'll pass."

"Wise choice," Mike says.

———〰———

Tom finds Sammy in his office. It's what he expects: a small cavern of loose stacked files whose organization would confound anyone but Sammy. "Who spoke to Jacob last night in addition to you? Maybe before you?"

"Am I supposed to talk to you?" Sammy says.

"Your call. But talk to Mike first, if you like. He just sent me down here."

Sammy thinks about this only briefly before picking up his phone. Mike must have been waiting for the call, since he takes it immediately. Tom hears Mike's voice boom, "Tell him what he wants to know." Sammy hangs up and says, as if nothing of significance had transpired, "The cops who brought him, obviously. My boss, for a couple of minutes, maybe. The usual."

"Your boss, Foster Donachetti?"

"That's right."

"Is it usual for him to talk to suspects before you do?"

"Happens, sure."

"Were you there when it did?"

"Yeah, I think so."

"*Think* so?" Tom says.

Sammy rises. "What the fuck is this, Weldon?"

"Nothing, relax."

FIFTY

Tom gets to Rikers Island by bus. As an assistant DA, he's entitled to drive into the compound, but Tom neither owns a car nor commands one. The other passengers, all women, are older than he and get off first. He pegs most for visitors and one for staff. He'll never know. The trip to a place like this is generally uncongenial.

Dealing with a series of corrections officers, who regard him with resentment, he has Jacob brought into a room. It smells of disinfectant and fear.

Jacob, sleepless, is surly. He's still in the black workout clothes they brought him in with. Tom waves off the squat guard's presence and any necessity for manacles. The door closes on the officer's smirk. As an ADA, Tom can get what he wants here, but not without receiving some attitude.

Jacob says, "This place is a hellhole. You can't even fucking sleep here."

Tom gives him a look of indifference. "I thought we had a deal."

"You're an ADA? I'm supposed to have a lawyer."

"Right," Tom says. "And if you don't have one, I can't use anything you say. So. I thought we had a deal."

"You got outbid."

"That right? By whom?"

Jacob laughs. "By my civic duty. By the need to tell the truth."

"Think it through, Jake. If you do tell the truth, your story will hold together; your deal will hold together; and you'll get the minimum for murder one, or felony murder. Stick to the lie, your story will be challenged and come apart. They'll throw the book at you."

"You lied to *me*. You said I'd get the chair, but there is no death penalty in this state. I've checked with the jailhouse lawyers. And you're recording this fucking conversation."

"I told you. I can't use it. I'm a lawyer. You're an arraigned defendant without one." Tom gets up. "You know the name of the ADA who questioned you last night."

"Sure. Sammy Riegert."

"Who else? Same building."

"No one."

"You're sure? No one, no questions?"

"I fucking said."

"Talk to anyone else?"

"No."

"Sure of that?"

"Jesus! Yes! Fucking sure!"

"Thanks, Jake."

"For what?" he says.

"Time of day, man. Pleasure of your company." Tom signals the corrections guy to come back in.

—◦◦◦—

Yasim Maktoum, sitting alone in a park in Oklahoma City, calls Mike Skillan on a cell phone just purchased for the purpose.

"Put it through," Mike says, when learning who's on the line.

"I have information for you," Yasim says.

"I'm listening."

There's a long silence until Yasim says, "I really don't know what to do, so I called you."

"I understand."

"I just learned something terrible."

"About your girlfriend."

"Yes, how did you know?"

"She's a paid assassin," Mike says.

"How did you know this?" Yasim says, now even more agitated.

"We know more than you apparently realized. Has she confessed to you?"

"I don't know what I should tell you."

"Let me tell you what you should do," says Mike. "From wherever you now are—"

"Oklahoma City."

"Yes, I have that. My point is do not go back to your room. Go straight to the airport. Come back to New York. You called me, because you're an innocent bystander to this. Have nothing further to do with her. Go from Kennedy to my office at One Hogan Place. We will take your statement and protect you. You understand? If you stay out, you're in danger."

"Yes, I understand. I'm in danger, but not only from her."

"All the more reason," Mike says, "to get back here as quickly as you can."

Long silence, until Yasim says, "Okay."

"I'll look forward to meeting you," Mike says. "Ask for me when you arrive. They'll have word of you downstairs. And Yasim. What hotel, what room?"

After a long pause, Yasim says, "the Radisson, 906," and hangs up.

Mike looks up, and there's Tom, standing behind the chair in front of Mike's desk. "You know who that was?"

"Yasim Maktoum," Tom says.

"He's coming back here."

"Good," Tom says. "I'll want them all here tomorrow morning. Yasim, Rashid, Stamos, Jacob, Piet, Elena, Sofi, your original eyewitness—what's his name, Moon—and others I'll tell you about."

"*You* want them?" Mike says, with a laugh.

"I do."

"You're getting awfully high-handed, kid. Especially for someone who's been here two days. And now once again a suspect himself."

"Oh come on!" Tom says. "You're still on that—that bullshit story?"

"It's been confirmed," Mike says, with a straight face.

"Look, Mike." Tom grabs the back of the chair. "Stop dicking around, and I'll solve the case for you."

"We already know Stamos was at the center of it."

"Can you prove it?"

Mike hesitates. "Not cleanly. Not yet."

"And who was paying him?"

"Jockery, probably."

"Right," Tom says. "Probably. We know how far 'probably' gets. And who else? Rashid? *Probably?* For all of it? Part of it? Anyone else?"

Mike frowns. "Whatta you need?"

"What I said. Tomorrow morning."

Mike props his index fingers one inch apart. "You got that much."

"Thanks," Tom says. "I'll want them all in the reception room at the same time, so they can see each other. I'll need three interrogation rooms. And I'll do the questioning."

"Boy!"

"I know. High-handed."

"Beyond that, fella. You are an arrogant son of a bitch. No wonder she split."

"You think *I'm* arrogant?"

"Then you deserve each other."

Tom laughs, leaving the older man with a rueful smile.

—⌇〰⌇—

Tom is sitting in the upstairs hallway in front of Elena's door
when she returns to her apartment.

"How'd you get into this building?" she asks.

"You think that's a challenge? You choose to live in a building without doormen."

"The front door is locked."

"And often opened by people living here wishing to leave
and not particularly caring who comes in after them."

"I don't want to see you," she says.

"I know, but I do you, because I need you."

"Don't start, Tom."

"I'm not. I need you to talk to Mike Skillan. Tell him you
heard Jacob—the thug who abused you—admit he was working for Teddy Stamos."

"Why?" she asks. "Doesn't he believe you?"

"I need confirmation. Jacob is now claiming I was responsible for the plot to kidnap you."

"That's ridiculous."

"No shit," he says.

"And what?" she says. "Skillan believes that?"

"I doubt it. But he's got to deal with it. And I promised
him I'd solve his case for him tomorrow. You can help."

"Me?"

"I'm bringing in everyone, ten a.m. Even Sofi and your
charming sisters."

"My sisters?" Elena exclaims. "What do they know?"

"Maybe nothing. They'll be there so we can find out."

"And what?" she says. "You'll question everyone, and break
the case? You've done a lot of this, Hercule Poirot?"

"Never," he admits. "But it's not rocket science. The prosecutor holds all the cards. And the play is simple. You pretend
you know more than you do and let them tell you the rest of
it. You saw what happened last night. Jacob confessed in two
minutes that he's working for Stamos."

"So you don't need me."

"Of course I need you."

"I see that man again, I'm going for his throat."

"You'll be in a separate room."

"I won't be there! Aren't you listening?"

"I need you there."

"Why?"

"Because you know more than I do. You're smart. Two heads are better than one. I like working with you. You're beautiful."

"You just want to get laid."

"That too," he says.

"Okay," she says reluctantly after a long pause. "I'll be there tomorrow. But the other thing?" She shakes her head. "Not happening."

FIFTY-ONE

Tom wakes up feeling confident. He's always had that—a breezy expectancy of good fortune. Commuting from Red Hook to Foley Square, however, he's reminded of the paucity of material he has to work with, the cleverness of those he has to work on, and the consequences of getting it all wrong—or, just as bad, getting nothing.

Not a good time for a loss of confidence, he reflects. *So I damn well better not have one!*

Mike is already ensconced when Tom arrives at the senior man's office. "This is a highly unusual situation," Mike says. "In several respects. I'm allowing an assistant DA, who's himself a suspect, to interrogate a bunch of witnesses to prove his own innocence. Let me stop there for a minute. You have any idea why I'm doing that?"

"You believe I'm innocent."

"Must be that," Mike says. "But I could be wrong."

"You're not," says Tom. "Have you talked to Elena?"

"I have. I myself asked her to come in."

"So you know what happened with Jacob?"

"I know what she says. And all these people have come in, some without lawyers, all without the need for me subpoenaing them, seemingly happy to tell their stories. You have any idea why?"

"They want to lead you to believe that their stories are true."

"You think they're all guilty?"

"No," Tom says.

"But you know which ones are?"

"Reasonably sure."

"And you think you're about to prove it by the brilliance of your questioning?"

"With one more witness, yes."

"One *more* witness?" Mike says, beginning to get hot. "You need someone in addition to the seven suspects we've already assembled for you? Someone you haven't told me about?"

"Well, he's already here. He works for you," Tom says. "He's the guy who's been leaking stuff."

"You now know who that is?"

"I do." Tom sits. "Remember what I said? When I caught Jacob in Khalil's basement, he confessed he'd been working for Teddy Stamos. Later that night he talked to two people here and changed his story. One of them turned him."

"Not Sammy Riegert," Mike notes. "We've been over that."

"So we have."

"Okay. So what is this? I have to pull it out of you?"

"It's Foster Donachetti."

"What?" Mike says with a harsh laugh.

"Sorry. I know he's a friend, but that's the guy."

With blinking eyes, Mike rocks back a bit in his chair. "This I don't believe."

"Yeah, you do," Tom says.

"How do I know you're not just making this up? The change of story?"

Tom takes out his iPhone and plays the recording. Mike listens. Then thinks. "Where'd you get this?" he says.

"I went to see Jacob at Rikers."

"Outbid by civic duty was all he said."

"Listen to it again," Tom says, and replays it. When it stops, Mike sits there, says nothing.

"As you just heard, he admitted talking to Sammy—

obviously he had to, but said it naturally, no strain at all. He denied talking to Donachetti. Not only do I know he was lying, because Sammy told me Foster had spoken to him, but Jacob's an easy read. The lie was all over his face. And in his voice. Only one reason for him to lie about it. It was Foster who fed Jacob the new story."

"That's it?"

"That's it."

"Ain't as much as you're implying."

"I think you know better."

"I *don't* know, Tom. I've given you a lot of rope."

"And I need more. I want to put Jacob in an interrogation room now. Teddy Stamos in another. Then I want to cuff Foster and show him in cuffs—and pissed off about it—to both of them. When I'm finished with Jacob, put Moon in that room, but make sure Teddy sees that happening. After I've talked with all of them, and probably one or two more, we'll have what we need."

Mike is now staring, not at Tom, but into space. "Foster Donachetti has been my friend for more than thirty years. We were at law school together. And the only thing you have is that some creep lied about talking to him? On the basis of that, you want me to charge him? Humiliate him?"

"I think you've got more than that. And I think you know … Donachetti is the lance we need for opening this whole pocket of pus."

Mike blows out his cheeks. "Quite a metaphor."

"Quite a mess."

"What more do you think I have?"

"You're an easy read too, Mike. I think he's the guy you've been suspecting all along."

———

Tom appears at the door of Foster Donachetti's office with two uniformed cops—and with Foster's secretary screaming for them to leave. Tom formally addresses the thin-faced man. "We are charging you with obstruction of justice in the investigation of Robbie Riles's death, and this is your Miranda warning. You have the right to call a lawyer, and to remain silent, and anything you choose to say will be held against you."

Foster, smartly suited as usual, rises from his telephone conversation. "Are you outta your fucking mind?"

"Gentlemen." Tom beckons to the cops who immediately cuff Donachetti with his hands in front. "Please follow me," Tom says.

Stunned, furious, and literally being dragged, Foster lets go a scream that pierces the caterwauling of his secretary. "What the fuck you doing, Weldon?"

"What I'm doing, Foster, is enacting your worst nightmare."

They're at the elevator, and the door opens. "I'll have your ass," he snarls.

"That's it?" Tom says. "Pretty weak."

"Mike hears about this, he'll roast your balls."

"Who you think authorized this, Foster?"

"I don't fucking believe it! You're false-arresting me? It's you I'll have prosecuted!"

Tom gives him a pitying look.

Heading down, there's just glaring.

At interrogation room one, Tom opens the door, and the cops pull in Donachetti. Jacob, already seated and manacled to the table, looks startled.

"So sorry," Tom says. "Wrong room."

Closing the door, they then repeat the process at room number two, where Stamos registers equal shock to see Foster dragged in with cuffs. Tom then oversees settling Foster in the third room and returns to face Jacob. He takes the seat across from the prisoner.

"Just as well you saw that," Tom says.

"I want a lawyer," Jacob shouts. "Now!"

"Well, you see, 'now' is the problem. You will have a lawyer, but if you don't talk until he or she gets here, you'll lose the race."

"What fucking race?"

"I've told you how it works, Jake. First one in with the material evidence gets the best deal."

"You've already lied to me is what you've done."

"About capital punishment?" Tom says. "Not really. There's quite a range in this state when it comes to prisons. Some ... staying there long term? You'd rather die. And you ... felony murder, sexual assault ... you're definitely long term."

Jacob tries to read Tom's face. "You got something more to say?"

"You're listening now, are you? I have your attention?"

"What's the fucking deal?"

"Depends on what you have to give me."

"Suppose I could give you that guy you just brought in here?"

"Well," Tom says, "we already have him, as you saw. But ... corroboration? That's useful, I admit. So you'd get something for that."

"Like what?"

"Like maybe dropping the sexual charge. Would make a difference on sentencing. Certainly on the facility they send you to. If you want to be caged with a couple of hundred other sexual offenders ... well, wouldn't be my choice. Nor something a guy like you would likely recover from."

Jacob looks a little sick. "You said you'd drop that charge."

"You reneged on the deal. Now, you've got another chance."

Realizing what he'd just admitted, Jacob puts his hands to his face.

"Hey, it's up to you," Tom says. "No pressure from me. You do what's good for Jacob. All I know is, I've got other witnesses in other rooms here waiting to talk to me. You've got a chance to jump in first, because right now I'm in this room, talking to

you. I get up off this chair, that chance is gone. So you tell me,
Jacob. Are you cooperating now, or do we burn you in hell?"

"I dunno, man."

Tom gets up. "Suit yourself, man."

"Sit down," Jacob says.

"I'm outta here."

"He's the guy."

"Donachetti?"

"Yeah."

"Guy who did what?"

"Told me what to say, night before last."

"And what was that?"

"That you were in on it," Jacob says. "Thought the whole
thing up. That we were working for you."

"Which is untrue."

"Yeah."

Tom blinks, when he knows he shouldn't. The case against
Donachetti had been hanging by a thread. It just became a
cable around the man's testicles.

"And the truth is what, Jacob? Who were you working for?"

"Hey," Jacob says. "That's different."

"Why? You want to stop? Make half a deal? Give this one
to Donachetti? He'll be all too willing."

Jacob says nothing, twists his mouth.

Tom says, "Look, man. You shot a guy down in the street.
Murder for money. Cold-blooded, premeditated. You're not
walking. You want to go up forever with no possibility ever of
parole, you clam up now. And you may have noticed. I'm not
even asking you to admit this. I don't need your admission. I can
prove murder one without you. I'm only asking who paid you."

"A woman. Birdie."

"Birdie O'Shane?"

"Probably. I heard her name once. You said it. In the cellar."

"But she wasn't the boss," Tom says.

"No," Jacob replies.

"So?"

"I don't know his name. You seemed to."

"Describe him."

"Little guy. Expensive threads. Looks like a frog."

"How little?"

"I dunno. Maybe five-two."

"Teddy Stamos?"

"That's what you said. He didn't give me his name."

"How much did he pay you? Through Birdie, I'm sure she gave you the money."

"For the first job?" Jacob says, then realizes what he's done.

Tom laughs. "As I said, Jake. Didn't need your admission to the murder, but nice to have it from your lips." Tom gets up. "Sit tight. Someone will pick you up in a minute."

FIFTY-TWO

Foster Donachetti, believing Mike and the team to be assembled behind the glass, is trying to reason with its reflection. "For Christ's sake, Mike! This is insane! You don't know this kid! You know me! Whatever the hell he's told you, if you think I've done anything wrong or disloyal, have the goddamn decency to come in here and tell me yourself."

Tom walks in on the end of this speech. "Decency?" he says. "Nice point. You're in here, Foster, because you sold out a friend. Then, night before last, you fucked up, big time. Put your life in the hands of a thug, who just sold *you* out."

"You think I'm talking to you?"

"He is," Tom says, sitting across from him. "The thug. Jacob Wozniacki."

"And what? His word over mine?"

"So you know who I mean?"

"You just pushed me into his room."

"Right," Tom says. "He identified you too. And Mike believes *him*. Or you wouldn't be here. And guess what? Teddy Stamos? The guy in the next room? He's my next interview. Jacob Wozniacki has nailed him too. So Teddy needs something to trade with. For his own deal. And the man kisses up. Maybe he's not giving his clients away so fast. But kicking down? Those who *took* his money? So what's it to be, Foster? Is Teddy giving me you, or are you giving me Teddy?"

Donachetti is speechless and sullen.

Tom adds, as if offhandedly, "Whatever large sums he paid you—now that we know to look, we'll find them. Some bank somewhere. Cayman Islands, maybe? Popular resort for dirty money."

Donachetti now looks sick.

"You have a minute," Tom says, and studies the clock on the wall. "Then I leave and do business with Teddy."

They wait, Foster staring straight ahead, Tom still looking up at the clock face. When Foster also turns to the clock, Tom knows that he has him. As the second hand approaches the minute mark, Tom's eyes shift to Foster.

"You're not scaring me," Foster says.

"Too bad," says Tom and gets up.

"No one's going to believe that creep."

"I'm about to get three creeps," Tom says and starts walking. "You top of the list."

"Stop," Foster says. Tom does, turns, looks.

"This is too fucking crazy," Foster says. "You just got here— what? Two days ago? You're running a sting now?"

"Add it up, Foster. Wozniacki is gushing. On you. Can't stop. Piet's heading in here. Right here. This room. Can't wait to sell you, FOB. Like Teddy next door, who will deliver you in seconds. And the money he paid you? You didn't stick it in a box, Foster. Not a guy like you. It's earning interest somewhere or invested wisely. You probably never saw it, other than on a bank statement. You think we won't find it?"

With an expression of sympathy, Tom heads to the door. "All right," Foster says.

Tom stops. "All right, what?"

"All right, tell me what the fucking deal is."

"You know the deal. We won't push for the maximum sentence, but you'll serve time. Probably a minimum security facility, five years in, three on parole. You'll lose your license to practice. For how long? That's up to you and ultimately,

I suspect, the Court of Appeals. With no deal at all, you go to Attica for twelve years minimum, and you'll never practice again."

Foster looks homicidal. "Not much of a deal."

"Best we can offer. You should know that. You're a high-ranking public official whom judges like to smash."

"I'd be giving you a very big fish."

"Correction. You'd be corroborating the fish that someone else has already put on our plate."

Foster reflects. "I'll need the deal in writing."

"Sorry. I don't have the time. Once I get what I need from Teddy, while you wait for your writing, there goes your leverage, and there's no deal at all. And you don't need it in writing. You know we're recording this."

"You're a real prick."

"No doubt. But how else would I nail one?"

Silence and an exchange of looks. Tom's says, *one last chance.* It gets a grimace from Donachetti.

"Have fun in Attica," Tom says.

As Tom opens the door, Foster says, "All right, already."

Tom turns and tilts his head inquiringly. Foster, looking miserable, says, "You got it."

"It?" Tom says.

"Sit down, will ya?" Tom stands his ground.

"I've been taking from Teddy Stamos," Foster says.

"How much?"

"Several hundred thousand."

"Several?"

"Five," he says angrily.

"Dollars, I presume."

"Yes. Dollars."

Tom comes back to the table. "Over what period?"

"About half the year. When the takeover plans started, I suppose—way before they became public."

"What did you give Stamos?"

"Nothing at first. Not for months. Then information on the status of our investigation of the Riles murder."

"Leaks? To the press? You do that?"

Big sigh. "Yeah."

"Did Stamos ask you to talk to Jacob Wozniacki night before last?"

"Yes, yes." Now he's impatient to end it.

Tom sits. "And did you do what Stamos asked? See Wozniacki before he was shipped off to Rikers?"

"Yes."

"What did you tell him?"

"Basically … to blame everything on you."

"Which was false."

"Yes."

Tom stops for a moment. Gives Donachetti a chance to realize how far he's just gone. That there was no reason now, and no way, to turn back.

"Piet Dvoon," Tom says.

"Same thing," Foster admits.

"Stamos asked you to suborn Piet with the same story, which you did?"

"Yes."

Tom says, "Victor Contrares, the gun dealer? According to the file, he came in fast, claiming to have sold a gun to Elena Riles. Did Teddy Stamos procure that testimony?"

"Yes. It was false."

"And who was he working for, Stamos?"

"I assume Jockery or the UAE, or both."

"You assume?"

"I don't know, is the point. If I did, you think I wouldn't use that?"

Tom smiles. "Guy like you? Yeah. I'm sure you would."

———◦◦◦———

Interrogation room three.

Entering, Tom says, "No lawyer, Teddy?"

"I am a lawyer," Stamos says. "Besides. I assume I'm here only as a witness."

"Target, Teddy."

"You can't be serious."

"You have the right to remain silent and to call a lawyer. Anything you say now can be used against you in a court of law."

"You're Mirandizing me?" Teddy says, as if the very thought were preposterous.

"We're charging you with two homicides. Murder one in each case. And two kidnappings. We already have two witnesses against you, with more on the way."

"You suborning their perjury?" Teddy's now laughing.

"No, Teddy. They've been quite willing to help out."

"Really? No carrot and stick? No train's leaving the station? You guys still do that, right?"

"Hardly coercion."

"People bullied into confessions they later recant?"

"And how does that work?" Tom says. "The recanting? Especially when a witness is the third-ranking ADA in the county."

"Oh, ho!" Teddy's lower lip slides up in a parody of being impressed. "You have Foster, you're saying. That should make a splash. Helping himself at my expense?"

"You think Foster Donachetti isn't credible?"

"If he's tried to implicate me, he's lying. Shouldn't be difficult to prove."

"He's confessed to accepting your bribes. And you mentioned subornation of perjury? Happens to be one of the things you paid him to do, he says. You may deny that, Teddy, but you're not going to be able to disprove it. And Foster ties you into everything. So does Jacob Wozniacki."

"I did not murder or kidnap anyone," Stamos snaps.

Tom says, as if losing patience, "It was you who hired Jacob, Piet, and Birdie to murder and kidnap. Wozniacki has sworn to that fact; Donachetti further substantiates it; Birdie has just been flushed from a hotel room in Oklahoma City and will doubtless reconfirm it."

"And what? Now we start playing carrot and stick?"

"In your case, I'm afraid, not much left to that carrot."

Stamos looks wary.

"Here's your situation," Tom says. "It's pretty obvious you wouldn't have paid anyone to kill Robbie Riles or kidnap Elena, unless someone had paid you a lot more to do it. So your leverage, normally, in making a deal would be to identify that person. Or persons. However, one of those guys, Lowell Jockery, is dead. You've no leverage there, since we can't prosecute a dead man. That brings us to Rashid al-Calif, who obviously paid you to kill Jockery."

"You're dreaming, Weldon. I've never met anyone of that name, much less had any dealings with him."

"Sorry, Teddy. Won't work. We know he's your client. Can prove it ten different ways. And then a funny thing happened this morning. Filmed by our cameras in the reception room. He took one look at you and—would you believe it? As soon as you were taken in here, he flew right the hell out of the building, claiming diplomatic immunity."

Tom stops for a moment to gauge Teddy's visage, which seems a bit quivery. "The thing about diplomatic immunity," Tom says, "is that it's political. The country—here the United Arab Emirates—can waive it, if they want, which of course depends on a lot of factors. How important is Rashid to them, now that he's been discredited? What would they be getting in return? And from the U.S. standpoint: would we even ask for a waiver, if Rashid is willing to cooperate? By, for example, giving us you. Dunno, Teddy, but would seem like a no-brainer for

Rashid, adding his testimony to the others against you. Either as a chip to get the immunity to stick, or as part of a plea bargain if it doesn't."

Teddy says nothing, but his concentration is not wavering.

"Of course," Tom says, "you do have a few remaining bargaining chips, yourself, don't you? They're sitting outside; you've seen them. I'm going to call them in next. Because they also have the ability to offer us you. To lighten their own sentences. Question is: do you trust them to keep their mouths shut? They *are* being represented here by a lawyer. Or do you think they, like Foster, Jacob and no doubt Birdie and Rashid, are ready to help themselves at your expense? Maybe even at that lawyer's advice. You've seen them close-up now. How would you assess their loyalty to you?"

Stamos's silence matches his now totally grim face.

"So, Teddy—you give us them? They give us you? You have the choice. For at least—" Tom looks up at the clock—"another minute."

"I want to call my lawyer."

Tom brings forth an apologetic look. "Of course you have that right. While you exercise it, I'll just pop into the next room. And you mentioned a train? What do you know? Looks like, right now, it's leaving the station."

—◦◦◦—

In the observation room, Elena is crammed between Mike Skillan and Joe Cunningham. Sammy Riegert is crouched in front of the glass. She's been sensing their surprise at the two confessions already exacted. And they're now all observing a third—Teddy Stamos's—with evidence pouring out of him. To Elena, it's like watching Grand Guignol. To the three men, it's embarrassing taking even furtive glances at Elena witnessing her sisters and their husbands being caught in her lover's net.

"Okay," Tom says, "let's get it now in sequence. Who first approached you?"

"Lawton Sergeant," says Teddy, struggling to get a grip on composure.

"The husband of Elena Riles's older sister, Constance Riles?"

"So I understand."

"And was the approach by phone or in person?"

"He called my office."

"Saying what?"

"He wanted to set up a meeting. At their apartment. I suggested we meet at a midtown hotel."

"You already suspected what this was about?"

"Let's just say, I suspected they wouldn't later want evidence—from doormen or anyone—that I was ever in their building."

"Did Lawton Sergeant tell you how he'd gotten your name?"

"I asked, but he didn't. And it didn't matter. I knew who he was."

"Where did you meet, and when?"

"Hotel Pennsylvania, about five weeks ago. I took a room. It's not a place frequented by anyone any of us would know."

"And did the two sisters ask you to kill their father?"

"Ha!" Teddy says. "To begin with, Lawton monopolized the conversation, so no one else had much chance to say anything. The younger sister, Patricia, never opened her mouth. Lawton, however, speaks gobbledygook. Constance cut in and expressed their wish in one sentence. They wanted the deed done so that it would appear it had been perpetrated by Elena."

"Which you arranged for."

"Yes."

"For which they paid you $2.5 million."

"Yes."

"Who put the money into your hands?"

"We live in a digital world, Mr. Weldon."

"Right. So wire transfer?"

"That … would be Constance," Teddy says.

"From her to you?" Tom asks.

"Don't be ridiculous."

"Okay," Tom says. "Why don't you tell me?"

"It was a transfer from her charitable foundation to my bank."

"Was there an exchange?"

"Yes," Teddy says, as if now getting bored with the subject. "The appearance of one."

"And did you tell Constance you were also being paid $2.5 million by Lowell Jockery?"

"I saw no reason to divulge the names of other clients."

"You used the term 'deed done.' You mean—"

"Riles … terminated, yes. And, of course, done in such a way that evidence would point conclusively to the youngest daughter. You understand, I'm simply a middleman. Had they not found me, they would have found someone else."

"One more thing," Tom says. "How did I figure in their plans or yours?"

"You didn't. No one had any idea who the hell you were. But you had a wallet full of identification. And fit beautifully into the frame."

FIFTY-THREE

As Sofi Harding is ushered into the interrogation room, Tom takes a moment to join the observers. Approval marks every face but Elena's.

Mike says, "Well done," which has a ring to it, given Harry Stith's use, not so long ago, of the same term.

Tom says to Elena, "I'm sorry about your sisters."

"Yeah?" she says. "Really?"

"Probably a mistake, asking you here."

"How the hell did you know?" she says, voice strained.

"I didn't … know."

"You concocted all this out of suspicion?"

"Not entirely," he says. "It was what Sofi told us."

"About Stamos?"

"Yes. And the personalities involved. Connie and her husband."

"Whom you've met only once," she says.

"It was enough."

Mike says to Tom, "How the hell did you know about Rashid?"

"What? That he'd skip? Claim diplomatic immunity?"

"I just heard two minutes ago," Mike says.

"You weren't surprised, were you?"

"You just made it up?"

"Something wrong with that?" Tom says.

"So that's what you do?" Elena says, still thinking about

Connie. "Just imagine the worst about everyone and make them admit it?"

"I've never done it before, El. And it's a murder case. Committed by people who were also gunning for us."

Awkward silence, until Elena says, "What exactly is Sofi doing here?" She has the look of someone feeling a grievance but still thrashing about for its source.

"Helping more," Tom says. "No harm will come to her."

"Like that Jacob creature," she says, with acrimony.

"Christ, El." He looks at her sternly.

"Forget it."

"What he got from me," Tom says, "and we've been over this—is life imprisonment."

"He should burn in hell," she says.

"Beyond my skill set," Tom says.

"Or," adds Mike, "mentioned anywhere in the penal code." He turns back to Tom. "Get in there, she's waiting."

——⟗——

Sofi Harding says, "I can see why you wanted to question me downtown—all this paraphernalia, recording devices, and so on—but does it have to be in one of these—" she looks around—"rooms? With the two-way glass or mirror, whatever you call it? And people staring at me from behind it?"

She turns away from him, and he observes her outfit: cream-colored turtleneck blouse and light tweeds, as if for a day in the country—an odd selection, Tom thinks, and wonders whether her mental association had been with hunting. But her oval face has a formal composure, especially in profile, as though she were sitting for an ivory silhouette.

"I don't have an office on this floor," Tom says.

"What's so important about this floor?"

"The reception room," Tom says, "and the direction in which you left it."

She turns back toward him. "You wanted the others in that room to know you'd be questioning me?"

"I did."

"Meaning you suspect them. Or some of them."

Tom says nothing.

"Are you aware," Sofi says, "one of them is a relative of mine?"

"Lawton Sergeant. Your sister's son."

"Yes," she says and studies him. "Elena mention that?"

"No," Tom says. "I looked it up."

"Why?" Sofi asks. "Why in the world would you have?"

"Something you said. About Teddy Stamos. That he would happily work for both sides and approach either. I'm trying to figure out whether he approached Lawton and Constance, or they him."

"Why would you think they'd want the services of a Teddy Stamos?"

"Ah," Tom says, and nothing more.

"You're not going to tell me?" she says.

"I'm hoping you'll tell me."

"And what difference does it make?" Sofi asks, somewhat defensively.

Tom says, "Let me ask you straight out. Did you ever discuss Stamos with Lawton or Constance?"

She lets out a sigh. "Yes."

"Why?"

"Because Teddy had called them, and they thought I might have some idea who he was."

"Thank you, Ms. Harding. That's all I need."

"You called me down here for that?"

"You haven't saved your nephew, Ms. Harding, but believe me. He'd be in for much worse without it."

—◦◦◦—

Interrogation room two.

Logjam.

Both Lawton and Jasper Kane trying to get in at once, with Harrison Stith right behind them. Lawton is the tall one: slender, groomed, face a fine oval like his aunt's.

Tom says, "I asked for Jasper."

"I know more than he does," Lawton says.

Tom turns to his former boss. "And whom do you represent, Harry?"

The older lawyer, suited, vested, gazes inward for guidance. "The family," he says.

"Looks like you may have a conflict."

"Looks like, yes." He turns to his now-former clients. "It's Constance who called me, and it's she I will represent. I advise both of you to say nothing until you each have your own representation." Whereupon Stith departs.

Neither young man seems to notice. Lawton grabs the witness chair and Jasper, also slender, but short, bird-like, curly-haired, perches on the edge of the table. At a deliberate pace, Tom resettles in his seat, then stares at both of them. "You two want to do this together? A bit unconventional, but it's okay with me."

"I'm not leaving," Lawton says. "I've seen the cop shows. First in, first out, right?"

"You're a little late for that," Tom says.

"Whatever you got, I can add to it."

"And you want to?"

"Sure."

"No waiting for a lawyer?"

"Don't need one. I've been to law school."

"And what about you?" Tom says to Jasper. "You been to law school too?"

"No, but I'm fine. Frankly, I'm just curious what he's—" pointing at his brother-in-law, "—got to say."

"All right," Tom says. "Floor is yours, Lawton. Tell us what you know about the murder of Robbie Riles."

"Sure," says Lawton, as if he'd been waiting impatiently to tell his tale. "It was entirely the idea of Teddy Stamos. He thought it up, and he carried it out."

"And how do you know that?"

"Because he propositioned us."

"Us?"

"The four of us. My wife, Jasper's, him, and me."

"Propositioned meaning—"

"He tried to sell us on the whole idea. Get us to finance it. Assassinating Robbie."

"And?" Tom prompts.

"We threw him out of the room."

"But he carried it out anyway? The killing?"

"Presumably, yes. It happened just as he said it would."

"So if you refused to pay him, why'd he do it?"

"Presumably someone else paid him," Lawton says, as if explaining the obvious.

"Definitely not you."

"Definitely."

"When he approached you the first time," Tom asks, "why didn't you go to the police?"

"No point. He would only've denied it."

"Would have stopped him from doing it."

"Who knew he'd actually do it?" Lawton says. "We thought we *had* stopped him."

"By refusing to pay for it?"

"And because we knew about it. Before the fact, as it were."

"But you didn't warn Robbie?" Tom notes.

"Connie may have said something, I don't know. Robbie and I were not on the best of terms. But y'know how many death threats that man got? Probably two a week. Why add another one?"

"Okay, then," Tom says. "Why didn't you call the police when Robbie was murdered?"

"Me? Because I thought the person Stamos got to finance the killing was Elena."

"That's your story?"

"Yeah," Lawton says, apparently disappointed it didn't seem to be going over that well. "Everyone knew she and Robbie didn't get on, and, of course, she had the most to gain."

"You decided to say nothing out of concern for your sister-in-law?"

"That's right. You heard the press reports. All the evidence pointed to her."

"Okay," Tom says. "So now I want to talk to Jasper. Alone."

Lawton looks from one to the other. "That's not happening."

"We'll let Jasper decide, shall we?"

Sergeant gets up, then says invitingly, with his hand extended, "Jasper? Coming?"

Tom asks, as if really curious, "Do you have a dog, Lawton?"

The only one laughing is Jasper. "I'm ready to continue the conversation," he says.

"Conversation?" says Lawton. "Are you fucking crazy? This guy's trying to nail your ass."

"I kind of doubt it's my ass you're worried about."

"Well, I'm not leaving," Lawton proclaims.

Tom gives him a wan smile, picks up the phone and says into the receiver, "Ask someone to come in, please. Witness removal." He looks at Lawton with a benign expression.

"Fuck you," says Lawton. As if having made some sort of point, he leaves.

Tom goes to shut the door. "So, let's just start with who called whom."

"Stamos called Constance," Jasper says. "Lawton wasn't lying about that."

"What was he lying about?"

"Is this really going to matter? I mean to me."

"Yes. We get the truth from you, it will help. In sentencing, definitely. In the charge against you—if there is one—maybe."

"You realize, I don't believe I've committed any crime."

"Tell it honestly," Tom says, "we'll see."

"Okay." Jasper slides into the chair. "I'm going to trust you on that." He nods for a moment as if collecting his thoughts. "The idea—to … take out her father—came entirely from Constance. It shocked the hell out of me, Patty, even Teddy Stamos. Lawton said nothing, but I could tell—he wasn't surprised, maybe even ready to go along with it. Teddy—well, after that first reaction, you could just see his mind clicking away, starting to figure out how much money there was in it for him and having trouble not showing excitement."

"Did he tell you he had other clients willing to pay him for the same result?"

"No," Jasper says, "and I don't think he did, at least then. He had other clients on the takeover. He told us that at the start, but put it forward as a plus. He thought we owned a big block of Riles stock, and he had some idea of brokering a deal between us and his other clients. That's why he called in the first place. But then Lawton and Connie started to work on him. Asked how well-connected he was, not simply to businessmen, but to mob figures, and she sort of taunted him into admitting that he actually knew an assassin-for-hire. I tell you—when she finally came out with what she wanted him to do, he was floored. Like the rest of us."

"Did he mention a fee?"

"Not then," Jasper says. "Not to me, ever."

"Do you know what it was?"

"No. I know nothing about the fee."

"Did your wife pay any part of it?"

"I don't think so."

"Did anyone ever ask you to?"

Jasper laughs. "No."

"What's funny?"

"I've no idea of the fee, as I said. But it's hardly surprising no one would mention it to me. I have no money. The rich son-in-law is Lawton."

"Okay," Tom says. "Anything else? Any other conversation with or about Teddy Stamos?"

"I never saw him again, until he showed up this morning. Nor did I ever talk about him. With anyone. Patty included. Connie especially. I wanted to get as far from that subject as possible."

"How 'bout after Robbie was killed?"

"Particularly then," Jasper says. "She raised it, Connie did. Said it looked like Elena had dealt with Stamos or done it herself."

"To which you said?"

"Absolutely nothing."

"Why do you think Constance raised the subject with Stamos while you were there? You and Patty?"

"I think she wanted us implicated, but to understand that, you'd have to know the sisters. It's not simply that Connie is the dominant one. She treats Patty as some kind of alter ego, like a special lobe of her own brain constantly telling her how wonderful she is. And even weirder—from the first, she's treated me the same way."

"You've given her cause?"

"Why not?"

"And she trusted you?" Tom suggests.

"Obviously."

"Or maybe she just wanted to share the blame, if there was to be any?"

"Also possible."

Tom thinks about that, then picks up the phone. "Constance Riles," he says into the receiver. "Room one. And bring in another chair."

"Off you go, Jasper," Tom says. "But others will want to talk with you before you leave the building, so sit tight outside."

FIFTY-FOUR

Constance glides in, as if on a runway modeling her designer skirt and trim jacket. Right behind her, her lawyer, the large, fleshy Harrison Stith, with an expression of perpetual pout. Then, his tight-lipped nod, and, with shuffling of feet, all take their seats at the table.

"For the record," Tom says, "you are Constance Riles and are represented here by your attorney, Harrison Stith?"

"That's correct." No resemblance to Elena, Tom is reminded, in manner or appearance, and little capacity for fun, although this is hardly the occasion for it. Constance is a solemn, high-cheeked beauty whose humor, on any occasion, comes mainly at others' expense.

"As he's doubtless explained, you need not say anything to me, and anything you do say may be held against you."

"I understand that, yes." She looks at Tom sharply. "And what do you understand, Mr. Weldon? Do you understand how conflicted you are? Investigating a murder in which the woman you're involved with is the principal suspect?"

"Well, that's changed, you see," Tom replies. "You're now the principal suspect."

"Me?" she says, managing to look both surprised and amused. "Whose nonsensical notion is that? My weasely brother-in-law's? Or did you come up with this on your own?"

Tom says, "So, when was the first time you talked to Teddy Stamos?"

Stith intervenes. "Constance, this is a good time to reiterate that you need not say anything to this man. He's just accused you of murdering your father. An appropriate response to any of his questions would be for you to decline to answer on Fifth Amendment grounds."

"Of course, Harry. And I will take your advice. After I've made short shrift of his ridiculous accusation. The fact is, Mr. Weldon, that evil little man came to my home some weeks ago and made a grotesque proposal. I threw him out and have never spoken to him again. Including this morning when I saw him in your reception room."

"Did he just arrive on your doorstep unannounced, or did you invite him?"

Stith breaks in. "All right, Weldon. No more questions along this line. My client declines to answer on grounds specified in the Fifth Amendment."

"That the answers might tend to incriminate her?"

"If it pleases you to put it that way."

"Not my pleasure that matters here. I'm reciting the accepted interpretation of the constitutional amendment you're relying on, and simply asking whether it accurately describes your client's position. And she should answer that herself."

"You won't bait me, Mr. Weldon," says Constance. "I did not hire anyone to kill my father, and it's hateful what you're doing here. I'm taking my lawyer's advice. No more answers to these trick questions of yours."

"Hired?" Tom muses out loud. "What gave you the idea that someone had been hired?"

"I'm not answering," Constance states. "Fifth Amendment!"

"Then you should know this," Tom says. "There are ample grounds to conclude that you were responsible for the murder of your father and the kidnapping of your sister. If you have something to say in your defense, we will listen. If not, you will be taken into custody and arraigned."

"Yes, you're trying to pressure me. It's all right. I've been warned. I'll be out of your … *custody* within the hour. And as for any trial, Mr. Weldon, you'll never prove that absurd charge. I see who your witnesses are. They won't stand up. Every one of them has a motive to blame me. Mainly to take blame away from themselves. My lawyers at trial will destroy them. And they will destroy you."

"You know who the witnesses are?" Tom asks innocently. "Would you care to name them?"

"Just one minute—" Stith starts.

"See!" Connie breaks in. "More trick questions!"

Tom sits back. "You will take advice from your own people, Connie. But when they see the evidence against you, I doubt seriously they'll let you have this case tried."

—⁘—

Stepping into the observation room, Tom asks, "Where's Elena?"

"Left," says Mike. "As soon as you brought in Connie."

"She say anything?"

"Nope. Just took off."

"Upset?"

"Very."

"Hmm," Tom says.

"Look." Mike stands. "You're doing great. Really fine job."

"One more witness."

"You really need him? There'll be a cost."

"A slightly reduced sentence? Does it really matter whether this guy spends four years in prison or two?"

"He cooperates," Mike says, "he'll get out in less than one."

"Even better," says Tom.

—⁘—

Interrogation room three. Across from Tom sits Horace Moon in his best clothes. "Where'd you get the suit?" Tom asks. "Looks like Saville Row."

"Mr. Riles," Horace says with pride. "We were friends."

"That so?"

"That's a fact. And I'm here to tell the truth. Don't even need a Miranda."

"You could have a lawyer, Mr. Moon. Paid for by the state."

"I know that kind of lawyer. Not what I need."

"What is it you need, do you think?"

"A deal. What *you* think? No time. Community service, okay, but no prison."

"Can't promise that," Tom says.

Takes Horace aback. "Should I be talking to you? Seems to me you're personally involved."

"How's that?"

"Come on. I watch TV, man."

"You're right," says Tom. "I am personally involved. But you give me what I need, I can be your best friend."

"Oh, yeah?"

"Yeah, Horace. I mean it. I'll get you the lightest sentence I can, but it will involve time."

"Like what?"

"Months. Instead of years."

Horace goes into a thoughtful head shake. "I don't know why I trust you."

"Glad you do," Tom says. "And you should."

"Yeah, hmm, well … I know I owe you."

"Yes," Tom says, "you do owe me."

"Okay. I know what you want. Who paid me to say what I said."

"That's right."

" 'Cause it wasn't true."

"What you said here? To Sammy Riegert, the man questioning you? About the shooting of Mr. Riles?"

"Right," Horace says. "It wasn't true."

"What is true?"

"I didn't see anything. I heard gunshots and hid."

"So who paid you to say it was Elena Riles?"

Big sigh by Horace. "Her sister. The older one, Constance."

Tom says, keeping his voice even, "Were you surprised?"

"No, man. I asked her for it."

"Just went up to her and asked?"

"I've known her since she was a baby. Nasty kid. Just got nastier. At thirteen, she already hated her father, and Elena even more. Because they loved each other and not Connie."

Reappraising this guy rapidly, Tom asks, "So you knew she, Connie, was responsible?"

"Not then, no."

"Okay," Tom says. "From the beginning, one step at a time. Right after the shooting, you figured out that Connie, whether or not she was responsible, would like to cast blame on Elena?"

"I wouldn't say, 'figured out.' I just kind of guessed it was possible."

"So you approached her, Connie Riles, for money, is that what you're saying?"

"Right. At the time, I needed money bad."

"What made you think she'd give you any?"

"I took a chance, but it wasn't that big a chance. As I said, I knew she hated her sister. If she went for the deal, then I'd guessed right, and I had my money. If she didn't—well, look at me, I'm just foolin' around. Not so nice, so what?"

"How much did you ask for?"

"Twenty thousand dollars."

"Which she gave you?"

"Next day. In cash."

"When did you learn Connie herself was responsible for the murder of her father and the kidnapping of her sister?"

"Same time."

"She actually told you?"

"That's right," Horace says. "I mean, who am I? A janitor.

And let's face it, I took the money. I talk, I got lots to lose, so it's a safe brag for her. Also, pretty obvious when she paid so fast she was tied up in it somehow, so she wasn't telling me that much."

"Pretty cagey of you, Horace."

The janitor shrugs.

"Except for one thing," Tom says.

"Yeah, well, I figured that out too."

"Your false statement accused an innocent person."

"There was wiggle room. I said I 'thought' it was the woman in the photo."

"And you planned to take that back? Confess it wasn't?"

"When it mattered, yeah," Horace says. "Like now."

"Have you spent the money?"

"Oh, yeah."

"How you feel about that?" Tom asks.

"I needed to spend the money. To live, I needed to spend it."

"And to live with yourself?"

"That's why I'm here, man."

FIFTY-FIVE

It's a charity event at the Colony Club: two hundred rich people in their finery, standing around or shuffling about, trading chitchat, holding drinks. Mike Skillan arrives late. Dottie is introducing the mayor, but heads turn Mike's way. *He* is the flavor of the moment. Though the press conference isn't scheduled until the following morning, no one is unaware of what Mike has reputedly pulled off. Or the deliciousness of it. Society queen paying assassins to murder her father! Notorious gumshoe ringmastering the crime! High-ranking G-man sabotaging the investigation! And Dubai slithering beneath it all!

Mike is mobbed when the speeches end. The mayor, an ungainly man with a stately nose and preoccupied stare that always roams elsewhere, clasps Mike's hand and rushes off to the next party. Dottie finally pulls her husband into a corner of the room.

"So you'll make the announcement, right? I mean you personally."

"Of course," he says.

"And who will be your Boswell on this—Joe?"

"Boswell?"

"Someone has to tell the press how brilliant you were."

"I wasn't particularly."

"Of course you were," she says. "But you can't be congratulating yourself. And the mayor will be in Albany tomorrow. I've already asked him."

"Cool down, baby. This wasn't my play."

"What are you talking about? You're the fucking DA."

"Acting," he notes.

"Not after this! That's what I'm saying. Mayor's ready to remove that stupid qualification."

"This was a one-man show."

"You're saying Weldon?"

"Yes," he says. "Brash, arrogant son of a bitch. Took crazy risks—pushed *me* in with him—but it worked. In short, brilliant."

"So who had the judgment to let him do it, huh? *Who?* That's leadership. In our world, the credit goes to the boss."

"This kid doesn't live in our world."

"No?" she says. "Well, it's time for him to move there."

"Tell you what, baby. May be time for me—us—to move a bit closer to his."

———

Every day, every hour, Indian summer in New York brings a different look and feel to every street. In Red Hook at six-thirty, with the sun low off the water, Bowne Street is sultry and hot. It appears to Tom like a Hopper painting, with colors so deep they seem melted into the stones.

Bowne Street is now home for Tom, so it's the last leg of his walk from the subway. The houses line up: fronts somber, backs blazing. On the stoop of his building, a young woman in a summer frock sits motionless, looking his way. He hopes it's Elena; in three steps he sees that it is. He eases down beside her, without causing any noticeable change in her contemplation of the sidewalk.

"When I was six," Elena says, "Connie was thirteen. I loved a cat, so she killed it. Sprayed it with lighter fluid and set it on fire."

"That's a horrible story," he says.

"Got lots of 'em," says Elena.

"Including today's."

"Today," she says. "Well, today was extreme. And a surprise. Even for Connie."

They sit in silence, until Elena says, "So today I learned how my father got murdered. Banner day."

"I'm sorry."

"Why should you be?" she says. "Just doing your job. I had to know. Eventually. Might as well've been this morning. Might as well've been you pumping out the whole mess."

"Still," he says.

"Forget it. I mourn here and there. In my own way. I'll get over it."

"You have reason to mourn. I understand that."

More silence.

"And you?" she says. "What are *you* going to do now?"

"With my life?"

"Let's start with your job."

"I think I might stay a while," he says. "With what I'm now doing."

"Yeah," she says. "You're pretty good at it. By the standards of that office."

"Thank you."

"It's not a compliment."

"I got the nuance of your statement," he says.

"Nuance?"

"And what about you?" he asks.

"I think I'll run the company," she says. "With Sofi. We're going to merge."

"Good idea."

"Yeah. We worked it out today. Over lunch. While you were handing out deals."

"There was," he says slowly, "a bit more involved than that."

"Some," she says, not giving much.

"You're never going to forgive me, are you?"

"Me? Never."

"The deals were not as generous as you think."

She says emphatically, "Any deal, in these circumstances, was generous."

"It's the way that office is run, Elena. Has to be run."

"Great. So you should do well there."

"Okay," he says. "You don't like it. Not much I can do."

"No."

"Can we live with it?" Tom asks.

"You and me?"

"We are the people I care about," he says.

She blows her cheeks out. "You think I don't?"

"So what are we doing, El?"

"Tonight?"

"I had in mind more than one night," he says.

"How many?"

"All of them?"

"That's a lot of nights," she says.

He spreads his hands to acknowledge it.

"Well," she says, "I don't see much alternative."

"You could sound happier about it."

"Is that me?" she says. "Look hard! Is that me?"

He does look and smiles. "So shall we go upstairs?"

"I suppose you want to have sex again," she says.

He blinks, as if stunned, and she laughs.

"I didn't come all the way out here, idiot, so I could spend another hour going back on the fucking subway."

ABOUT THE AUTHOR

Alan Hruska is the author of the novels *Pardon the Ravens* and *Wrong Man Running*, the writer of several plays produced in New York and London, and the writer and director of the films *Reunion*, *The Warrior Class*, and, most recently, *The Man on Her Mind*. A New York native and a graduate of Yale University and Yale Law School, he is a former trial lawyer who was involved in the some of the most significant litigation of the last half of the twentieth century. *It Happened at Two in the Morning* is his third novel. Hruska resides in New York City.